I0771495

Abandoned They Wake

Absolution

Rebecca Kropp

To my family and friends who encourage me every step of the way.

I love you all more than you know.

Also by Rebecca Kropp

<u>Abandoned They Wake Series:</u>

Dissonance

Absolution

As Aiden walked, all became clearer. He was headed where the misty tendrils pointed and his flyer noted: a place where children are left, a place where they hope, and a place where they wish and dream.

It might've been his home, were he worse off.

Either way, it was someone's home, and it was someone he needed to collect, to return.

The grass dampened his trousers, waving in the night's breeze, glistening under the moonlight. It was all so comforting, how the land seemed to gently push him along as though he belonged with it.

He very well could, but he himself was not sure, fogged and vague in his own mission – that being all that was clear.

In his head, a small voice rang as he moved, "They take that which bless' us, renderin' us over-encumbered. Our gifts stripped away, we are left to wander." It was a woman who spoke, though the voice he could not place. It was sweet in its rhyming.

He smiled.

The trees cleared as the grass became patchy; old cobblestone, overgrown, bulging, uneven, was now underfoot as he pressed onwards towards a large structure. It was bigger than a cottage, smaller than a manor, and covered in glorious vines seeking to lay claim.

The voice whispered, then, carried on the breeze, asking him to witness a story, then to take them home.

ONE

The knocking was hesitant and in the next instance boisterous. There were two people coming this night, one most assured, one more timid. It was late, a peculiarity, but not uncommon. The matron of the Orphanage allowed any and all to visit at any time of day since they resided in such a rural area, Southwest of Draeden, surrounded by wood. One would think it'd be a horrid area for business, but being the only one in the land allowed it to be tucked away.

This *residence* needn't a name due to it being the single place allowed for such a purpose – King Huxley made it clear there could be just one, giving whatever gold and resources necessary to keep it running and keep the matron happy.

Happy she was, for she did the talking, the selling, and the setting. The children were brought in and adopted at a decent pace, full capacity never being reached and never being a worry.

Her tongue was gilded and her name was Miss Camille, her last name lost to the ages.

The matron called from a separate room to her underling, the one who cooked, groomed and was made to do all Camille did not wish to do herself, "Go along and let them in, I will be but a moment longer!"

The girl abided, her feet heavy and solid upon the floor, no matter how lightly she attempted to walk.

She fumbled with the locks, one a chain, a deadbolt, and then a key of weighty iron was needed for the third. Her matron gave it to her earlier for this such occasion and its heft was a pleasant comfort. The knocking grew more insistent now, as she struggled to slip the key into its proper spot, "One m-moment," she mumbled as she turned the key, and with the sound of the latch coming free, the door swung open to reveal a man and a woman. It was raining outside and the husband clutched an umbrella with a pale hand.

"About time! We were worrying over sleeping on the stoop in this piss-poor weather," the man crooned, stepping inside and shaking droplets off the umbrella just outside the door.

The woman's hands were clasped at her stomach, her back hunched as she stepped inside. She appeared short until she rolled her shoulders back, standing regal and elegant before the girl at the door. "Dear, do not take him to heart. The journey here and the weather made him so crabby."

"The lengths we go to adopt a child. Why must there be but one orphanage so far from the rest of civilization?" He shot a look at the girl in front of him – just fifteen, she was. She closed the door and faced them, giving a light bow. The man responded with a raised eyebrow, "Well then?"

The girl fumbled at her sleeves, tugging and stretching the already taut fabric. She met their eyes and watched their demeanors soften as she did. Her lips parted and she spoke with practiced words, "Matron Camille will be about shortly. Please follow me to the guest area." She picked what was said with care, what her tongue let her say with ease.

Without another word, she turned on her heel and plodded into another room with a blazing fire and low-backed sofas and chairs for guests. Hot tea was already prepared and sat atop a table, centered between the seats.

She stumbled when she remembered their coats, holding out her hands like a poor child asking for coin. "Apologies, I will take your overcoats and put them up to dry."

They nodded, removing their outer layers and then sitting down. The girl rushed over and began to serve them their drinks when the woman's voice cracked as she spoke, "Is there any honey?" She cleared her throat as her husband side-eyed her before taking a sip.

The clumsy girl paused, her mind struggling to come up with the right words, her mouth pursed, her tongue ready to say what she could not, would not speak.

The guests looked at her with expectation as she began to shake her head back and forth, her cheeks flushing with embarrassment, "N-no. We've sugar."

The woman shrugged, giving the girl a careful look before her eyes dashed to the doorway. Camille made her way in, her dark hair sat in a bun atop her head, silky and perfect. Her dress was simple: black with a white sash at the waist. She was in her thirties, at least, "So sorry to keep you waiting in the rain. The door can be a pain to open but we must keep the children safe. I am Matron Camille." She curtsied and the couple smiled, copying the lady's grin.

"It is a pleasure my lady, I am Mark Faust, and this is my wife, Dara," the man beamed. He must have been in his forties and his wife, her thirties. Lady Camille and Dara shared the same hair color, the latter's temples showing trickles of gray. The girl stood by, idle, dutiful, and wondered if the grays were a testament to their marriage.

Camille took her seat across from the guests, the fire lighting up the right side of her face, the left side cast in shadow, "We've readied a room for the two of you, whenever you wish to retire. Did you travel by stagecoach or on your own?"

Dara began to speak when her husband cut her off, "We took a stagecoach, paid him well enough and told him to be around late afternoon tomorrow. I suspect we'll pick a suitable child by then."

Camille nodded and glanced at the wife, who gave a small smile and asked the matron, "Do you think that is an adequate time frame to adopt a child? We are of the mind that we will know which child we'll take when we see them."

The girl shifted side to side as she listened, absentmindedly whispering, "Like love at first sight?"

Camille's eyes darted to her then back to the couple, Mark's rested on the girl as she stared at her feet, uncomfortable to be of one's attention. The husband added, "Of a sort, yes, but within consideration."

"Of course that will be enough time to choose. We educate all the children so they are of general competency; we pray and read our teachings thoroughly; everyone contributes and takes responsibility of their lodgings whilst here as well." She crossed her legs, took a cup of tea for herself, and continued, "We also discipline them accordingly to ensure proper behaviors are learnt."

Dara's glance, soft and kind landed on the girl as she raised her head. For a moment they held each other's sight as the young one attempted to straighten out her skirt. Mark was fully engaged with Camille now, leaning forward. "When will the children be awake?"

"A sharp eight, so there is time for you two to rest before we can begin the process."

Mark purred, "Excellent."

The girl stood by the fireplace now, basking in whatever warmth wafted to the side, keeping herself hidden. She wanted to hide away again, to sleep, but the matron would tell her when it was appropriate to do so.

"Marion, what is it that we are out of?"

The fire's light flickered across the young girl's face as she stepped forward, pursing her lips and trying to settle her tongue, settle her mind as she over-enunciated, "H-h-huh-honey."

Camille closed her eyes and gave a curt nod. "We'll need to get some come morning."

The young girl listened as her head drooped further and further down. She felt the eyes of the guests on her as shame flared her cheeks to a deep crimson – she could never get used to it, despite how hard she worked, how hard she tried.

Camille believed it to be stubbornness, an inability to adapt and grow. The girl accepted it as weakness.

"Prepare a fire in their room ahead of time, then you may see yourself to bed."

The girl scuttled away before Camille's cool voice cut through the air, her hand outstretched and her gaze still on the man and woman across from her, a pleasant smile sat on her face. "The key, Marion."

She had forgotten she had it, her heavy feet dragging as she made her way to her matron's side, lifting the iron key from her apron pocket and laying it in the palm of the outstretched hand.

The comforting weight left and the girl felt herself grow more unsteady as she walked away to the guest room, the conversation in the other room fading beneath her loud footsteps.

Dara's voice held a genuine pity, "Poor girl, a stutter?"

"Well, we surely would not be adopting *her*. We need a child in good health, mind, body, and whatever else."

As she began to ascend the stairs, she heard Camille chuckle, "Marion is much too precious to me. Whether you fancied her or not, I wouldn't be able to let her go."

"Is she your child?"

"No, but she does belong to me."

Too far away, she could no longer hear them speaking as she creaked open the guest room. It was plain, decorated with a dull and unvarnished wood garnished by touches of gray fabrics. The only color was from a red painting of a sunrise hanging above the fireplace. Opening a drawer and taking out the matches, she struck one and let it burn down. The warmth reached her fingertips when she blew it out, her breath silent. Another was struck, and the fireplace roared to life soon enough. She looked at the rising sun and wished to burn it.

She turned on her heel; making way to her room, she listened to the steady sounds the children made as they slept. There would be one less tomorrow afternoon, whisked away to a family she hoped would love them, care for them. There weren't many to choose from, and many appeared dull and uniform, the glow of being a child snuffed out through rigidity.

They were perfect, something she would never know. She wondered if it came with more freedom in that it offered a peaceful mind, a sounder future.

Her bedroom door clunked open, the hinge and wood coming apart as she lifted it by the knob and forced it shut behind her, taking up a seat in front of a mirror and bowl. The three in the main room could be heard chatting and giggling. Mark was loud, Camille was calculated, proper, and Dara was hesitant, speaking when her husband quieted.

Splashing cool water on her face, the girl sighed, patting her cheeks in an attempt to drain the heat of embarrassment. It clung to her painfully as she looked in the mirror, illuminated by the moonlight that filtered through the heavy trees.

"H-h-," she dragged out the h's, her tongue curling. It seemed so simple, a letter pronounced with a simple exhale, but that didn't stop her mouth from disobeying her. The more she tried, the more her tongue was like melting dough, her throat beginning to constrict and her eyes squeezing shut.

She reached into her mouth, pinched her tongue still and pulled at it, making it taut like her sleeves. She huffed, trying to say the simple word, "H-h-hu-honey." She continued until she began to gag, letting her tongue slip from her fingers. Saliva dribbled from her mouth as she sniffed back tears and congestion. It was a visceral act she did every night, but with different words that attacked her throughout her days.

She wiped her mouth and stared in the mirror, "'Oney."

She crawled into her bed and pulled up the multitude of weighty blankets she had collected over the years, ones she mended, some she knitted. They made her heaviness feel less lonesome, lulling her into feeling safe.

Footsteps made their way upstairs, and Camille's voice was light as it echoed through the wood. The girl could picture her Matron pointing out of which rooms were whose, her thin finger flourishing with grandiosity. The steps stopped at her door and she could hear faint knocking: it was Camille, "Goodnight, Marion."

She didn't wish to answer. Mark and Dara whispered goodnights and for the sake of politeness, she replied, gritting her teeth, "Goodnight."

The blankets were tugged above her head, holding her down and steady as she curled into herself, hoping for all the world that her parents couldn't see her betraying herself.

Two

Clockwork, that's what she was, rising at a quarter to eight. She slept, deep and heavy, without dreams and without memories, just like every other night.

Pushing away her covers, she patted them in thanks before loudly pacing towards her vanity. It was different in the morning: there was no time to practice, no time to loathe as she washed her face, smooth as stone and with a warm, reddish hue. She smiled at herself and took in a deep breath. Her mother taught her about love and kindness, how everyone deserves it, at least in the beginning.

Smoothing out her brunette waves before tying them up, she eyed herself, up and down. She stroked her arms, feeling the bumps in her skin but not looking at them. She had believed her mother once, struggling to believe her again, finding herself torn with who deserved love and kindness the most.

With a brown, plain gown, tied tight with an apron, she continued to leer at herself.

Shorter, with a solid build, her shoulders on the wider side, her body with slight curves. She was fifteen but had already hoped she would look more like her mother than father. He was broad and barrel-chested, hearty and full. He was well built, and so was she. There was still time to grow.

Leaning in, she traced her thin lips, a bright red for as long as she remembered. Moving up to her nose, she pinched the small bridge and ran a thumb along the slight outwards curve of it. Her eyes were next, not too deep-set, but not protruding. Leaning closer, she lowered the bottom lid to get a better look of her eyes and smiled.

Camille had repeatedly called her intriguing in look and stature, not ugly, not beautiful.

Eyes like warmth, red and gold. They were lined with shades of other joyous colors appearing as her favorite stones. She opened a drawer and touched the armlet her mother left with her before reaching next to it, plucking one of several stones. Dipping it in her water, she held it next to her eye, turning it about, letting the cool trickle run down her sleeve.

She was yet to find a stone that matched her eyes, but of all the gems, rocks and minerals her mother had showed her, red agates matched her the best. She rubbed the stone dry and placed it in her pocket for the day.

In her room, alone, she believed her mother, but outside, it was difficult to trust the words she heard ten years ago. In that room, looking in that mirror, it was as if her mother stared back, telling her that love and kindness was most important to oneself. They shared the same eyes. Her father's bright amber eyes had no lines.

All the same, those eyes made her feel loved.

Once, she believed her eyes made others feel so.

She winced at the thought.

A few minutes to eight, she gathered herself and trudged to her door, strong-arming it open and closed, announcing the morning to all of the Orphanage and announcing to herself that the comforts of her room were far away.

She began to knock on the children's doors, asking them to be ready for breakfast and tidy themselves extra well today. Descending the stairs, she wondered if the children were excited at the prospects of being adopted, of leaving this place. Of everyone that left, their smiles seemed practiced when they looked at her, forced. She did not wish for appeasement, but knew it was taught. If anyone fell out of line, they were punished, and she knew the punishments most intimately.

She missed how genuine everyone once was, but, it could not be helped.

She gathered water from the well enclosed by tall walls in the back garden, ancient laid stones casting heavy shade from the morning sun, not an imperfection to be seen: no chips, no cracks, all smooth, gray surfaces. The chamomile, daisies and roses sucked up all the sun they could throughout the day, blessing her with their pleasant smells as she made trips to fill her pots of water.

She wished for a river instead, knowing there was one just outside of the woods, running alongside a plain full of prairie flowers, tiny and bright. The desire to go to it slowed her gait to that of an elder as she tip-toed, looking above the wall, watching the trees scratch and groan at each other in their proximity. A crow called out, followed by a mourning dove.

She stepped inside.

Time passed quickly during breakfast. Every morning was similar, and she allowed herself to go blank the entire time. It was a different kind of peace from what she knew in the morning when she woke up. Soon, she would be done and the children, prim and proper, would be waiting in their seats to eat in near silence.

"What is it you are making?"

She jumped, the wooden spoon splashing some of the food onto the counter.

It was Dara, "I do apologize, I did not mean to frighten you."

Taking the large pot off the flame, the girl wiped her hands, facing her surprise visitor. "I was merely surprised, no-" a voice in her head stopped her. *Harm*, forbidden. She gulped, looking at the floor then back at Dara, "Do not worry yourself. I was m-" She stopped again, "Porridge."

Dara gave a large nod, as if to acknowledge the difficulty the girl faced.

"Marion, right?"

The girl turned and bit her tongue, placing the pot on a rolling cart along with a wooden ladle, "Yes, it is."

"May I help?"

"No." She did not mean to sound so coarse. "I do not wish for you to get burned, thank you." She was awkward and forced. This day would be exhausting. She pushed the cart out into the dining hall as a quiet Dara moved away and watched as the children at the table followed the girl with their heads. One by one, their bowls were filled, and they hesitated before being directed to eat. The girl sighed. She did not know how to feel in moments like these. Their lack of spirit, their need to be told to act, their living deadness – it frustrated her and saddened her own soul. She gripped the stone in her pocket, rubbing it with her thumb, wanting to go back in her room, wanting to see her mother staring back at her and telling her she was okay, that her entire person was good and she was beautiful and loved. Behind that wretched door, she belonged, she was free, she could say and be just as she was.

Out here, she was a monster.

As the days passed her by, it grew harder to keep that thought out of her bedroom and out of her heart. Her walls were thinning.

They ate without a slurp, without words, without clanking spoons into bowl, and in the silence, the girl felt herself sinking, her head a weight, falling deep in herself down to the pit of her stomach and further into the center of the world. All was caving in.

It all meant nothing, including her.

"Thank you."

Eyes wide, her head snapped up, some of the children flinching as her shining eyes flicked from one child to the next as she came out of her blackness. An automatic grin graced her lips, not reaching her eyes, not anymore, "Welcome, always welcome."

A small boy, new to the Orphanage, twisted back in his chair to look at the girl behind him, staring at her eyes until she met him with hers. He smiled, a full and beautiful smile, and the tears pricked at her eyes. How she wanted to drop to her knees and hold him tight and tell him how wondrous he was, how lovely. How he was alive and genuine and real. He reached out and tugged at her apron as the other children sat, stunned silent, their backs aching at the effort they put into sitting straight. He mumbled to her, "Thank you, sister." His voice was sweet, his little head covered in perfectly kept hair, combed to one side - how bad she wanted to ruffle it, to make him look how he sounded.

She held her hand back, her smile changing and as she held back a gasp and cry, it quivered on her face under her crinkling eyes.

He was so innocent and pure, still a five-year-old, not a doll, not some puppet. How she loved him in that moment, how she, ever so slightly, envied him for it, her warming voice grew strained with control as she choked out, "You are most welcome, little sweetin'."

He grinned before his face fell, tightly paced click-clacks of heels echoed and vibrated throughout the bottom floor, making way to the dining area. The children stiff as they became the spitting image of flawlessness, though, calmer as the matron came closer. They did not fear her: they only wished to make her happy, a constant struggle. The boy whipped around and straightened up as best he could, his face fluctuating between a small smile and a larger one as he struggled to maintain face with the others.

Camille stopped in the doorway, her black hair braided into a tight bun, her thin, bird neck straight, and her hands clasped in front of her hips. Her dark eyes perused the room, and her full lips were pink and smiling. High cheek bones, rosy cheeks and not a strand out of place or a wrinkle to be seen.

She was perfection.

"By His Royalty, I bid you all good morning, my dear children."

In unison, "Good morning to you, Miss Camille."

Beaming brighter, Camille continued, "Today, someone will be adopted, as you know. I want you all to be aware of this as you go about your day." She motioned to Dara in the corner, near the girl and Mark made his way in from behind Camille. The dining room was small, there being only enough room around a full seated table for a food cart to be maneuvered around. The fireplace was inlaid in the wall and so were the shelves. Camille flicked her wrist towards Mark, who gave a large smile, "This lovely couple is Mark and Dara Faust. They will make their decision by noon." She brought her hands up to the side of her head and gave two claps. The children were organized, passing down their bowls and spoons to the girl at the cart, the little boy in front of her fumbled a bit with his bowl and smiled when he handed it away, he grinned just like a child should.

Troublesome, the girl thought, biting at her lower lip as she stacked the dishes, the orphans standing up and making their way through the main parlor where Mark and Dara had tea the night prior, to the library and classroom that connected to it. A child approached matron Camille, his hands folded in front of him, he lifted his eyes to meet hers, not a hair shifting. "Lady Camille?"

"Yes, dear?"

"May we play at the front today?"

She hesitated, placing her hands on the slope of her jaw, drawing out her thoughts and the silence. "I believe that would be alright today, just after Marion finishes cleaning."

The stuttering girl nodded and made her way past Dara, who watched her and her shadow pass by.

She tolerated the steaming water as she cleaned the utensils, fretting over what might come today. She tried to loosen her tongue practicing words in whispers and listening to the doves outside the window.

"What are you mumbling?"

She bit her tongue, turning to face her shadow, or rather the boy who stood in it. She winced for several reasons, "What are you d-," she paused, her tongue stiffening, "Why are you in the kitchen?"

The boy stood on his tip toes as he walked to the counter she worked at, his eyes level with the surface. He began to hop foot to foot. "I wanted to see what you are up to! The other kids are boring!" He reached for a small wooden spoon, his little fingers just grazing the handle.

The girl looked behind them, peering through the doorway to see if anyone watched. She sighed, took a breath, and held it before giving him the spoon. He clapped it against the counter quietly, and then took a step back, twirling in a circle and holding his wooden piece aloft, "It is a sword, sister!"

She giggled as she washed, about done with her work. The sun seemed to shine brighter in the window as though the trees backed away outside. The little boy totted back and forth and around the small room, leaping in an attempt to reach the drying herbs above him.

Flicking the water from her fingers, she felt something hard tap her rear, spinning around to see the little boy holding the spoon still, a playful grin reaching up his face and cuteness crinkling the corners of his eyes as a chuckle and small shriek escaped his lips. She couldn't hold back and lifted him high above her head, his grin blossoming into the purest of enjoyment and his laughter filled the room. She spun around, remaining bound to her spot, the boy stretched out above her head breaking his constant laugh to suck in a breath and then give more laughter, deep and jolly. To her surprise, she too was laughing, her lids growing heavy with joyous tears.

Her sleeves began to slip away from her arms, and she lowered him to rest on her hip as he laid his head on her shoulder, tapping her collarbone, then forehead with his spoon. She gazed down at him, remembering being a child, remembering how it felt to love and be loved.

He shifted and kissed the corner of her eye.

She smiled at him, her voice delighted. "And what for?"

His head swiped side to side, full of giddiness. "I think your eyes are so pretty."

"Thank you, little one."

"They make me feel loved, like you care about me and, and you are nice, very kind."

Her face fell, her lips tugging down her cheeks as she felt the thin skin around her eyes puff. She set him down, patting his head. "Thank you. Now, we must be quick — the others wait." Holding out her hand, the boy returned the spoon before jaunting out the door, his footsteps coming to an abrupt halt.

Spoon set with the others, she cautiously followed him, entering the dining room to see him standing in front of Miss Camille, "Run along." Her words were short and sharp. All at once, the girl's stomach dropped deep within her, dread left in its midst. The boy walked off.

"You keep us waiting by indulging in little games?"

"The boy followed me and it was only a bit of fun, only a few minutes."

"You give an inch, they take a mile. Of course he followed when you lapsed in your boundaries. Marion, you are the adult, meant to guide."

She held her breath and clenched her arms as Camille looked down her nose at the girl before turning to leave the room, producing a key to open the front door. Like a whipped puppy, the girl followed after.

Inside, she asked her parents for help, knowing what may come. A small voice answered her, and out of her periphery, she sought Dara.

* * *

The front yard didn't begin till one met the edge of the forest and cobblestone—a short walk, but a walk nonetheless. Where the trees cleared, the land was long and wide with grass that tickled one's ankles. A faint, sweet scent of flowers carried on the breeze. The sun set in this direction, but it would be several hours before they were greeted by the sun and later, the moon. It was warm now, the children spreading out to squat in the grass, exploring the undergrowth. One propped her face between her small hands, gazing at the small blue and pink flowers. A boy with a leather ball began to toss it to another. Sticks were tapped in play fights whilst others sat, reading amongst themselves.

The laughter was muted, as were the voices, but this was done by the children themselves, not by loud breezes or creatures singing songs.

She saw Dara walking alongside her husband now, nodding along to him speaking and pointing at particular children. Dara's eyes glanced around before catching sight of the girl staring back at her, and then she tapped her husband's shoulder before making her way to the girl. "How are you, Marion?"

The girl exhaled, "I am... well. Yourself?"

Holding up the hem of her yellow dress, Dara looked at the children, "Well, enough. Quiet, are they not?"

Awfully, the girl mused before replying, "As Miss Camille would say, behaved."

"You look as if to say something?"

Capturing her curious gaze, the woman tucked a loosed strand of hair behind her ear as she examined the fifteen-year-old's face.

"The small boy, what do you think of... the boy?"

"The one who smiled at you and followed you to the kitchen?" Her voice was pleasant as she cast a glance towards the boy gallivanting in the grass and trying to get a hold of the leather ball being tossed about.

Mark was talking with Camille now, both of them watching the children with scrutiny; they appeared quite engaged with who to pick.

"Yes, that boy."

"He is quite a little darling, with more energy than the others, more like a child in my mind as opposed to these," she paused, turning the words in her mouth, "Little adults. I want a child to play with."

"If he captivates you so, I think that is the one you should choose," her words were slow and meticulous as she avoided stuttering.

"Yes, but Mark must agree as well, and time is growing short."

"Please take h-h-him," she could not hold back her desperation, as she looked away from Dara, hiding away her flushed cheeks.

"Why?"

"Deserves a lovin' family and a good huh-home." Truly she believed such, but also wished the boy to remain as a boy.

"I'll speak to Mark about it, but," Dara walked to the girl's other side, bending her back to catch the young girl's eyes, "why do you avoid me? Is it the stutter?"

A pained, muffled breath escaped her lips as Camille made her way through the grass towards the two, accompanied by Mark. Dara stepped away and joined her husband's side, lacing her arm through his. The Matron pressed, practiced and gentle, "Have the two of you made your decision?"

Dara looked at her feet, then out to the children before sweeping her head to meet Mark's, then Camille's. "I enjoy the little boy with the blonde hair who cannot stop dancing."

Camille's eyes shifted; she side-eyed the girl tugging at her sleeves and looking at the ground. Mark huffed, "I want a child who will be well behaved and mindful of themselves, like the boy reading over there."

"I want a *child*. One who plays and smiles."

"He *is* smiling, Dara." His tone was confident. "He is content in what he is doing and is no nuisance in the process."

A cool voice cut through the air, "The little one, Martin, has only been with us a short awhile. I'm afraid he is not yet disciplined or educated like the others. It is your choice, in the end."

"Oh, Mark, the name Martin, does it not sound so sweet to say?"

"Martin, *Martin*. Sounds as though I speak of an uncle," he quipped.

The girl stood silent, eyes screwed shut, as she held back the bile in her throat.

"Please, my love?" Dara pleaded with him, holding his arm with both hands, looking up at him, attempting to reach him.

He pecked her forehead. "No, I am afraid we wouldn't the time to teach him proper." He began to walk her towards the boy who sat alone. His voice trailed off as Dara stole a glance at the young girl, sadness marring both their features. The soon-to-be mother's expression turned apologetic, then faced away.

"Marion." Camille stood next to the girl now. "Look at me."

She struggled to control herself, trying to calm her muscles, tensing like stone. She swallowed hard. "Yes, Lady Camille?"

Camille gently wrapped her thin hands around the girl's wrists. "I told you not to meddle with the adoptions. Were you trying to sway Dara?"

"She liked Martin and I simply encouraged—" Once more, she swallowed, leaving her words to drift in the air, unfinished.

"Encouraged who?"

"Dara."

"Finish your sentence." Camille was cold, squeezing the girl's wrists.

"Encouraged h-h-" She was in knots now, her stomach flitting in a deep pit, her tongue flicking the roof of her mouth, her teeth. It was too hard to say: she was too tense.

One last squeeze and Camille began to walk away, without giving a second glance. "Tonight, you both will be punished."

The girl watched the boy, wishing to whisk him away in her arms, running to any place but here. It took all her strength not to crumple, not to fall into the grass and cry. She was doing well, no one had been punished in so long, yet, he was the first child in a long time to grace the Orphanage's steps.

No, no, no, please, spare the boy.

No one would hear her silent pleas, locked up in her mind.

Mark and Dara held hands with the boy they chose to take with them, Camille beaming at the three and their apparent joy. The adopted child had a smile brighter than he ever had at the

Orphanage. He was as free as his parents would allow, as much as his teachings and mind would allow.

Little Martin watched them go before running to the girl's side and embracing her legs before stepping back. "Sister, look! It is pretty like your eyes!" He held a tiny red flower up to her, the petals edged golden and black.

He couldn't know it was diseased.

Collapsing into the grass, she pulled him into her, sobbing, grasping his hair and trying to quell her breathing. He wiggled enough to face her. "Why are you crying?" He was confused, holding up his flower and wondering if it was too ugly, a poor gift.

Shaking her head, she plucked the dying plant from his fingers and tucked it behind her ear, letting out an exasperated chuckle before stroking his soft cheek. "You may not understand for ten o-or twenty years," her voice broke, her gasps ragged, full of sorrow, "You may never even forgive me, but, please know this—."

He stared back at her, frozen, not knowing how to comfort the girl in shambles before him, unable to comprehend her words. His eyes bright and wide in shock and confusion.

"*I am sorry.*"

THREE

Dara and Mark had left a week ago, but it was hard to tell for the girl had not been in her room, her safe place, for quite some time. She had been in the basement, her and Martin, for their punishment. Camille was there as well, but she stayed hidden and quiet behind the heavy curtains, just out of sight.

There were minimal candles lit and all was dark and dreary there, a place where the young girl's eyes seemed to glow in whatever light they could capture. Brilliant reds and yellows, with deeper colors still that danced in lines, becoming more vibrant when wet with tears. To one, a sight to behold, and to others, something much more sinister and malicious.

It was still as dark as it was for her in the past week, just past dusk, but now she plodded through the halls, making way to her bedroom for the little rest and comfort she could squeeze from the space. The silvery moonlight through the few windows lit her way as she gripped and massaged her aching arms hiding under her dress' fabrics.

The orphanage was silent at night, and her mind was beginning to match it. Once her head was a cacophony of conflict, of shame, dread, hope and promise. She had to steel herself over her lackings, over that which she could not control, which seemed to be all.

A begrudging acceptance, but acceptance the same.

She heard whimpering behind one of the doors and recognized it as Martin's. She had heard such sorrow for most of their time in the basement. No matter how blank she was making herself feel, a terrible rumble shook within her belly, wanting her to remedy something, to try.

Her hand hesitated over the doorknob as she steadied her breathing, slowly in and slowly out. Her fingers twitching as she tried to control the spasm of her muscles before letting them fall, heavy, onto the knob, to twist it and push.

The room held its breath as the door swung open, the shapes under the blankets tensing one by one till all were solid mounds. Save for the quivering one who had suffered in the basement.

She tried to walk without sound, but failed as each footfall emanated wholly and thoroughly through the floorboards, solid and flat. Barefoot or not, it was all the same.

Reaching Martin's bed, the young girl sat on the side of it, her hand hovering over the covers as she rocked with each beat of her pounding heart. She rested her fingers first, feeling the rough-hewn linen against her numbing skin. So cold she was.

Carefully, she pulled the blanket down to expose the small boy who shook and curled into a fetal position, covering his head and crying as quiet as he could.

She whispered his name, and his shuddering stopped as he retreated farther into himself like a roly-poly bug hiding its soft spots. She laid her hand upon his head, smoothing his blonde hair in an attempt to soothe him, already knowing it was too late. He hissed out his breath, "Go away."

"Martin, I mean no ill towards you." Once more, her words were careful.

He peeked at her between his fingers and she could see the swell of his face, the bruises deep blues and purples, his eye bloodshot as it glared at her. She pulled her hand back, unsure what to do, what to feel. He sat up and spat at her, "I hate you! Leave me be!"

She held out her hands, pleading with him, "You called me sister once. I still am that."

"You are too horrid to be a sister!"

Outside the wind picked up, pushing aside the curtains, the moonlight pouring in and illuminating the girl's eyes. Martin winced and shrunk back, pulling his legs to his torso, lips quivering as he struggled to speak, to make her leave.

Her hands were still outstretched as a different voice chirped through the quiet, "Marion, if you do not leave, we will all be punished again."

Another, a boy. "You are not welcome in here, Marion, he does not want you."

Another, still. "Haven't you done enough? Marion?"

Their voices were piercing. It cut her through, but she understood why they said such things.

They all felt the same hatred as Martin now did. They all resembled Martin, once, both before and after discipline.

She stood and backed away as one of the children's feet slid in silence across the floor to tuck Martin back in, the boy's eyes holding pity that changed to ire as soon as they were cast in her direction. Soon enough, the room was filled with such looks, a few handful of children holding fear, pain, and anger within them aimed at the girl as she, filled with much the same emotion, retreated from the room, shutting the door behind her and squatting down to catch her breath, letting rivulets of tears fall from her eyes.

She sat motionless, a statue, for quite some time, listening to Martin's crying drift into exhausted sleep. It sounded like a good idea for her too, to climb under all her blankets, to fall into a comforting darkness, to fade, if even for a few hours, into nothing, devoid of pain and misery and the physical sufferings that plagued them. So, with exertion, she pushed off the ground and resumed her plodding to her own bedroom not much further down the hall.

* * *

The door was gone. The heavy, lopsided door, no longer separated the orphanage from her space. The hinges sat, empty and clinging onto the trim nailed into the pale walls. She marveled at it, touching the space the door used to sit, trying to feel the difference in the air between her room and the hall. Was it cooler? Warmer? Heavier?

She could not tell, only seeing the darkness that covered everything of hers gently spotted by the moon's glow through curtains speckled with holes.

She touched the inner walls just beyond the threshold, wondering if it rested on one of the walls, something to fix. She tapped the floor with her toes, waiting, anticipating hitting solid wood that was not the floor.

Stepping inside, she felt the pit in her stomach sinking deeper as a glow from behind her began to flicker some of her surroundings into illumination.

"This is *your* punishment, Marion," Camille said, her long locks draped over her shoulders, her dark eyes looking down at the girl. "If you do not actively maintain boundaries, then you will not have them in any regard."

The girl wanted to run through Camille, to throw her to the ground so that she would know pain. How all that was within these walls was false, how all the control and all the perfection was a human lie that should be the problem of her Matron, not hers, not the children's. Perfection was cold and unyielding, tormenting those in its wake – but Camille was pristine, untouched, unbothered.

Instead, she could only look at the ground and nod in agreement, her knowledge of the outside world stunted and utterly lacking. There was only the Orphanage.

"Do you have anything you wish to say?"

The girl shook her head.

"Say it."

"No, Lady Camille."

Camille stepped closer at this, gripping the girl's arm and pulling her closer into the candle's light. "Say it in a full sentence."

Hadn't this week been enough? Her throat convulsed as she tried to control her tongue, "I h-ha-h-have nothin'-n-nothing to say."

Camille sighed and released the girl's arm, her exhale expressing disappointment, her slight smile speaking volumes of other feelings. "Ten years, and still, you have a tattered tongue. Oh, Marion, Marion, Marion, whatever am I to do with you?" She produced a match and lit the end on her candle before holding it out to the girl. "Use it before it runs out. As I have done and always will do, I will give you light, but only if you continue to use it."

The girl took the match, watching Camille walk out her room, down the corridor and away, the light she carried fading into the distance.

The match burned down to the girl's numb fingers as she let it snuff itself out.

She cast it into her fireplace, walking to her vanity and producing her own matches. The box was hefty, comfortable, and she pulled out her own match, striking it into a beautiful combustion that hissed in the air – like a summoned spirit. She marched to her fireplace and let it come to life, setting a pot to boil over it, staring until it was ready.

Setting cloths into the water, she watched them bulge and bloat before looking at the gaping, open doorway, sneering at it. Her bed had less blankets and above her fireplace was a tapestry of a sunrise. She was surrounded, exposed and smothered all at once, wanton to shatter like glass.

She tugged at the tapestry without thinking, harder and harder still until it ripped loose from its fixtures and she held it before the roaring flame, bringing it closer and closer still.

If the building was to catch fire, would she survive? Would she care? If nothing mattered, did those questions matter? Her mind flashed to Martin, when he would smile, and then to the rest of the children before their basement ordeals.

She even saw what she once looked like in her mind's eye, how she used to smile and laugh before her first punishment.

Taking the tapestry, she hung it to cover the hole in her room, figuring it was all she could do to replace her missing door. The motif faced the hallway while the knotted back faced her room. She smirked in defiance, knowing she may need to explain but that it would have to do for now. It was fine now, it had to be.

"Straighten up, chin up and move forward," she whispered words of her parents, keeping her eyes down, unsure what to do with them.

The cloths were gingerly removed from the burbling water, and she waited a few minutes for them to cool before placing them along her bare arms. The hot, sopping rags settled into grooves and bumps as they loosened her up, gentle and comforting as she stood in front of the flickering firelight.

She swayed, her eyes closed, listening to her mother and father hum to her in a far off memory, applying subtle pressure up and down her covered skin. She was getting heavier, feeling as though the floor sank beneath her as though soft clay or sand, sinking into a pit and taking her along. The world, the room, everything began to melt away as she felt tears running down her cheeks, neck and collarbones.

She could no longer keep count of the horrors she endured, that the children suffered. She couldn't remember how many children had come and gone, their faces blurring together until no features remained. Even Martin's would fade.

Who was first?

Her eyes snapped open as the thought crossed her mind. It towed along a myriad of others she never gave credence to. As a little girl, she paid no attention to who else was around and how they behaved.

Were there any others at the time?

These were questions for the matron, but whether or not she would answer in truth was another matter entirely. The girl was not afraid to ask, not afraid of the scars she may come to bear because of it, rather the children that may be dragged into what may come made her second guess everything.

The rags had gone cold, flat and weighty now, time passing without hindrance. Wringing them out, they dried on the windowsill as she crawled into her bed, hiding underneath what was left of her blanket horde. Her eyes drifted closed as her parents began to sing songs to her, and the prior week's exhaustion dragged her into a dark sleep in which she dreamed a memory.

* * *

"Come now, my sweetin', your pa is waitin' in the woods to play."

"Mama, I want to play 'ere in the flowers!"

Short like a prairie flower, her mother scooped her up into her arms before holding her high above her, spinning once, twice and more before her arms buckled, dropping the toddler back into her bosom. She planted a kiss on the girl's cheeks, nose and forehead, who sloppily mirrored her mother's affections. After a playful grimace, the spit was wiped clean onto the little girl's tummy before they both giggled, and her mother held a finger to her tiny lips. "With the trees we are safe, if we are to wander, we must wander safely. The woods are better to 'ide in."

The little one grumbled as she was carried into the shelter of the trees, "I do not want to 'ide, mama." She pouted as a deep grief welled up inside her, too big and deep than what is meant for someone so small. She watched as her mother's eyes, deep, warm red with darker rings abound, drooped to watch her own footsteps. She pouted too, nodding. They'd had such a conversation before.

"It is what we must be doin'. Our lands will take care of us, but only if we do as much as we can."

"'Tis true, darlin'." it was her father, stocky and strong with a curved nose and thick brows who weaved his hands under his daughter's arms, taking her into his. "Someday we can go 'ome, but that may be a long, long time."

"B-but I thought it was all our 'ome?" The little girl was spilling over now as fat tears dribbled down her face and drool collected at the corner of her lips. "I am tired and I want to go 'ome!"

Her parents began to hum something simple now as her papa rocked her, holding her right and tight. "We've not to know when but we do know 'ow. For now, we live 'owever we can." They continued to walk through the thick trees as the crying quieted, her parents knowing time could quell such pain.

A clearing, brief and sunny, lit up a patch on the forest floor. Thick tendrils of lichen coiled around the oaks and walnut trees, and as they came to stand in it, her father held her out, laying on his wide forearms. The sun illuminated her rosy, swollen cheeks, and cast a light that danced in her eyes, riding the bands of colors in her irises. Her mother cooed over her four-year-old, "You are full of kindness and love. No one can ever take that from you, little Edda."

Then Edda was falling to the cold, hard ground, her mother's face contorting as the golden sun above her grew speckled in crimson.

"Marion!"

"No..." she cried, paralyzed in sleep, her eyelids unwilling to open.

A hand clapped her cheek and when she didn't respond, it came down upon her face once again. Her eyes snapped open as she glared at Camille who cradled her hand, gazing at Edda in disgust. Touching her own face, it was cool and smooth, whereas Camille's palm was beginning to swell. Edda cocked a brow. "Yes?"

Camille stepped back, clasping her hands in front of herself before clearing her throat. Her voice cracked, "The children have informed me that Martin is missing."

Eyes wide, Edda looked at her tapestried doorway, seeing several legs and feet waiting on the side of the sun, unable and unwilling to move it. In their stillness, she could not tell which child spoke, "We looked about the house first, not wanting to cause a fuss, but could not find him."

Another voice, almost the same. "Our window is open."

And another. "He's gone."

FOUR

Edda rushed from her bed, pushing Camille by the arm, then tearing through the fabric separating her from the children. They all stood staring at her, before mechanically stepping aside, one by one. Some showed worry and concern whereas others wore masks of stone. They stared at her in her sleeveless gown and paled. She thundered through them, down the hall and stairs in haste. A vague fear of punishment loomed behind her panic. It couldn't matter now, it shouldn't matter.

Martin could still be saved, and perhaps, she could be forgiven.

The front door was unlocked. She gasped in gratitude and thrust the door open, hearing the hinges of the door rattle with her strength. On the stoop, she let her jaw drop as she yelled for him, screaming from deep inside, "Martin!"

The others were behind her now, watching as she continued to yell, pausing to turn to them. Camille was behind the children, rubbing her arm, her face contorted with pain, anger and fright. The children shambled in front of her as a sorry shield of sorts. Edda's voice carried as she narrowed her eyes, "You cower behind them while 'e is alone. Why are you afraid?"

Camille flinched at her words as Edda flashed off the stoop and into the dark night, screaming for the missing boy.

Cobblestone cracked beneath her as she ran clear of the path and into the field they played in not long before. The long grass was wet beneath her bare feet as she dug her toes in, turning about, projecting her voice as far as she could, loud enough for the world to hear, "Martin! Come back! I will protect you! Please!"

The wind roared past her as she continued to bellow into it. She turned in the direction it blew and weaved back and forth into the woods, scouring the grounds and roots and lichen encrusted tree trunks. Round and round the orphanage, outside the backyard's stone wall to the window outside the children's room. He could have been hurt while climbing down, wood scarce to grab onto. She looked nearby, high and low, but found nothing.

Now, she walked amongst the trees, her fingertips glancing them in hopes they could tell her something of the boy. Dim light poured over her in a clearing as she sucked in her breath before letting it go once more, along with the boy's name, "Martin!" She fell to her knees as the light above her grew warm, and she began to cry in desperation as his name slipped from her lips. Over and over, until who she called began to change along with her ragged voice, "Mama, Papa, please."

She sat and cried, no longer speaking, resolving herself to prevent this again. A dove began cooing nearby, a crow began cawing, then another and another until a murder of them sang disjointed and hoarse. The beings of the wood lamented that which seemed lost.

She knew it was her fault.

"No more," she whispered in the loudness around her, planting her hands on the grass beneath her, pushing herself up, rubbing her eyes and smearing dirt along her cheeks. Hollow and shambling, she walked back to the Orphanage's main entryway, having to knock at the now locked door. She rested her head against it, numb and unable to think, firmly rapping with her knuckles.

After some time, the door came away as she was handed a shawl. "Cover yourself, the children are already distressed."

"Martin is gone, I could not find-"

"Put it on, now."

Edda swiped the shawl from Camille, wondering why she obeyed with such complacency. She looked up at the perfect woman, her face lined and eyes downcast. Edda had seen such a face before. Anger stirred as she recognized what she so often saw in the mirror, what she saw in her arms, scarred with red ribbons.

"What 'ave you done?"

Camille stepped back, glancing all around Edda, not meeting her eyes, "How dare you speak with such accusati-" Then, she was on the floor, blood dappling the stone as she sputtered, her cheek swelling in the shape of a young girl's hand.

"I know that look, you've made me live with it!" Edda fell to her knees, snatching up Camille by the front of her gown, shawl falling off her shoulders, twisted scars that matched her agate eyes visible to the world. "I've seen it before! When I was brought 'ere, to this forsaken place! Where is Martin? Where are my parents?!"

Camille's expression twisted as she gripped Edda's wrists. "Your parents? No, no, not me. I took care of you after they abandoned you here, Marion!"

"Do not call me Marion! That is not who I am!"

Through bloody teeth, Camille sneered, "Here, you are Marion, here, you are mine!"

Edda whipped her hand back, drawn to let it collapse into Camille's face when something shattered and glass shards fell down both their faces, gliding down Edda's nose. A child rushed her, taking hold of her arm while a few more pried at her fingers, trying to free Camille. A wooden bowl crashed against Edda's back and shoulders until it frantically found her head. "Let our Camille go!"

She abided, and Camille along with the other children fell back as the younger ones began to sniffle and scorn Edda, "You're cruel! How could you hurt her? She protects us!"

On the ground, attempting to shield her mouth, a small smirk crossed the matron's face as she caught her breath and shuddered, regaining composure. "I will send word for the King, and he will arrive within days. You best get to the basement and mind yourself, else he will do worse by you than you've ever done to your dear children." She spat a clot into her apron as the children around her fawned.

Edda rose, weighing her options as she felt the pain of obedience clasp onto her once more. To disobey and truly be a monster to the children, to potentially lose her life, or to once more fall in line, prey to those who are bigger than her, who are far worse.

Or to run, never stopping, like when she was a small thing and her family something that had to be hidden.

She traced the scars on her arms before she made slow, plodding steps into the basement. Camille called to her, her tone gentle, "A smart choice, Marion." A child closed the door behind her, fiddling with the lock. Edda could hear voices just beyond the door, speaking with the poor Camille.

"What are the red lines all on her arms?"

"Child, those are the marks left by the evil that controls her when she punishes us. She is wicked and we must stay strong against her, lest she'll hurt us all."

"D-do they spread? Will I be like her?" Panic.

"No dear child, do not fear. She is locked away in the basement now."

"Can we not send her away forever?" An older child now.

"We cannot. There is strength in numbers, both for us and for her."

The stairs creaked beneath Edda as she descended, having heard enough. The dirt floor of the basement was clean and cold as she shuffled to a corner, feeling the walls to guide her in the utter blackness. She ran fingers through the grooves in her arms, feeling the stiffness; opposite the skin on her hands, the depressed scars were as hard as the ground below her.

She curled up and closed her eyes, wishing time to stop and for herself to turn to stone, to feel nothing.

To be nothing.

* * *

"My sweet, when you were born, you 'ad no eyes and beautiful agates were slipped in."

As a child, Edda would tap around her eyes and her lids, feeling the softness underneath them.

"You're to make 'er think they'll pop out."

Her mother would giggle at her father's retort, the small child still in shock and awe at what she was told no matter how many times she heard it. It was one of the many fables her mother spoke of, but in her bones, Edda still believed they held truth.

She relived those memories in her isolation, not knowing how much time passed.

"More people, like us, mama?"

"Mhmm, many, many more," her mother's voice echoed.

"Where, mama?"

At this, mother would turn to father as he would shake his head heavy with mourning. Her mother would smooth her hair and kiss her head. "We are of love and kindness, do not forget." Edda, in her stupor, pet her own hair and pressed gentle fingers to her temple.

"Others, too?" she whispered into the dark.

"Yes, of all kinds, child, all across the land."

In the corner, she mimicked the movements of her mother of the past, spreading her arms wide and then taking on her role, touching her eyelids and asking more and more questions as though she were living the memory when it first occurred. "Their eyes stone, too? Are they love and kindness?"

In the basement, her mother's and father's chuckles reverberated, her papa answered, "Not quite, they ..." he would pause, searching for a word a child could understand. "They show other things and are of other things?"

Edda cocked her head, as a child and as an adolescent.

Her mother's voice perked her up, her tongue dancing, "Some are of a passion for life and family, some are dreamers, some curious, others creators! Some do not 'ave a mama or papa. They simply are."

"What 'appened?" Edda's question hung in the air of the basement.

The door lock clicked and light flickered down the stairs as Edda hugged her legs, squeezing into herself, trying to blend into the wall. A man clanked down the stairs wearing all but a metal helmet, his chest piece emblazoned with a rising sun. Inwards, Edda groaned, stiffening as he spoke with resolution, commanding, "Come, girl. The King waits for you. Do not keep him."

FIVE

Edda wobbled up the stairs, her footstep belying how weak she truly felt. She shielded her eyes as the daylight assaulted her gaze, slow in warming her to world above. The man she assumed was a knight gripped her arm, tugging her forward, his voice hoarse, "Do not be so dramatic. You were merely down there a couple nights."

From the stories she read and was told, even prisoners had light, some food, and drink. She decided it best not to answer as they rounded a corner into the sitting room. Camille had her back to the unlit fireplace, her eyes flashing from anxiety to fury as she spotted Edda, her cheek still swollen. Across from her sat a man, the top of his head a golden blonde.

King Huxley.

Forced around the chair and made to kneel before him, Edda glimpsed a young child beside him, perhaps nine or ten at most, his hair a sun-kissed brown. He eyed the young woman with curiosity. As she knelt, she kept her head lowered, before the king commanded otherwise. Upon meeting the king's amber eyes, she wondered if they were once stones, despite knowing the two of them were nothing alike.

"Lady Camille has told me of your..." King Huxley turned his tongue about, clacking his rings together. "Sins and misbehaviors." Edda kept her eyes on him, his large, fox fur lined robe, shining red and clashing with the plain chair he sat in. Out of her periphery, she noticed the teapot and cups had golden décor, twisting and creating elegant vines – a set Camille kept in her room for such an occasion. If a stranger meandered into the midst of everything, they could tell who belonged and who did not. King Huxley's voice vibrated through the room, "What say you, little Marion?" His voice dripped with poise, power.

A hint of malice.

Edda tried not to think on her answer, knowing that if she spoke ill, her life would be forfeit. "Yes, your Majesty."

The king chuckled, leading his boy by the hand, in front of Edda. "Tell me, Alastair, what do you *feel* when you look into her eyes?"

The boy strode forward, placing his hand under Edda's chin, raising her eyes to meet his light brown ones. His face flickered with conflict as he dropped his hand, turning to his ruler. "Father, I feel warm, as though loved, like how mother made me feel."

"Be wary, child. *This* is the manipulation of their kind." Huxley stood, pacing the room before producing a large vial of clear liquid, placing it in front of Camille. "If she is to ever be less than willing and obedient, make her drink some to placate her. We cannot be letting a wolf run free." He nodded to the knight who took Alastair's place in front of the kneeling girl.

"Look here," the knight gruffed, and she stared into his dull blue eyes. He hesitated before bringing his gauntlet down across her face. She barely moved, feeling next to nothing, her face unchanging as she looked at him. So he struck again and again with both sides of his gloves, until her cheeks bore discernable lacerations.

The slaps echoed in the sitting area, only adults and Alastair present to bear witness to what Edda deemed a light punishment. When the knight withdrew, she turned her gaze to Camille, whose face was marred with sick retribution that drowned under the shock of Edda's unshaken eyes.

This, the King paid notice to.

"What does she care for?"

"The children."

"Then bring one." King Huxley's voice was tempered and cold. Arrogant, he was.

Camille rose and scuttled out of the room. Time stretched as Alastair looked between his father, his knight, and Edda who could see an anxious fear and temper build in his eyes.

A small girl was brought in, one who was already fearful and ireful of Edda. She, who wore an orphan's plain linen dress, could not have been much younger than the prince decked in a royal crimson garb. The disparity was disgusting.

"Little girl, close your eyes and know that what comes is because of Marion."

The small girl glanced around her before swallowing. She began to tremble. "She is wicked."

"Indeed she is. Now close your eyes and do not move."

I am good, I am kind, I am of love. I do not hurt you, I never have. You are too young to see the strings, the wires orchestrated. I do not blame you. I have a gift and these people wish only to conquer and taint.

The girl locked eyes with Edda, flinching, arguing with herself, to run or accept, to know the pain and hate or accept the truth in Edda's eyes. She scowled as her mind reminded her of the traumas inflicted on her littleness, and who wrought them. She closed her eyes.

The knight took the flat edge of a blade, settling it to the side of the girl's head, above her ear, pulling the ear taught with his other hand. His face was uncertain as he bit his lip.

Unbeknownst to herself, Edda began rocking, forward and back, more and more rapidly as tension grew as with the king's impatience: "Do it," he commanded.

"No!" Edda flung herself catching the knight by the legs, his knife only managing to cut off the tip of the girl's ear. She began to fall as Camille rushed to her, comforting the girl she would not stand up for.

Edda pulsed with adrenaline, the deafening pulse of her own heart filling her head as the knight scrambled to his feet. Alastair grabbed the knife, pointing it at Edda where she lay at his feet. "Should we not kill such a demon, father? Others will cease to suffer otherwise!"

"Like flies to rot, they always find each other. There are worse out there, believe it or not. We require her alive. What better place than here?" The question was rhetorical as he snatched the weapon from his son, walking to the girl in Camille's arms. "Besides, we are not brutish enough to slaughter."

Edda began to weep and claw at her arms. Camille began to beg, "Your highness, please, I beg of you," her voice was firm, "Marion has learned her lesson. She will not misbehave again, you have my word."

King Huxley stared hard at the woman before glaring at the crumpled girl he knew by another name.

"Very well, I'm sure it will not be the last time we will cross paths." He handed the blade back to his knight and clapped his hands together. "Thank you, Camille. I will write you in the coming days."

Camille bowed her head as the royal party made their leave, the Orphanage quiet as a tomb. Some of the children appeared in the doorway, one with a bowl of warm water, another with clean cloth – Edda had taught them how to treat injuries. They gathered around the wounded child as Camille poured gratuitous, honeyed and encouraging words from her lips.

Edda remained curled up, sobbing.

The children sent nasty looks to the top of Edda's head as she shielded her face, all whispering to the injured girl that all is better and will be well, that to behave is of utmost importance. That the better they are, the more likely they would be adopted and the less likely they would ever be at the hands of the demon in their midst. It's a necessary evil they've been told.

Camille instructed them to bring fresh water and cloth after the girl was cleaned up and ushered away. When they arrived, their Matron took the bowl and sat on the floor aside Edda and began cleaning the marks along the broken girl's cheeks. Her wounds looked like cracks.

"Lady Camille, why do you care for her?" One voice expressed what the other children wondered, bewildered.

"She is mine, and it is my burden. I am of love and kindness and cannot let her waste away."

Her words made Edda stop breathing for several moments as they stabbed her deep inside.

Camille motioned the children to leave as they awed at the saintly nature of their Lady. Once out of earshot, she leaned over the agate eyed girl, her voice just audible, "This is much bigger than us, Marion. The children must be protected, and without you, they could not be. We all must sacrifice." Edda nodded, powerlessness ebbing back into her being: she had to do all she could to protect the little ones, it was all she was meant for now.

Hefting Edda to stand on her own feet, Camille led her up the stairs to her bedroom to rest. Several heavy blankets were laid over her and the curtains were tied shut, washing the room in black. Camille placed a kiss on Edda's forehead, both of them wincing at the forced motion, and then departed with few words, "I'll need you strong in the morning."

The dark of the room filled Edda's eyes, and she took the time to rest.

* * *

This was her life, but at least she had her door back. There was no longer a rising sun to view on her entryway, but it was once more tacked over her fireplace. The door no longer was a struggle to open, but now her room was sullied by the Kingdom's and the dominant religion's motif. She could not remove it: that was one of the new rules. She saw it all once she awoke from her long sleep after the King's visit, so many months ago.

Everything was normal once more, whether it was a comfort or not, she could not decide. She cooked, she cleaned, she minded the children with care and distance and did the more strenuous tasks as the children did their study under Lady Camille. She was never allowed to sit and listen, although as she grew older, it was something she grew to be grateful of.

She hung wet laundry to dry in the back garden, large enough it was to accommodate all the linens, the children inside now as she was able to enjoy the sun that seeped into the backyard through the trees for a few hours of the day. Next she would begin dinner, for the children were drained after their handful of hours studying and rereading the many texts they were meant to absorb.

She took the time to roll up her sleeves and observe the way the sun glinted off her scars, how they were hard and concave. Looking closer, the light from above her showed darker lines in her scars, a small variety of colors and warm hues.

She tugged her sleeve down, glad no one could witness her deformities, glad no new ones were created since Huxley and his brood were there.

Letting her cool fingers graze her cheek, she was pleased no scars remained on her face.

Glad she could find a small nugget of contentment in her complacent existence, she whispered in between the drying linens, "Mama, papa, am I doin'-do-doing well?"

No one answered her and after disappointment rang through her, it disappeared into the endless void of her belly. She sighed and turned to enter the kitchen, wishing she could revisit old memories or dream of times since passed. It was difficult to recall anything that was etched into her mind as a little girl—anything there surfaced on its own will.

All that played in her mind now was a mantra she chanted in silence: *get through the day and then the next, find solace in between.*

It helped her avoid any trouble so far, the sentence coming to her in a dream, spoken by an old woman, reverent and omniscient.

She had no reason not to trust her as she cast cut potatoes into a boiling pot, followed by garden greens and meat gifted to them by a family who recently adopted a child. Camille had been busy with requests to visit the children of late, and several families left satisfied. The dinner table was half empty at this point.

A relief to all, even the girl missing part of her ear was now part of a loving family. At least, one could hope so.

Stirring the pot, she felt more at ease with less eyes on her, less eggshells to walk on. Camille seemed so tired that Edda could even take deeper breaths, a small but noticeable reprieve. She even caught herself smiling now, given she was alone and not looking in a mirror. It was the smaller things in life.

She stacked her trolley with utensils and full bowls, the remaining stew left over the flickering flame of the cook top. She set the table, the children able to sit and eat without her watch and her without theirs whenever lessons were done. It was abnormally silent today, but it let her focus on the absence in her mind. The only bother was how late the children were today.

Shrugging, Edda made her way to the kitchen once more, busying herself with crushing herbs and salting meat for storage in the small space below a kitchen hatch. She hummed to herself, senseless notes that echoed deep in her throat. Once more, she caught herself smiling.

"Marion?"

Edda jumped, wiping her hands on her apron, turning to face Camille, her under eyes darkened with fatigue, a gentle smile on her face. The smile both sparked curiosity and wariness from Edda.

"Yes, Lady Camille?"

From behind the woman, she led a small boy who Edda recognized. Not knowing whether to smile or remain stoic, she glanced at Camille, who nodded and parted her plump lips to say, "Martin was returned to us."

Edda planted her hands on her thighs, leaning forward and looking the boy in the eyes. He was thinner, glancing between the nearby wall and the girl's eyes. "Martin, 'ow grand it is to see you. It brightens my day," she smiled. In the months he was gone, she felt she had matured more, better controlled herself and her affectionate gestures. It was what she needed to learn.

That, and she had turned sixteen.

Camille patted Martin's back and he mumbled, "It is good to be back, Marion."

All Edda could do was smile, regardless of how he must still hate her. She straightened up, stretching her shoulders when another boy, a few heads taller than Martin with black hair, stepped out from behind Camille. His eyes held twinkling embers. They were warm, playful, and curious.

"This is Lowell. He found Martin a ways away and brought him here. He, too, is alone."

Trying not to show her inklings of the boy, she held her smile, greeting the newcomer who strode forward, grasping her hand to shake it. "I am Lowell, I am fifteen, and I am very much starved, yeah? May we eat?"

Edda's eyes darted to Camille, who looked just as surprised as Edda, perhaps even amused, but the concern was evident in her eyes, a paler impression of what marked every feature of Edda's face.

"Let us eat, Marion. Please, gather some more bowls for our two additions, and why not join us yourself."

Lowell beamed at all of them in turn, holding up his hands to help carry his portion. Camille side-eyed him as she gave an approving nod, Edda giving him a portion of stew, before taking a bowl for herself and Martin, who had fled the kitchen seconds before.

Awkward, they all sat, the resident children dumbfounded by Martin and Lowell, but most afflicted by Edda eating with them at the table. Lowell sat next to her and at either side of them were empty chairs. Camille sat at the head of the table, surrounded by the ones who had not yet been adopted. Slow in their movements, they ate as Lowell took gracious spoonfuls in between looking at his new companions, locking eyes with near each one.

Camille cleared her throat. "Everyone, as I previously introduced, the young lad at the far end next to Marion, is Lowell. He has just arrived and is not yet privy to our rules here." Lowell waved and grinned with all his teeth, bits of green stuck to his front two. Camille gave an exasperated smile and continued, "And tonight, we welcome back Martin." All clapped as Lowell gently rapped the table with his knuckles before turning to Edda, grinning ear to ear.

She almost tapped her knuckles on the table too. How dangerous this could be, to all of them. Her arms began to tingle and ache.

Soon as it started, it ended; they continued to eat in near silence. One of the older children, about twelve, broke the quiet, "Marion, I have a question for you."

The girl paused, her brows furrowed. Across the table, Camille looked between the two, squinting, "Yes?" Edda's voice was tentative.

"If we call something that is difficult 'hard,' why do we not call something that is easy 'soft?'"

Camille and Edda paused. Conversation at the table was not forbidden, but rare was it to occur, and for it to begin with such randomness! Edda saw Lowell smirking next to her. She shrugged. "Curious indeed, but I am afraid I cannot answer."

The child nodded, resolute. "Marion," he sucked his teeth, "what is sugary sweet and sticky? What comes from bees?"

Edda sighed, "You know very well what it is."

"I wish to hear you say it, tattered-tongue."

Looking to Camille, who appeared not to care, Edda found herself at a loss. Martin squirmed in his seat.

"Do you get called that often?" Lowell interjects, wanting to be heard not caring who listened.

She whispered back to him, "Not often. Do not worry." Indeed, it was true. Camille had first called her by the name while she was young, only using it sporadically as Edda grew older. One of the children must have overheard.

One of the quieter children piped up, "Marion, you have grown far too quiet. Perhaps you need to remember your place beneath us. The teachings say you are inherently evil, opposite us. A lesser demon, but easily controlled. How does it feel for the shoe to be on the other foot?"

Once more, Edda looked to Camille, afraid of impending punishment, not wishing to bring it on herself. Once more, Camille looked down at her bowl, containing herself and her own thoughts.

"Should we not pester her? She may punish us again…" It was Martin now, letting the words ooze from his mouth.

Lowell slammed his fists in disgust. "'Ow rotten, you all. I may 'ave been wanderin' without me parents for a while, but I know 'ow to proper treat someone! Where is your shame? You all ought to be punished!" He glared at the children, some of whom let their spoons fall, jaws dropping in shock. Edda reached for the young man's hand, resting it on the table and shaking her head, her eyes wide.

"Lady Camille, he's one too!"

They began to panic, unrest and unease spreading from child to child.

"Together, they'll both hurt us!"

They began to get up from their seats, trying to crowd their matron.

Camille cast knowing eyes at Lowell and Edda, gripping her spoon tight as her pupils began to cower behind her, "That is enough. Take your seats and finish eating."

"But—"

"The teachings tell us to be aware, strong and unafraid." She relaxed her hand, her knuckles regaining their color. "Then be so."

With reluctance, they obeyed, keeping their heads down, sneaking peeks at the evil at their table, one of which vibrating with fear. Lowell began to open his mouth in protest, but Edda squeezed his hand, tan beneath hers. He resumed eating until they were all dismissed.

* * *

Lowell was made to sleep in the same room as the others, although they insisted he take the lone bunk on the farthest wall from the rest of them. It did not concern him one bit as he was able to shift the bed how he liked as he would throw his pillow to his feet and flip about, gazing out of the window he had to himself.

He tugged at the heavy curtain, letting moonlight spill in as he laid on his stomach, knees bent and feet in the air, swaying. "Stuffy, yeah?"

No one replied.

Lowell snorted as he began to tap at the glass in front of him, using his fingertips as though he played a piano. He was not tired in the least bit, reaching for the top of the window and undoing the curtains. Someone stirred, silent eyes watched the newcomer as he somehow fastened the curtains to the top bunk.

Hopping down, trying as best he could to drag his bed in silence in front of the window.

The moonlight disappeared from the room, trapped behind the curtains and filling the bottom bunk of his bedframe. He crawled in, giggling and basking in the silver glow.

"What are you doing?" Martin stood outside the heavy fabrics, little fist held awkward and aloft, wondering if he should attempt a knock.

Light greeted him, along with Lowell's large grin. "Come sit with me!"

"It's bedtime. If you are caught, you will be punished."

"Were you punished for runnin' away?"

Martin grumbled, "No."

"Then come sit."

"If he is to interact with you, you will sully him and his soul. You are a bad thing," a voice retorted from the darkness, hiding beneath blankets.

"Who says? An old woman, an angry man, or some damn book?" Lowell taunted the hidden voice, holding out a hand to the young boy he'd returned. Martin smirked before letting his face fall once more, rubbing at his chin. "If we are to be punished, we will be punished."

"You do not know what it is like."

"Perhaps I would like to find out, yeah?" Lowell was cool, playful.

Martin crawled in next to him, lit up by the moon. The curtain fell behind him in the little fort as he pulled his knees to his chest, resting his chin on top. The two sat in silence for what seemed like an hour.

Time can fly or crawl in a child's mind.

"What did you do to get punished?"

Martin strained, remembering his time in the basement, trying to recall what led to it. "I visited Marion in the kitchen and later, I brought her a flower in the field and played too loudly."

"Those are nothin'," Lowell proclaimed, shifting his weight to his side to face who he thought of as a friend. "Did Marion do anythin'? Before your punishin'?"

Looking out the window, then to the moon in the sky, Martin pondered again, his mind and himself young and still unable to grasp most of life's experiences. "She played with me. Picked me up and spun me round. When I gave her the flower, she cried and told me she was sorry."

"For?"

Martin's shoulders rose as he shook his head in utter loss, letting them fall after. Lowell remained silent, looking behind himself, peeking through the curtains, gazing into the blackness of the room for minutes on end.

Martin grew uncomfortable, "What are you thinking?"

"Mmm? Oh, that for 'ow 'orrible the children at the table acted today, you'd think they'd be punished. You received a swattin' for much less, that is sure." He let the moonlight encapsulate them once more as he turned to the younger boy. "Maybe it was not meant for you. Maybe you were just a means to an end."

"What does that mean?"

Lowell shrugged, "I know what it means but I cannot explain it. Maybe someday you'll just get it, hm?"

Martin snickered, "You are odd."

The older boy smiled back at him. "And you are my friend."

Six

As days turned to weeks and weeks turned to months, Martin and Lowell became thick as thieves. Edda watched every day as Martin spent more time with the boy, sitting closer at the dining table, reading together, and even leaving their religious teachings together.

Lowell did not stutter, but he did not care who heard his true voice. He wasn't made to fear it, and he was above being shamed for it. He would roll his eyes and scoff at anyone who made unfavorable marks towards him. He did the same as he walked out of the study after hours of what he called nonsense. Edda was surprised he was even allowed to attend.

She played a minimal but necessary role in everyone's lives of late. She kept a large distance from everyone; most made it easy. Lowell tried to play with her but she had to shoo him away many occasions, the wall around her heart easier to build than erecting one over his.

Martin still eyed Edda with suspicion and fear, and as though he always had a question flitting about his head. His mental scars ran deep as he spent the longest being punished in all Edda's time.

There was turnover in the orphans once more as most of the children were new and of varying ages, all younger than Edda, of course. With this, more were disciplined, as ordered by Camille.

Edda had the blessing to witness each incident firsthand before making her way to the basement.

One child was inconsolable, tugging Edda's dress, distraught until she scooped up the child, bouncing her atop her hip and shushing, humming, in an attempt to calm the wailing girl. That girl stayed in the basement for a couple days for not controlling herself better.

Another was a small boy who had run through the Orphanage, tripping on himself and bumping into Camille as she sat drinking from a teacup. It slipped from her hand and shattered. The boy stood shocked, just as Camille was. With urgency, Edda began to clean the mess, instructing the little one to help. He did, and when he began to apologize profusely, Camille watched on, looking between the two of them as though they were colluding. Edda noticed Camille's face and her lack of reaction to the boy, and attempted to reassure him, "It is alright. It was an accident that will not repeat."

"Indeed, it will not! This must be punished."

That boy was in the basement three days. She felt heavier each time she walked the steps.

The next day, a child spilled food on themselves and when Camille called for the child to be reprimanded, Edda stood steady and immovable. She just escaped the basement and refused to return. A child lay upstairs, sobbing because of her. There was no time for Edda to recover, to distance herself.

She stood, an immovable a statue, Camille tugging at her limbs before slinging her arm around the girl's throat, pouring a viscous liquid into Edda's gaping maw as she sought air. Her eyes began dancing to bright sparkling stars she could see inside the walls.

Her body went limp and she woke in darkness, a frightened child in front of her, vomit running down both their torsos. Her mind reeled.

That was the first time the King's elixir was used.

Closing her bedroom door after the recent bout of being away, Edda could not focus on where she was, unable fathom what she was.

Torn as a caretaker and as a punisher, forced to be both.

She peered in the mirror, gazing at her dulling eyes. Not believing in what she saw, she wiped at the mirror, hoping to see vibrancy once more. Yet she stared at herself, not recognizing what she came to be. She whispered for her mother and father, knowing she would hear nothing.

She hadn't heard their voices in what felt like forever: no resurfacing memories, no dreams.

Her parents would forsake her as the demon she became, her choice or not. She was a rotten thing to let live.

Reaching into her drawer, she pulled out the armlet her mother had hidden on her thigh last she saw her. Turning it over in her hands, she let her fingers glide over the gold, smooth and pliable with the right give. The smooth surface interrupted by bulging strands of gold that wrapped around like a vine. The inside was flat as she moved to place it around her upper arm, never having done so before.

There was a shine in the mirror as she watched herself, motioning with the arm band from her arm to her neck. She wondered if it would fit, fingering the outer prongs to bend them.

The armlet was warming with her touch, her vacant gaze drifting from her face down to the stone that sat centered in the heirloom. It gleamed like her mother's eyes did.

Striking a fresh match, she held it over the almond-shaped gem before lighting a candle on her vanity. From every angle, she observed the red stone, the engravings inside too perfect to be natural, too impossible to have been done by hand.

The stone was an agate, the center boasting a large black spot, a golden outline separating it from the deep red that surrounded it. From the very edges of the yellow, lines of white emerged. Edda held the armlet in what she assumed was the correct orientation, observing the thin marks that sprouted from the center spot. On both sides, they curved up then down, like a wing of a regal bird in flight, with several smaller lines splitting off, following a downward swoop.

She hadn't paid much mind to the piece before, not caring for gold, the sunny, rich man's metal. It could not change her life, it could not bring her parents back, and it could not save her. Today, however, she needed the reminder of her parents.

She squinted at the stone further, scrutinizing it, just making out a black line that shot straight down from the yellow ring, a thicker wave of a line cutting perpendicular to the straight one, riding along the bottom of the visible stone.

Tender and hesitant, Edda outstretched her thumb to caress the intricate agate. Grazing the surface, she paused as it appeared to react to her touch, a slight dampness to it. Swallowing, she pressed, feeling the stone flex beneath the pad of her finger.

Sucking in a breath, she snapped her right hand away, cradling the piece in the other. She stared as the stone glistened, moist.

The door opened at the corner of her eyes, her periphery playing a trick before the figure in the threshold became clear. For a moment she saw the silhouettes of her parents.

"Marion, I'm afraid I've made a bit of a mess. I have to ask you to clean it for me."

The armlet found its way into its drawer, closed inside in a single motion.

Camille quirked a brow, opening her mouth to question. Watching the girl, she closed her mouth. Edda tugged at her sleeves, no longer doing anything to soothe the aches that spider-webbed her arms, and stood to follow her matron.

Down the stairs and into the parlor, Camille motioned to broken porcelain scattered on the floor, sticky with a drying liquid.

Camille leaned over the fireplace, feeling the heat dance over her long features, the flicker lighting up her face as she stared at it. She listened to the scrapings and clinking of broken glassware as it was deposited into a wooden bucket before being tossed out.

A child could be heard giggling upstairs, past bedtime. Both the women knew who it was.

"I'll dispose of the porcelain. You can set it aside."

Hesitant, Edda nodded and set the bin on a table along the wall before standing still. Her arms twitched as she awaited dismissal, wishing to leave of her own accord.

"Why not take a seat, Marion?"

Stunned, the girl plodded to a low-backed chair, setting herself down at the very edge, and stared at Camille's taut back.

Rocking her head side to side, Camille rolled her shoulders, her back oscillating between straight and hunched, between control and release. She raised her hands to rest on the mantel, aware of the warm eyes on her back, set into the cold exterior that surrounded them. The juxtaposition in the orphan girl's body was not lost on Camille, nor were her own feelings of want and dutiful loyalty. Fear and love. Nature and teachings. Then there was the hate and envy, unopposed.

"How do the children fare?"

Edda swallowed. "Well, I believe."

"Do you believe the last boy has learned his lesson?"

Edda shifted her weight and straightened up as Camille turned to face her, the light from the fire turning her to a black void with the slightest glisten of her eyes showing. Edda spoke to the darkness, "I do."

"And you?"

"Pardon?"

Camille strode forward before kneeling next to Edda, taking the girl's hand into her own before letting her fingers glide up her arms, tracing the grooves underneath the fabric, touching fresh marks and making Edda's arm burn as she tried to hold herself steady.

How she wished to shove Camille away and run.

Edda could only stare as she watched her matron, who seemed fixated. Camille's head raised to meet Edda's eyes, the fire now casting half her face aglow as the other half remained black past her nose. Dark circles and exhaustion made her eyes appear to sink deeper into her face as she repeated her question with an empty voice, "How do you fare, Marion?"

Edda gave a subtle swallow. "I am well."

Camille scoffed and pushed the girl's arm away, weaving around the small table and sitting with her back to the flames, her face becoming a shadow once more. "I report to the king weekly. I tell him you are doing well." Camille's voice did not lend a positive light to her words.

Edda clasped her hands and fiddled with her fingers.

"I tell him the children behave well after your disciplines."

The girl's fingers slowed as she listened. She wished to sleep and sink into herself.

"He knows about Lowell, how he is of your ilk. He wishes to be here for his discipline."

"No h-heh-he is not." The words slipped off her tongue without thinking. She kept her hands firm in her lap, trying not to show her apprehension at the statement.

For the longest time, Lowell evaded the basement despite his behavior being the 'naughtiest' of all the children. With purpose he disobeyed, pushed boundaries and spoke out against the teachings that were hammered into the orphans for hours each day. Edda often wondered why he was not brought down to the deep, dank place.

He was being saved.

"Oh, my tatter-tongued girl, I have to remind myself how deceiving you can be. We both know the truth of things to come."

"When?"

"Soon enough, he tells me."

The pit in Edda's stomach pitched and spat at her, telling her to run, to fight back, to gather herself and to tear through the plans ahead. She pushed the feeling down, pushed herself back into her proper place, knowing how small she was, how powerless.

The quiet strained the forever tense air between them closer to a breaking point. The fire cast flickering shadows into corners of the room, the tall ceiling enshrouded in bouts of endless darkness before light illuminated its recesses for split moments of time, letting them fall back into bleakness.

Edda wished to be swallowed by it, for whatever way the future led her, she would fall hopeless and alone in suffering, wishing for only a cold and empty end.

She quaked in the cushioned seat, unable to act.

Camille broke the silence, "I wanted children of my own."

Edda's eyes were drooping in exhaustion and overwhelming futility, but she managed to drag them to the abyss of Camille's shadowed face. Her lips parted on their own. "Why tell me this?"

"Because I wish to tell someone of it." She leaned back, resting her long limbs on the arm rests, the horizontal hems running along her dress sleeves reminding Edda of a crow's legs, her imagination playing with the dark shades before her, transforming the stretched limbs of Camille and her dark features into a biding crow who does not wait for their meal to die before dipping their beak in.

Camille turned her head, the illusion of a beak dissipating before Edda's eyes, the sight almost humorous. A small chuckle escaped her lips.

"Amusing, isn't it? How the one I turn to is you."

"Not at all, my Lady."

Camille eyed her curiously and continued telling her plight, an overlay of a cawing, crooning crow echoed in her words; a bird only Edda could hear in her state of internal rot and decay. "I was too perfect to be married, too intimidating, too unrelenting. It was my far removed cousin who gave me the orphanage to live out this 'fantasy.' Somewhere, a little distant in my lineage, was the name Huxley."

Edda gave no response to the revelation much to Camille's continual ire.

She sighed, "I lacked a *maternal* warmth. Though many children came to my stoop, they were difficult." Her voice cracked as her eyes grew moist. "Orphans are hard to care for when they misbehave, and I hadn't the heart to do a thing. I was more rigid than now as well, and no one dared approach me. Yet I do love them, I truly do, each one."

Edda watched a wet streak glisten down Camille's cheek through faux feathers she imagined. She wanted to feel something for the matron.

Camille continued, "I wanted love from them too, but I am afraid I was unsure how to give it. My cousin instructed me to remain true to the teachings, to hold a discerning eye for what children came through." She wiped at the wetness on her face, inhaling deep, "He brought you to me."

Edda raised her head, trying to recall her first night at the Orphanage.

Camille kept her head lowered. "You were so small and *dirty*. He knew who you were the moment he saw you. The royal family and members of the church are keen, attuned to know how, well, *different* you are." Her tone was fluctuating now, between admiration and a deep, dripping hate. "As young as you were, the other children adored you, doted on you and listened to you. Even I did, once."

Camille began to chuckle to herself as the fire dimmed behind her, sending a request for more fuel to burn and gnaw into. The two sat in stalemate, allowing the fire to die out, daring the other to resupply it. Edda heard something creak as the crow woman gave in, thrusting herself out of her seat and tossing more wood into the flames with belligerence, watching them grow back to their original brilliance. Her gestures were sloppy.

"What changed?"

"Some of you are more difficult to deal with than others. The teachings dictate that to deal with your wretched kind, one should turn that which benefits you, into what ails you. In some cases, it's easier spoken than executed. The king helped attune me to your manipulations and he helped foster this..." Camille's hands bent at the knuckles, choking something unseen, "...innate hatred I held towards you. He justified it. I wished, too, for you to die, but then you had a use."

Camille swayed in front of the fire, a hand pressed to her temple as she grumbled something about being exhausted.

"Why do you tell me this?"

"I'm so tired, and you refuse to break."

Edda watched as Camille stupored about, a poker in one hand, tip glowing hot. She plodded to stand by Edda, the poker's tip hovering over her opposite hand, treacherously close to her long fingers. Camille played with the danger, watching the tip glow as Edda watched the reflection in her eyes. The tip cooled as Edda spoke, "What changed?"

Camille replied, entranced, "What the children gave me because of you, was false. They did not need me. I realized this and the teachings illuminated me to what I had to do. The King *applauded* me, how clever I was."

Edda's open palm seemed to raise on its own accord, becoming a resting spot for the dulling poker tip. She could not feel it burn her as it hissed upon her hand, a small, wisping smoke rising above it. Camille watched as horror crept into her eyes. Edda watched with apathy.

"I love the children. I deserve their love in return." The words fell from Camille's lips as she moved the cooling tip of the metal poker away from Edda's hand and to the crook of the girl's neck. They both wondered if the tip could pierce her flesh.

"You need me."

Camille pushed as the fright spilled from her face, Edda's flesh giving nothing to the light poking. Her voice trembled, "I needn't a monster like you. I control you, Marion."

Edda laughed, wiping the black soot from her palm, showing untainted skin where the hot poker once sat. "You *need* me. Either way, their love for you is through me."

Something in Camille broke in that moment as she let the poker drop from her hand, clattering heavy on the floor. Reaching in her pocket, she produced a vial - the one the king had given her. Lashing out with her taloned hand, she pinched Edda's mouth open and poured the liquid into her, down her gullet. It was the most she had ever imbibed.

Everything spun as the woman in front of her twisted into the flickering shadows of the room. A gentle, deep voice erupted from the back of her mind. Her father, appearing vibrant and large, came to her and cradled her in his arms, whispering, "Sometimes, love and kindness is tellin' truths, the 'ard ones most of all."

Fading out, Edda began to giggle, drool dripping from her mouth, realizing as she spoke that her words came out slurred, "Camille, I could never 'ate you, for I am nothin' but love and kindness." Camille's face was a contorted flash as her ward breathed out the words she always held back: "My name is Edda."

SEVEN

She stirred, groggy, one of her leaden eyelids working hard to open. Her head was pounding, her limbs felt all but dead, as though her control over them had shrunk. She was tiny in a large, empty shell. Clammy, damp skin and eyes that burned to the trickling sunlight that found its way into her room—that was her entire being now. She had some hope that she wasn't to remain like this forever more, but part of her didn't care, resigned to lay in her bed forever.

Small tears escaped her eyes as she wished to purge her belly. A damp, warm cloth was laid over her brow, and she winced.

"Edda, yeah?"

The voice was far away, playful and prodding with its question as it cared for her. Slow recognition crept in from the back of her mind, and she struggled to grasp at it as her recollection seemed to pitter in and out, filling in the gaps that had chipped away.

"If you're Edda, why is it you're Marion?"

Her voice was hoarse, her words cracking in and out as an audible answer struggled from her dry throat, "H-h-how long?"

"You can talk 'ow you should talk. Drink." A cup was pressed to her lips as a hand gently raised to her head, nimble fingers tangling with her matted hair. "You've been out, what, a week now? Camille is run ragged with 'avin' to run the Orphanage. I find it amusin'. She wanted nothin' but all this work, and she can't even do it what with 'ow much she's makin' you discipline the others. You were right in tellin' 'er she needs you."

Edda drank, water spilling from the corners of her mouth. She sputtered, "Lowell?"

He grinned down at her, his toothy smile lighting up the room, "That's right! Been takin' care of you, I 'ave. Mother would be proud of me, yes she would." He paused, tilting his head as he looked at the ceiling, thinking something clever, "I knew you wouldn't forget little me."

"Why?"

He tapped her nose. "Someone 'ad to! Besides, we need to stick together. You keep me at such a distance, I 'ad to jump on the chance." His tender eyes glittered. "It beats listenin' to that dribble Camille tries to teach us. They don't miss me none anyway."

Edda struggled to sit up, and Lowell forced her to lay back down as he replaced the cloth on her head. He placed a folded blanket under her pillow to help ease her into sitting, remarking at how heavy her head was and how tired his arm was from it.

"Where is-?"

"Well, I'll tell you, they're eatin' now, some slop Camille could barely make edible – my ma could make better things out of berries and nettle, stingin' or not."

Edda glanced around for Martin, knowing the two ran together near all the time. He followed her gaze, eyes dashing between her and where she looked. Her throat clenched as she forced out another word, "Martin?"

His head snapped back to look at his patient. "Oh, that is why you're lookin' about. Well 'e is eatin' with the rest of them. As good as a friend 'e is, won't budge regardin' you." He shrugged, then dropped a shoulder, leaving one raised, then began to alternate between the two, chuckling to himself once more.

Edda grinned.

"That's it now! 'Ow about some more light, then, yeah? I love the sun, sorry what 'is *Royalty* did to it." He mocked as he walked towards the window. Edda caught a glimpse of him sticking his tongue out and shaking his head side to side, adding to his tone.

"Fun, you are," she managed to squeak out.

The room was alight now as Lowell giggled, "Oh, I know. My mother told me not too long ago."

"Where is she?"

"She disappeared along with my younger sister, so I came 'ere." He sat next to her and took a handful of her hair, beginning to braid it. "My sister and ma 'ad the straightest, darkest 'air you ever seen, with dark eyes to match. I take after pa more." He paused in his weave, "Pa's dead now."

"Sorry," she crooned.

He continued his work. "Don't be, not your fault now, is it? You blame yourself enough. My pa and ma 'ad different eyes, and you know 'ow that can turn out. We are a mixed bag of things. All of us are curious, but I like to poke and push, like pa. My sister and ma, they dreamed, eyes full of stars. Taught me to plait 'air, they did. Feels nice to do it again, even if I cannot do it as right and good as I once could, but we do what we can."

"Thank you."

"Mhm."

They sat in silence as he continued his work, undoing braids and repeating them on the same locks. Edda fell asleep at some point, waking to Lowell sitting on the other side of her, braiding a new section of hair. She let him, helplessness seeping in as her memory and recollection of the other night crept back in. Knowing she couldn't keep him from the basement any longer, she chose to enjoy the blessing and kindness given to her.

She drank as water was presented to her and fell asleep again, coming to when the sun was replaced by the moon and the fire by her bed was now alive, a new cloth placed over her head and water dripping onto her bare arms. Shame and panic filled her as she struggled to move, wanting to cover herself. A dry rag wiped the dew from her arms.

His voice continued, nonchalant, "I know you cannot give me all the answers I am wantin' to ask, but I think I can figure it for myself. It's in my nature, I think you've figured that. Only way to control that 'demon' is to lock me in a room, but even then I 'ave a knack for thinkin' up things."

Edda was more coherent now, more lucid, and better able to hold onto Lowell's words.

"'Eaded to the basement soon, I know I am. Frankly, I cannot wait."

She shot him a stunned look that he giggled at in response. "Why would you? 'Ow do you?"

"I sat on the stairs and listened to you both. I watched Camille drag you up the stairs. I believe she was a bit drunk," he smirked. "I believe she needs a good chastisin', yeah?" At this point he propped his elbows on her bedside, chin perched between his palms, fingers tapping at his cheeks. "Truth be told, I want to go and see what 'appens down there."

"No, you do not." Edda's voice was stern, frightened.

He patted her head. "I like knowin'. Besides, I'd never fault you. I 'ave a good inklin' on what goes on there." He held her hand, watching tears gather in her eyes. He took the corner of a blanket and dabbed the tears, a kind shimmer in his gaze, "I miss my family. So, we 'ave to look out for each other."

Nodding, Edda sniffed, hoping his temperament toward her wouldn't change. "I miss my mama and papa."

"You lose them too?"

She tried her damndest to hold back her tears. She so wished she could find all her family and go home, wherever that may be.

He patted her head. "You can cry, it's alright."

Something in his voice, this young man's voice, broke her, and a wretched sob tore through her being as torrents of repressed tears broke through her eyes, pooling in her collarbone and wetting her neckline. She gagged in between her words, catching her breath whenever she could, "I do not wish to be 'ere anymore. Once I did, but now everythin' is meaningless."

Lowell sat, listening as her gown dampened with all her mourning, her eyes swelling and breath hitching for quite some time. She sputtered little things here and there, how she could no longer hear the voice of her parents, how her memories and dreams have all faded with time. How she held less and less hope that she would see them again and be free to roam the land once more—even if that lifestyle made her feel a fugitive as a child, it offered more freedom than her current standings.

Now, people got hurt.

The fire popped as a log collapsed, and the boy stood to place another. Edda watched him as he struggled with the wood, trying to situate it proper with the poker. She looked at her palm where a burn should have been, but her skin was smooth and unblemished. Lowell kept at the fire until it fit his liking. Wiping at his brow he grinned at Edda. "I remember stories my mom told me and my sister. My pa 'as been gone for quite a while so I do not 'member much of 'im." He shrugged and took his place next to the girl once more. "Ma told us that 'e went fightin', sayin' pain and struggle can beat us, makin' us fall, or it strengthens us, makin' us stand taller than before."

The fire crackled as it picked at the new log. Lowell fidgeted with his own dark hair, short and straight, rolling strands betwixt his fingers. Edda looked between him and the fire, her mind blank after purging herself. She wanted to feel well rested again and began to cry a little more.

Using his sleeve, he dabbed at the new tears, giving her a comforting smile.

"Did your ma ever give you anythi-thing to keep?"

"Anythin' to keep?" He paused, hand on his cheek while he looked towards the moon. "Aside from stories and 'ow to do what I feel is right, no, nothin' I can 'old."

Edda's head drooped, wanting to relate more with Lowell than she realized.

"She did give my sister this intricate 'airpiece." He held his hands aloft, fingers arched and encapsulating the air, the size of an egg. His eyes squinted as he gathered dusty memories, "'Bout this big and flat. 'Ad a pretty carvin' on it but I don't remember much aside from glances when I fixed it in 'er 'air."

"Are you upset?"

His head swayed side to side. "Not at all, I understand why ma gave it to 'er." He held his hand out as a closed fist, raising a finger to count. "She is better at mindin' trinkets, women are better at 'iding anythin', and they are more," he paused, looking for the right word, his mouth opening and closing as he grabbed at it, "they are more... attuned to what we can do."

Cocking her head, Edda pursed her lips, "What we can do?"

Lowell lowered his fingers. "I am certain you know. Even if you do not believe you do, you do."

She stared at him, scrutinizing his words. "You make no sense, Lowell."

He giggled, "What are you made of?"

Taken aback, Edda shrunk into herself, lolling her head towards the fireplace. Lowell skittered over to block her vision, gently cradling her cheeks between his palms, rocking her head so that the firelight lit her irises, allowing him to better see. She attempted moving away, to avert her eyes, but she could not fight her growing curiosity, nor her tiredness.

"Aha, I can see it now." His grin grew wide and his teeth caught hints of the fire as he moved his head to examine her warmed eyes. "A bit dull now, but I can see the love and kindness there. Some of us men can evoke it as easily as women, but we are confined to action more than not."

Edda let her head settle in his palms. "My parents told me when I was small that I was of love and kindness."

He tapped the corner of her eye, the skin red and puffy, and then tapped the same spot on his own growing face. "I ask you the same. What am I made of?"

"You are curious, playful – I can see little sparks of light."

He blinked at her, still smiling. "My sister's eyes were starry, and when she was around, I would dream day and night, explorin' everythin'. We worked well together, feedin' off what each other could give." His face began to fall now, his lips closed, pulling to the side.

Edda was small when she was with her parents. She couldn't remember all they told her. She raised a hand to Lowell's face and stroked his cheek, how she remembered her mother and father doing for her. This young man, only a year her junior, was giving up so much to her now, whether he felt it or not. The sadness in his face was not something she could fix now. He missed them. Even if he played himself to be impish and unbothered, he was still in pain.

He raised his eyes to meet hers, his smile coming back. "There it is."

At his words, she felt herself smile. "I want to show you somethin'. Can you get it for me?" He stood up and began to walk to her vanity as she raised her finger towards it. "In the drawer on the right, there is an armlet given to me by mama."

The candles spread throughout her room gave a fair bit of light; an hour prior, Lowell lit them as the sun descended and Edda slept. Opening the drawer, he could see inside well enough. He hesitated, eyes darting back and forth. "Pretty thin' it is."

"Am not too fond of gold but the stone is my favorite part of it. You can h-hold it. If you look well enough, you can see lines in it, but I cannot see 'ow anyone could have carved such a gem."

He leaned over the drawer and reached in as Edda watched, straining her neck, feeling the muscles tightening and pinching, begging her to lay back down. Giving in, her head fell back into the pillow.

"You should rest more. Camille will be pullin' you out of bed any day now. She's at 'er wit's end."

Edda forced herself to resign, knowing that her consciousness would elude Camille for a short spell. Time was of the essence, the length she could rest being constrained. Echoes of their conversation in the parlor began to whisper to her like little fingers peeking underneath a closed door. "Camille told me she loves you all, the children."

"She does, does she?" He closed the drawer and walked to Edda's side again, his mind both elsewhere and with her, torn in two. "Funny way of showin' it."

"Yes, but, she dislikes me."

Lowell reached out, tapping the side of Edda's head, next to her eye. She believed she understood the motion, wondering if she should speak on it. He decided to go elsewhere. "Camille reminds me of a story ma told me. It was about birds."

The sight of Camille shrouded in shadows, the semblance of a beak phasing in and out of existence, rushed back to Edda. "Oh? Why not tell it?"

The boy stepped back, reaching his hands up high and clasping them before stretching, bending himself left and right. "Can't recall it too well. Maybe later I will, yeah?" he teased.

Edda sighed, sinking into her pillow, realizing the pit inside her was no longer as deep as it once felt. "Off to bed?"

A curt nod and he leaned down, surprising her with a gentle hug. She embraced him, still careful of the wall inside her. He smiled down at her, stepping back towards the door. "You didn't tell me why you are called Marion."

"I am afraid you will find out soon enough."

His fingers danced at his sides, rising and falling as though he were playing a piano. "On that note, goodnight, Edda."

He stepped out before she could answer. Closing her eyes, the sound of her name filled her ears, heart and room. She fell asleep with a smile on her face.

Eight

Edda was given respite for another day before Camille started up her demands again, pressuring Edda more than ever before: waking her earlier, allowing her retiring to her room much later, having her clean more thoroughly, and if there was any punishment, she was not allowed rest after, but was made to continue to care for the children. Camille took the pleasure of caring for the child that went down to the basement, playing the saint and savior.

The silver lining was there were less punishments given as Camille tried to stretch Edda thin and get all the use she could from her.

King Huxley kept them on their toes, taking his time to arrive for Lowell's punishment. Edda spent evenings looking over her shoulder, checking outside and listening for the rattle of wooden wheels and clicking hooves on the cobblestone. The anxiety and anticipation were kept at the highest pitch, the king sending a letter at even paces to keep it in place.

Camille grumbled at the letters, her deteriorating appearance sometimes improving before fading once more. Her eyes gathered blackness around them, seeming to sink into her skull as her neck thinned, looking stretched. She was growing gaunt, her apron tied taut around her thinning waist.

She could not sleep, Edda knew, for something gripped her inside that would not let her rest. Edda could—it was how she lived for the longest time. However, now, since Camille could not rest, why should her little pet?

Lowell spent his days smiling and laughing louder, staying up with Martin to watch the stars winking at them. The young man disappeared often, only to be seen strutting about near Camille's door. No one spoke of it.

Not Lowell, not Martin, and not Edda.

Camille was too frazzled to notice, her grip over the Orphanage exaggerated through her heightened use of the girl, yet it was slipping, her palms too sweaty to keep a proper grasp. Despite this, no one rebelled, maintaining pace and figure, keeping the status quo. It was easy and simple, allowances taken advantage of when they arose. Rest was enjoyed here and there, moments of respite, glances and smiles exchanged, wanderings.

Martin knew of Lowell's future fate, fretting over it despite the constant delays. Regardless he never gave into his elder's prodding, quiet as a corpse. He enjoyed the increasing freedoms with his friend, taking full advantage of their stargazing and banter. Lowell made his life seem more enjoyable, a release from a prison of which he could no longer remember who locked him in.

All Lowell did was turn the key to his cell, for it was always left in the lock if Martin found himself brave enough. Out of everyone there, Lowell had the most courage.

Edda still caused him unease. Watching the small exchanges between her and his best friend caused his innards to twist and groan. They could never be of the same kind, the demon in the girl shown to all but Lowell - Martin wished him to know, to see it but shamed himself over the thoughts, hoping no harm would befell his only happiness in this dismal place.

He shunned the others, ignoring their glances, their judgement of his friend, undeserved and all over how he spoke and interacted with others. How he wished to be like Lowell, to have his gusto and swagger, this older boy turning into a young man a good handful of years ahead of him. Inside, amongst the twists of his innards, he knew he could not and never be the same, so he decided to protect him instead. He could die for his friend, and he found enjoyment and pride in this feeling.

* * *

When he escaped over a year prior, after his week in the acrid underground with Edda's glowing eyes, he wandered to the front of the Orphanage, finding the stony path under his soft feet. Turning back, he remembers a lit candle from the parlor, pinprick eyes shining as he jogged as well as a child could, away and far.

He found the field where he once brought Edda a flower and watched her cry to him, apologizing for what was to come, to what passed and whatever else would be. The thought made him cry as he passed through, long grass filling gaps between his toes as he rubbed his chilled arms in the moonlight. He kicked at the small blossoms he found, cursing Edda, filled with both the resentment of a child and the begrudging nature of an adult. He would forever see her words as meaningless.

He dashed through another wooded area, small clearings where the light of night watched over him, and found a larger stream. Dipping a foot in, he found it too cold, huddling near it until day broke ahead.

This was how he passed time for what felt like weeks, scrounging for berries, little things to eat with the stream to drink from. His clothes hung on his little body and he wished for his mother and father, Lady Camille, and even Edda – anger flooding him whenever he realized what she'd done to him. His body vibrated with illness, cold, longing, and frustration – but he did not, *could not* understand it all. He simply felt it and let it consume him as nature seemed to do to him.

Far away from the Orphanage, lightheadedness began to overtake his consciousness as he stared at the water, following it to nowhere until he remembers nothing but an older boy grinning down at him, the widest smile he'd ever seen.

It was Lowell, alone and wandering himself, who found Martin and cradled him within his larger frame, speaking without end although Martin could not answer.

"Good day to you, little one. My, 'ow small and frail you are! 'Ow did you find yourself 'ere? Where did you come from? Why did you walk this way?" He would laugh to himself, a brightness in the dark. "Who are you? Come all this way to find me, yeah? You shouldn't 'ave."

Some nights in his blinking recollection, there was warmth, a fire, and sometimes there was food other than berries, flaking fish flesh pushed between his lips. His jaw cradled and moved in an attempt to make him chew. He was cooed at and cared for, his caretaker calling him 'fascinatin'' as he tried to help him do acts he could once do alone.

One hot day, he was plunged in the water, held upright, hands rubbing cooling water over his face and hands. "The workin' of the body is interestin' to me. My family told me I was strange, wantin' to know all I could. From the small squirrels that fell and needed feedin' to little turtles stuck on their backsides – there is learnin' in 'elping, I told them, yes I did."

It was then that Martin's strength returned enough that he could look his caretaker in the eye, his lips dewed from the bath. "Martin," he croaked out his name, his sluggish finger pointing at himself.

"Lowell!" his friend responded, exuberant, hands held high and flailing, overtaken with the purest ease and delight.

Martin knew then, he wanted to keep him as best he could.

They stayed near their camp, miles from anywhere of importance, and talked to one another. They learned each other's names, similarities, reservations – of which Lowell seemed to have none. They were cut of the same cloth, both being without parents, abandoned by accident or on purpose.

"Ma tucked me into a tree one night, sayin' to stay put. She took along my little sister, too. She was none too good at hidin'. Wasn't the first time they 'ad done so. I fell asleep and the next day, gone they were, so I waited. Was there a long time, playin' with the critters I found, findin' berries and things." Lowell had gazed at the sky then, feeling the pressure from above bearing down on his eyes and face before meeting Martin's look once more. "They never came back."

Martin cried for Lowell many times, not knowing why but letting all the emotion flow out of him. His friend hugged him tight, patting his back like his mother did until a coughing fit and vomiting drained her of all life, leaving him to go elsewhere.

Lowell listened to him, undivided, his eyes large and full of twinkling kindness and inquisition, wanting to know more, wanting to understand. They sparked a familiar feeling in Martin, one full of happiness, joy, pain and conflict—his accent brought the same sensations. He tried to drown those feelings, shoving them below every time they bubbled, bobbing up for air.

They would play too, unlike at the Orphanage, with large sticks and tiny creatures that flew, emitting light from their backsides. Lowell showed his small friend how to block a good swing from his make-believe sword and to make the little bugs with four wings and long bodies land on their hands, allowing delicate fingers to pet them before zipping to a nearby plant on the water.

For days and days, they existed on one another's words and giddy fancies, scraping by on what a fifteen and now six-year-old could gather until Lowell was moved to make a decision. "We both know I 'ave lived out 'ere forever and a day, but we cannot continue. We need older people – you left such a place, yeah?"

Martin hid his face, giving a barely discernable nod.

"Come along now, we'll die like this, and that I want nothin' to do with!"

"I followed the river down."

Lowell dragged the boy up, dusting off his sides and rump before doing it to himself, gleeful in his question asking, "Now then, follow the leader?"

Rueful, Martin did so, worried about seeing that girl once more, about committing some sort of wrongdoing and finding himself swollen again, crying and helpless. He walked behind Lowell, both of them carrying along their battle sticks. Occasionally the long bugs Lowell called 'dargonflies' would land on the sticks, accompanying them as they walked for days.

Martin, filled with a sense of duty, walked behind his friend, ready to swing at whatever snuck up behind them.

The river thinned as they went upstream, and Martin knew they were getting closer. The river curved, bringing them adjacent to the Orphanage – he churned inside, wanting to prolong their adventure, even if his bare feet ached and his stomach gurgled. Dread built on the idea of seeing that girl again. Even the idea of Camille and the other children brought him some unease, despite how they cared for him after fending off his visitor when she heard him crying after his long discipline. He was imploding. Even if he couldn't explain the feeling, it was visceral.

"I am 'appy I found you." Lowell's voice was genuine, filled with serenity. "You are a good person. I did not think you would be savin' me 'ow I saved you."

Martin's eyes watered as he looked down – he could never betray his friend, never allow him to suffer more than necessary. Lowell would not do that to him – it was only right.

Fighting his inner thoughts and fears, he tapped Lowell with his stick, pointing to where the woods led to an open prairie. "That way."

"Then you lead, my friend."

Ditching the sticks nearby, Martin guided them through the summer grass and flowers, trampling some as he walked, turning about when he heard his friend's footsteps falter before coming to a halt. Lowell was stooped over the crushed flowers, cooing to the cocked-eyed and crinkled budded heads propped between his gentle fingers. His eyes filled with sadness as he willed them straight.

Martin approached, crouching beside him and watching the devastation wash over his friend's face over what he did. Lowell sniffed and smiled, meeting Martin's eyes. "You 'ave to watch your step, little Martin. Somethin's struggle to live, and many aren't allowed to, not really."

"I-I am sorry."

"Just remember it, and do better by the life around us."

Martin glowered, his face flushing and paling in turn, wanting to trample the flowers and cry over them all at once. Lowell straightened up, stepping over the small blossoms that would correct themselves in time, grabbing his friend's hand and squeezing it. Martin apologized more and more, holding back all his emotions, wishing his lost mother could guide him through.

"In time, understandin' comes to us if we cannot meet it before. It is quite alright. Let's keep movin'."

Martin swallowed and took care in his steps, finding cobblestone, then guiding his friend, he walked up the stoop he once ran away from. Swallowing hard, he knocked, pausing before tapping the door again, hoping no one was home when the familiar clinks of the locks came undone. When it opened, relief found him as Camille stood before him, surprise apparent in her eyes as she looked at Martin and the new face.

Her bewilderment was overtaken, her brows furrowed and eyes squinted, her jaw clenching to match. She motioned them in, whispering under her breath, "How dirty."

The two stepped forward, into the mouth of the Orphanage.

* * *

Lowell kept a keen eye on Camille, not acting terribly overt in his suspicions, but side-eyeing her in observation when given the chance. Martin grew cautious as well of her and everyone else upon his return, giving distance between himself and Lowell before realizing being close to his friend would garner no chastising. His loyalties were with his savior. He was fixated on Edda's whereabouts and jealous of Lowell and Edda's connection that seemed to surpass theirs. Some days, he could ignore it more than others. Other days, he glared with little awareness at them both – his friend giggling at his amusing face.

He hated it when Lowell insisted on aiding the girl when they overhead talking one night as they stargazed. Lowell snuck out of their room to get a better listen, reporting back when dragging and thumping rang throughout the stairwell. His friend could not help his nature, snubbing Martin's pleas to stay away from that thing, that girl. For a few nights, Martin sat alone in their nighttime bunker, watching the autumn stars and trying to focus on how they twinkled different from the summer ones.

He was elated when his friend crawled into their fortress of moonlight, worried when he saw his face. "What did Marion do to you?"

Lowell met his gaze with a dubious look. "Nothin', she appears better now." He pulled his knees to his chest as Martin shoved his shoulder. Lowell was never one to hide his thoughts or ideas, unreserved at the worst of times.

"You are never so downtrodden."

"Really? Odd, yeah?"

"What are you thinking of?"

Lowell traced invisible lines on his arms. "What 'appened downstairs? What 'appens when you are punished?"

It wasn't the first time Lowell asked, and it wasn't the first time Martin refused to answer. "I hope you never know. She is a monster."

"No, she is a person."

Martin scoffed and Lowell eyed him, without judgement, clinical and curious. His tone was edged with satisfaction, "Camille said the king will be 'ere soon and that I will be punished. I want to know."

"No, you do not! You should not!" A child stirred in a creaking bunk outside their fort, in the cold room kept out of the silver light. Martin was in shock, fearful, shaking with anger and pain. He had to stop it, needed to.

"Martin, out of all *poor* behaviors that sent the others to the basement, why not I?" His friend shook his head in response, shrugging as he stared with eyes wide in disbelief. Lowell smirked. "My time 'as finally come." He rubbed his hands together in an effort of warming.

"When?"

Lowell's mouth was like a fish's as he pouted his lower lip, eyebrows raised. "Eventually." He was much too calm, innocent, naïve. Martin's hands went to the window like they did months ago. Lowell pushed the prying hands away, shaking his head.

"Come now, it is much too cold. Besides, there is no fear to be 'ad by me."

"You are stupid, that's why."

"Ouch," Lowell's laugh was dry yet he smirked. He planted his hands behind him, lifting his face to the moon, gazing up as he turned ideas about in his head. Martin stared at him in anger, tense and helpless. The nonchalant boy's mouth opened and closed as he picked words out of his racing thoughts, devising, planning.

"Spit it out!"

"'Er name isn't Marion, it is Edda."

"Why should I care?"

Lowell's brows quirked and he sucked his teeth, smiling, his voice hushing, "I need to get into Camille's room. Can you 'elp me?"

"Oh, o-of course? Why?"

Ruffling his baffled friend's hair, he giggled, "There's somethin' in there that I need to get. I might need to go in a few times – little searches, like when we looked for bugs."

"What are you looking for?"

Resting his head on his own shoulder, Lowell's smile grew broader, his teeth shining in the light. Meeting Martin's eyes, he answered with only a wink.

NINE

It took a year, a full year of winter chilling the Orphanage in place and giving illness, spring casting down torrents of rain and letting little flowers bloom, of summer bringing bright, muggy sunshine and warming the skin. It was a year of anticipation, of eagerness, of angst, fretting, fright and growing anger.

Camille's rage built with each letter putting off Lowell's punishment. How could her own cousin, as important as he was, leave her to fend for herself against *two* of them? Moreover, someone had been fiddling about in her room, sifting through that which was rightfully hers. The children would never do so, and her *Marion* hadn't the time. She always kept a keen eye on her, and the orphans could be trusted. Lowell was always with Martin, and Martin was a good boy—he was on *her* side.

Martin was close to his enemy to better know him, she sufficed, questioning if she had moved the items around herself. She needed more help, she needed another like her to quell her growing suspicions and paranoia. Her supply of sedative was used up on Edda and, as of late, herself.

Sleep no longer welcomed her in her fearful state, regardless of how often she checked her door and windows and no matter how well-lit her space was. Her faith was a split foundation now as she teetered on the edge of sanity. The teachings, around for a hundred years at least, her tether in life guarding the innocent from demons while also controlling them, harnessing them, breaking them down, seemed to fail her of late.

She had never questioned His Royalty. Why did He not protect her now? She studied incessantly in her spare time, learning how best to prevent harm by these creatures, these *subhuman* abominations that ran rampant the land before the arrival of salvation. She had never questioned it before, but now, in her hour of need, was she left forsaken? The Monastery had *two* demons, one who had given into the teachings, obeying, compliant, and the other, quelled through blindness.

How abhorrent it was that she could not handle *one*. Now, she had *two*. Martin helped her, as did the children to the best of their abilities. They loved her, needed her as she did them. They were one another's saviors.

These thoughts clawed through her mind as she lay awake most nights, gazing at the rising sun tapestries that hung unopposed on every wall of her room. They once brought her comfort, but what was fabric to do against something so physical?

Camille was always afraid, able to hide behind her perfectionism and poise – her pride kept her aloft until the evil child had fought back against her, her precious children rushing to save her. Her heart swelled before the pulsing of her cheek overtook the pleasure in her heart. She taught her babies well, but the girl stared back at her, only dazed at being struck.

So, she tried another method, or rather attempted a different approach on an old technique: striking at the creature's emotions. A few glasses of her hidden wine and she opened up, hoping to appeal to the humanity of the creature. Part of her wished for the thing's love and understanding, having cared for her for over a decade. When she scoffed at the disintegrating Camille, having the gall to claim *she* needed *it*, all hope seemed lost.

Then the thing held the hot iron poker, unmoved, her reddish skin marred by the soot of the fire's ash left upon its tip. Terror seized Camille tight as she drugged the creature, dragging its limp body to its bedroom.

She could only destroy it from within; through the internal, sensitive, vulnerable bits, or the children. It was for the greater good, and, for years, she balanced her mind and body with the teachings.

Now she was abandoned, waiting for King Huxley to rescue her, to set the Orphanage right once more. Day and night, she withered in wait, unsure when a siege may take place. She was a prisoner in her home, surrounded by hapless children.

The King was her single hope now, since being stranded far away from others, from public eyes, meant she could not call on neighbors. The Monastery was much too busy to answer her pleas, her old home too caught up in their lovely and controlled realities to pay her mind.

So she waited as her insides felt ripped apart, her mind swimming in fog.

Over a year had passed before the carriages rattled along the cobblestone road. Her breath hitched as she took in a deep breath, feeling the weight of forever lift from her shoulders. She tried to better her appearance, applying rouge and tint to her lips, a powder around her eyes, trying to lift away the weeks of sleep she was sorely in need of.

Rushing down the stairs, she caught her breath as she straightened her dress, then hair, trying to keep her quaking hands from pulling her bun loose. She couldn't match her appearance from over a year beforehand, but, for His Royalty, she came as close as she could.

She swung open the door before anyone could knock, before anyone had even made it to the stoop, stepping out to greet her cousins as they descended the thin carriage stairs and onto the solid road. Excited, she curtsied, her thin cheeks and stretched skin making her grin skeletal.

King Huxley's brow quirked as he examined her, his son a step behind him cocking his head in cold curiosity. "Camille, how worn you've become."

She swallowed her pride, holding herself stiff and proper, wanting nothing more than to collapse and beg for their assistance, to hurl anger at them for making her wait, to curse them.

She was better than this, for she was no beast, no wicked witch.

Alastair had grown taller in the time since she'd last seen him, his sun-kissed hair growing down to his shoulders, his eyes holding the warmth of the sun but little else – the child blessed by God. He smiled at her, a small twinkle in his eye as he gazed upon his cousin, his small fingers lifting her chin aloft to meet him. Her blood ran cold as they held one another's eyes, knowing something had bloomed in the boy. Her eyes quaked as doubt planted itself in her breast, painful and throbbing as he dropped his hand and grinned with the teeth of a predator.

He was still just a child.

"He's grown well, no? I have only grown prouder of him since we've last seen one another. The dreams he has are like no other, guided is he to what his role is. He's a most engaging actor, as well."

Alastair beamed at his father as they stood side by side. "I have always liked the theater, father."

They both chuckled as Camille grasped at the teachings unravelling in her mind, the place she once stood firm now nothing but a thin weaving of cords and strings. The irony was not lost on her. "A pleasure to see you both again. Please excuse my appearance, as the rampacity of life has been more overwhelming of late."

"Rampacity?" King Huxley sucked his tongue, trying out the word. "I like it. Please, lead the way."

* * *

Edda felt the vibrations near the well as she fetched water, knowing before even hearing the horses that the day had finally come. The apprehension that filled her fell away as relief flooded her, before the grand pit in her opened, its maw wide and ever hungry. She no longer needed to wait, but now she needed to act, in more ways than one. It had taken so long for the royals to arrive that the threat loomed over her like passing clouds in the sky, remaining only a vague intimidation.

Life went on, and despite what may pass, it would continue.

"Finally, been waitin' long enough." Lowell stood behind her in the garden, walking up to lean against the well. He claimed to be sixteen now, but age seemed lost on most the orphans – however, he stood taller than before, casting a slight shadow over Edda. She stared at him as he looked down into the dark well and then at her, smiling. "No one 'as told me a thin' and I find it rather tirin' to be left waitin' for the answer to a puzzle."

Edda looked everywhere but at him, knowing he would never hate her for anything, but the shame inside pushed her to routine, letting the empty bucket down the rope into the water below, then bringing it back up, filled and heavy. She set it down next to her before she gathered the courage to look at him: his dark hair that had grown to cover his ears, his large grin, his glossy, ember speckled eyes. Her heart panged. She raised her heavy arms, gathering him in them, and holding him firm, his head rested upon hers.

"You're always so cold!" he jollied, returning the embrace. In the back of his mind, images of his mother and sister emerged, the hug reminding him of warmth, acceptance and love. He squeezed her, wishing to drain every last drop of that maternal feeling from Edda, to hold it in himself as a memory carved into his soul.

Edda cried onto his chest, the droplets running down his shirt. She kissed his heart, beginning to pivot them both as she turned from left to right, side to side, forward and back. A gentle, somber dance.

"It will be alright, Lowell." The words were tender, a comfort to him and herself.

"I know, it is simply 'ow some things are to go."

From the doorway of the kitchen, Martin watched, not wanting to spoil their time yet, wishing to fracture it with impunity. He heard Camille dash through the locks on the door, and he could see her throwing herself at the feet of the King. It disgusted him, but he understood her desperation. He knew it would be difficult after the punishment, but it may rid him of his competition. If the girl was like a moving statue, broken in mind and spirit, all could continue well enough, even if his friend would be melancholy for a little while.

It was a simple price to pay. He paid it longer than anyone, and more brutally than anyone, but it opened his eyes to the monster that wore the face of a loving, caring girl.

He watched them hold one another, as a mother might her son, or even a loving wife her husband. Remembering his punishment, unease pricked at his sides and soft spots. She seemed almost like a person, but he'd seen the lie firsthand.

"You two best finish up. They've arrived, and we wouldn't want to make it worse."

Edda pulled away, cupping Lowell's cheeks, standing tiptoed and planting a kiss on his forehead before letting her hands fall limp to her sides as she looked upon him with tears still stuck in her eyes. He just smiled at her before reaching out and holding her cheeks. Pulling her up, he pecked her nose, "That's what ma did to me and my sister."

Confused, Edda blushed as Lowell took her hand, leading her inside, clenching it tight so she could not let go. He reached a hand towards Martin, who stepped aside. Martin held out his arm, his fingertips brushing his friend's before he decided against it, letting his hand return to his side. Pain flashed in Lowell's eyes before he shrugged it away, pulling the girl along to the parlor.

Camille was already in the room. King Huxley and Alastair stepped into view, a nondescript knight behind them. Edda tried to wrench her hand from Lowell's, but his grip was tight. He drew comfort from her, using it to sweep away any trepidation he hid behind his genuine excitement. Martin stood close behind Lowell, his small hand reaching forth, hovering and hesitant, wanting to grab his friend's arm and pull him away from everyone. As the tips of his fingers grazed Lowell's elbow, Camille's eyes jutted open, stern with warning.

His fingers shot back, curling into fists as he tucked them behind his back, stepping away as the eyes of the royals watched him with temptation. The prince's eyes seemed to flicker with cruel creativity as his tongue licked his teeth, creating a bulge like a maggot under a carcass' skin. Little Martin retreated to the dining room, peeking around the corner.

"Father, I do not wish to wait. Can we get along with it?"

"Alastair, my son, patience is next for you to learn – remember when we hunt?"

The boy sighed, "If you are too quick, you lack wit, and then your prey may outrun you."

"If you act slow, all the better it will go, for then prey will walk beside you."

"Yes, father, but how does it apply here?"

King Huxley harrumphed, "It is a more satisfying win, child, delayed gratification and playing the long game. It stops most from being too smart."

Camille stood by them as they conversed, frozen in place, awkward at their words, feeling as though prey herself. Edda's hand clamped Lowell's as he rolled his eyes. "Your son is right there, King 'Uxley. I'd never walk alongside you or 'im. I prefer better company, yeah?" He shook his arm, trying to make Edda's wiggle with his to no avail. She gripped him tighter.

"Insolence!"

"Father, how dare it speak back," Alastair crooned, giddiness escaping his throat.

Camille interjected, staring at Edda, oddly wishing to apologize to her. "Your Highnesses, shall we begin?" She reached her hand out to Edda, pleading, wishing to make it quick, wanting Alastair to be out of the Orphanage. His aura bled black and seeped into her home. All the love and care she believe she imbued into the foundation would be lost if the boy stayed too long. She wagged her fingers, a bid to hasten the girl. "Come along Marion, let us prepare."

Edda stepped forward, her heel meeting the floor with a solid and hollow *thump*. One step, two step as she released Lowell's hand. She was mechanical in her programming, trained and solemn.

Lowell looked to her, swallowing his voice and feeling his legs begin to quiver beneath him. He glanced behind him, seeing the glint of Martin's eyes from the room behind them where he hid away from the danger. He tasted the fear that seemed to ebb off his friend whenever he asked about the punishments. Whipping his head around, he grabbed the back of Edda's dress and called for her, "Edda."

Something clicked in her mind upon hearing her name; her forward stride paused and she felt suspended mid-step. Like a dance her family once did in joy, she motioned her raised foot and planted it to her right, her arms raised like branches, their soft singing ringing in her mind, humming to her. She staggered. "N-no."

Alastair stepped ahead of his father, hand on the hilt of his little dagger. His father held his shoulder, pulling him back. "Temperance, child. Camille, what is it she says?"

Choking on air, Camille wondered if repeating those words would damn her. She shook her head in disbelief. "She said no, Highness."

Huxley scoffed, "Say it again."

Edda's barrel chest puffed, like her father's once did, the softness of her gentle curves lost as she became large and indomitable, emulating the strength of her papa. "No h-harm will befall Lowell!"

Alastair sniggered, "That is why you're tattered-tongue, eh? Speak proper, you evil thing."

Edda spat, "You will need to topple me, irreparable boy."

Ire flashed through the prince as he hissed, rushing the girl taller than him, better built than him: he pulled his dagger from its sheath and went for her neck. The knight hurried behind the boy, trying to hold him back, the child escaping his gloved hand. Huxley dug into his pocket, producing a vial that Camille eyed with want of her own.

Edda's arm raised to block her face as small sparks erupted from her arm, the knife in the prince's hand splintering, chipped. A gash in her sleeve showed the scarring underneath, her skin without fresh blood, no wound in sight. Camille let out a whimper and Edda's hand shot out around Alastair's throat. She forced him to his knees, her agate eyes staring deep, prodding into his mind. His face burned red as he beat on her hand, shock and panic in his eyes as the edges of his vision blurred. She purred to him, overtaken, "You are the scourge on *our* land. May you never know love or kindness, never filled by it. You shall be blinded by your rage."

His eyes bulged as his voiced croaked, "F-father!"

The knight pulled on the girl's hair and arms, wrenching her head back as the king forced fingers into her mouth, pouring an ample amount of liquid down her gullet. She held on, weakness filling her innards as she felt herself be sucked down into the pit within. The prince slipped from her grasp as she collapsed to the floor, the wood cracking beneath her, splintering from her heft. Lowell gazed down at her, pride and gratitude pushing away his fear. He smiled in love and thanks.

Her eyes fluttered closed as her hearing remained little longer. Alastair scuttled to his feet, damning the girl. The dagger, thrown to floor, cracked in two as he rushed to Edda's side. The dull thuds made her side shiver, her head rolling before the prince fell to his feet, crying over his bruised and swollen foot.

Behind her collapsed body, Lowell sank to his knees, shambling forth and taking her head unto his lap, his soft hands brushing hair from her face.

King Huxley sucked in an angry breath, annoyed over his boy, at Camille for her lack of discipline and control, and at Edda for her audacity. He sneered, "Well, then, let us begin."

TEN

Candles flickered, small jettisons of smoke trailing up into the darkness of the ceiling. Mirrors lined the walls, catching the gentle shadows that moved within the blackened room. Little warmth was found here aside from if one went to touch the flames scattered throughout the basement. The floor was dirt, fresh in the middle of the room, soon to be packed down only to be replaced and packed down again in an unending cycle.

Edda's consciousness slipped back to her, her eyes already open, held wide by device and set aglow by the placement of the candles. She was displayed before an audience now, King Huxley, his knight and scowling prince, whose arms crossed tight over his chest, his light movements hinting at the bruise about his neck – a purpling handprint. She knew it had been over a day from the coloring of it. She had been in the basement for at least a day now.

Groaning, she tensed her arms, feeling deepening grooves as the wires dug at her limbs, cracking her skin and carving out what could never be replaced. Behind her, she knew, was a heavy curtain that stretched throughout at her back, from wall to wall, ceiling to floor, with a gap where the heavy threading led from her arms to well-made cross braces handled time and time again by nimble fingers. Attempting to tug at the wires, she felt her arms cracking, begging to shatter should she pull more.

It was a pain she couldn't fight, a pain excruciating in every manner of the word that made her very soul quiver and scream.

Cloth, damp with saliva, sat between her teeth, fixed. Her head immobile, a metal cage clamped around it, suspending it from a straight rod that sat firm in the wood above her.

She was always to look in front of her, eyes ever wide and watching, encased in a terrifying machination. Whoever sat in front of her to always see the warmth of her eyes as she was made to commit atrocities she could not escape, ones that would haunt those who would be the recipient of her true nature – the one that hid behind the manipulation of her eyes.

Her victims would always see her loving, kind gaze while being beaten passed their limits, made to hate that which felt like compassion in its purest form.

This place created the pit in her as the pain grew larger than she could ever imagine or ever admit. She shoved it far below her until it changed, swallowing her from within, an insatiable creature never quelled for it needn't eat, only wishing to be seen and felt, being pushed deeper with all the other horrid aches she bore.

To face it would mean to shatter, and to shatter would leave her role vacant for another to endure. Instead, her heart petrified, more and more. She longed for the day she no longer felt, yet, over a decade has passed and she still did.

Behind the gag, she gurgled, hanging by her head, arms at upward diagonals, her legs limp and resting, bent at joints against the packed soil beneath her.

The prince's voice filled the room, "Father, is she awake now?"

"It appears so. With her eyes always open, it can be hard to tell." He shifted his weight as he leaned against a mirror behind him, candles dangling above his head in fixtures with wide bottoms. He smiled at the room and image before him. "Quite clever, I admit. Camille has outdone herself – in thought and execution."

The knight watched, standing straight like a tree, his eyes clouded with indifference, a sell-sword with little left of himself.

Edda's arm raised as pain shot through her, down to the bone and throughout all its ligaments inside her. Her open hand, fingers stiff and clawed, came down on what she refused to see in front of her. Eyes watering, she stole a glance at the boy at her feet and whimpered.

Chains kept his hands together, bound and chafing behind his back, keeping him tight against a wooden pole that ran from the floor to halfway up the ceiling, taller than he could ever manage to escape. Cuts ran down the length of his cheek and blood covered his face, a patch of hair missing and a shining protrusion from his thigh; enough to pain him but not to cause anything so severe that treatment could not cure.

Lowell looked up at her, spitting out one of his teeth, a globule of blood sticking to it. He grinned at her, the candles casting a sparkle in his eyes. "Edda, you're awake, yeah?" His voice was gentle, albeit strained.

She tugged at the wires, screaming behind the cloth, her arms threatening to rip from their sockets. She shook her head as best she could, feeling the stiff crick shoot through her neck gripping her from shoulder to scalp.

His visage was red and brown, his neck and naked torso streaked with dried blood and deepening bruises. He seemed elated at finally knowing what happened, as though physical pain didn't exist to him. He closed his eyes and sighed, groaning against the pole behind him. He looked like a man twice his age, his temperament aging him.

"Spirited, is he not?" Huxley commended. His son grumbled in response.

Lowell called out, his voice hoarse, "Camille, 'ow clever you think yourself to be! Marion*ette*, 'ow smart of you!" he ridiculed, letting a laugh slip his split lip.

The wires coiling Edda's arms tensed as the woman controlling them gripped the wooden pieces, moving her hand to strike the boy once more. He hacked and sputtered.

Where he sat, Edda could see the others that came before him. She could see Martin, the hate filling his eyes, the fear and distrust. The betrayal. This was why she was despised and she understood it, coming to believe she deserved it. The words her mother and father told her, repeated so many times, came to mean nothing as she wrought pain and destruction by her own hands. Whoever pulled the strings did not matter, only that it was she being pulled.

Ever since she was six.

"Look at me, Edda, I see you. Do not worry, I will never 'ate you."

All she could do was cry as the prince growled from his spot, "Shut up, filth."

Lowell laughed, unbreakable. "Look who speaks! I know, one day, you will look in the mirror and see what you really are!"

The prince began to stomp his feet, his anger coming out in grunts as his father held his child's shoulder and squeezed. Edda's hands came down upon Lowell again and again, heavy against her own will. The room quieted as the boy caught his breath, wheezing, huffing and cackling, "The teachin's are rubbish and lies. You all 'ide behind your virtues when you are the most villainous!" He scoffed as the prince broke away from his father, rushing to Lowell and swift in planting his foot into the boy's side.

Lowell coughed, his body shaking, betraying his taunting words. He was hurting.

Huxley swaggered to his son, tugging his ear to stop him. Begrudged, Alistair found his original place in the room. Watching with increasing wrath as the beatings continued, the prince tugged at his father's sleeve and spoke in his elder's ear. The king regarded what he said with interest, nodding in approval. The brat gazed at Lowell's back before smirking at Edda, sticking out his tongue. The wires trembled as Camille exhausted herself, setting down her controls. She stepped down from her contraption, for there was no point in hiding herself away. Lowell knew the truth of it all.

The lot left the two alone, pain larger than themselves, weighing on their young bodies. Lowell whimpered, readjusting, resting his head on his shoulder, his mouth gaping open and closed as he sucked in breaths that made his broken frame quiver. His ribs rattled in his chest as he spoke, a man before the girl, looking to soothe her. The very look in his eyes broke her heart in ways she never knew possible. "Did I ever tell you about the birds? What ma told me about birds?" His eyes rolled in his head and he closed his eyes, his words the same as his exhales, "I'll tell you 'bout the crows, Edda. Th-they are envious things, lookin' to take. S-some get ahead of themselves. Tired of waitin', they look to steal. 'Orrible what they do, yeah?" He sputtered, blood dribbling from his lip. Opening his eyes again, looking into Edda's clamped open eyes, he smiled sweetly at her.

She wailed, trying to say his name, spittle rolling down her chin.

"Take back what they took. M-maybe not now, maybe not even in ten years, but you c-can take it back. Crows are jealous creatures, but they are cowards. Shoo them away, Edda, I know you can." His toothy grin was bloody, and as his eyes closed again, he whispered, "Rest with me, I'll be 'ere when you wake. Think about it, yeah?"

She nodded her head, the metal about her clinking while Lowell's body limped with exhaustion, his chest quaking into a ragged sleep. She watched him and sobbed.

Eleven

owell and Edda stayed in the abyss for a few weeks, beating Martin's record that he had the privilege of creating when he was five. The cracks and grooves of Edda's flesh were deep gorges, the skin at the corners of her mouth rashing and red, her neck much the same from the cage holding her head upright. Her hands and fingertips were swollen, streaks of caked blood hidden in the cracks. Her eyes were the same as ever, unbothered, despite her inability to blink and moisten them – they shone as though polished to a clever sheen.

The young man before her spoke less as time went on. He was drained, exhausted, battered and fraying at the edges, muttering warbled words to himself when the two of them were alone. Edda knew his wrists were rubbed raw by his bindings, infected as was his leg, left to fester. She feared he wouldn't make it out of the basement at this rate, red swollen blotches spreading from his wounds, weeping along his legs, chest and face. His only clothing, torn pants made of coarse linens covering from his hips to upper thighs, the color of rusted metal, splotched with fresh blood that congealed and blended with the secretions that came before it.

The air smelled of copper, ammonia and feces.

Lowell spent more time in between the torture sleeping, trying to heal himself in whatever way possible. His chest heaved more and his sleep barely drifted below a cat nap. Edda felt a statue before him, as though he was cast there to worship a fallen deity, as though she were to grant him forgiveness through his sufferings and penance. She watched him breathe, whimpering to him when he stilled for too long, dragging him back to his present state when he might've wished to leave it.

He would look up to her, one eye swollen shut, and smile, sometimes showing broken teeth, other times keeping his lips closed as he regarded her. "Y-yeah, I'm 'ere," he would nod before passing out, only to be jarred awake by the royals returning with Camille.

The King and his son spoke with Camille, who was oscillating between haggard and put-together. She was alone in caring for every little thing and child - now having to save face and give to her distant family whatever ridiculousness they asked. Her face, in the light of the subroom they occupied, betrayed her exasperation - they knew nothing of running the Orphanage, only enjoying its results. "I cannot keep this up," she heaved out a sigh, glancing at Edda and Lowell as her pride left her. "I need her to return to her duties."

Huxley looked between the lot of them. Alastair smiled, nodding along, "Where shall we go?"

Camille was stunned, wondering if she could have stopped such senselessness earlier, the two prisoners well beyond broken. As much as she pushed herself to control her Marion, her heart ached along with her arms and hands for it was all beyond what was agreed upon. Her hands were well calloused, small nicks where she removed splinters; she wasn't meant to be punished along with the two. She pulled the strings but was removed from the acts – her hands were meant to be unblemished, clean.

Huxley motioned to the center of the room, commanding them unbound, the matron and protector of her orphans rushing to Edda and cutting the wires that were all but embedded into her skin. Aching, the girl's arms crumbled to her side, limp and scarred more fiercely than before. Camille pulled a small key from her apron, turning it about and letting the girl drop from the cage that held her upright. Dust scattered as she slammed to the dirt below, moist with what waste she purged. Edda laid there, urging herself to move, twitching her arms inch by inch to undo the gag, soaked and molding.

Hacking, she stared at the royals and their knight, their accomplice with all the tired malice she could muster, and removed the fixing on her eyes, careful not to twitch and tear them out. A gentle lift and curving pull freed the scooping restraint from her sockets, and her lids drooped, bruised. She tossed the piece to their feet, collapsing onto her arms, extending herself just enough to brush her hand against Lowell's foot.

He softened to her touch, his bindings released as he toppled to his right, head colliding with the soiled floor, mind reeling with pain and relief all at once. They both gazed at one another, wordless, their eyes fluttering open and closed as tears fell from them. They smiled at one another, coy, Lowell letting out a harsh chuckle as he seemed to sink into the ground.

A splash of bitter cold water befell them before a few bucket loads more drenched them. Edda gasped, shaking as her limbs seemed to burn. She turned to Lowell, as, he too, writhed on the ground, stifled groans of pain leaving his lips. The wooden pails resounded against a nearby wall as the young prince giggled to himself, "Shall we go now?"

Edda grasped for Lowell's hand, both their fingers cold as though they had just played in snow. She rubbed his palm with her index, a futile attempt to reverse what felt an eternity.

Alastair kicked at Lowell's back, both their faces contorting with pain. Edda hissed.

"Oh ho!" Alastair scoffed, brushing off the injured creature's attempt to hound him away. His father watched from the bottom of the stairs, arms folded, a disturbing smile on his face as his prodigy continued, "Come along, it is a nice day outside and we must hurry."

Hands came upon Edda, delicate and clawed, looping under her arms and hoisting her to an assisted stand. Camille's frame was little more than Edda's, and she struggled to hold the girl up. Alastair gloved his hands, gripping Lowell's forearm like a dog who bit into its first kill, and tore him from the floor, his smaller frame hiding an unknown strength.

With the smallest amount of aid, Lowell stood, staring at Alastair before mischief glinted in his only opened eye. Parting his lips, his tongue played with a jagged tooth as he purred, "Caw, caw, little crow."

"You contemptuous rat!"

"Temperance, Alastair!" boomed the king. The mirrors along the walls buckled as the dying candles flickered.

Lowering his fist, Alastair sucked his teeth, shoving Lowell to the knight, who nonchalantly pushed him along.

One by one they ascended the stairs, sunlight scorching their eyes, closed and opened, as it poured in through windows on the first floor. The air was fresh, smelling like a space where people could live, hospitable. Edda's legs buckled, threatening to bring Camille down with her. The matron braced against a wall, face red with exertion. "I require assistance, your highness."

Huxley regarded her with absent eyes before resuming to leading them all to the front door. "You are too soft, Camille."

She grumbled into Edda's ear, leading with a lurching shoulder as she tried to maintain her pace.

The entryway was empty, the children shut away for the convenience of the royals who were too pompous to look upon the lesser, save for one spoilt by friendship and taught curiosity through his friend. Martin watched as they exited the front door, leaving it ajar. Glaring, he followed, using the wide trunks of trees to hide. Camille dragged the loathsome Edda, some man in knight's garb leading his precious Lowell, his savior, his older brother.

Martin had seen what she did to him - he held back his bile with the pure hatred that grew beautifully inside him. All the small moments he witnessed between them, teetering on a friendship he could not fathom, blinded himself to the natural bond that flowed between them - how he wanted it and how she abused it, soured it.

Unforgivable.

He followed them to the tree's clearing as all were led to where the prairie flowers grew abundant and bright, a few tinged with the colors of Edda's eyes. Swallowing, he crouched, hiding as best he could in the tall grass, staying close enough to hear Alastair when he spun about, addressing his audience, practicing when his time to ascend the throne would come to fruition.

Camille released Edda, stepping back as the exhausted girl slumped to her knees, her head lolling side to side, eyes glossing over those who circled around her. The midday sun seared the serpentine trails on her arms, emitting a glow that warmed her beneath her skin. Lowell in view, braced and leaning on the knight. She found herself frowning, bemoaning all life had to offer.

"I gather you all here for a show!" Alastair was boisterous, proud in his exaggerated movements – hands held up and out, fingers splayed open as a malicious grin plastered his face. He stepped towards Edda, crouching to meet her eyes, placing his hand under her chin, squinting at her. "How interesting you are, how you look. Unlike my future bride, yet. That will be some time. Father said to have patience, so I have to play nice for now."

Edda glanced at the king, his hands resting on his hips, his mouth gaped wide in a yawn. She wondered what Alastair was like at home, in the castle, full of theatrics and wanting of everyone's attention and admiration. She met his eyes as he raised a single brow.

"For you, girl, I do not have to pretend. You know what I am and who I am – and I will play a rather large role in the future of this land, of Wyrd. His Royalty has willed it. Those at the Monastery have blessed my birthright, and I am ever so eager to collect it."

"What h-ha-happened to you?" Edda whispered, her curiosity genuine.

"Oh, how she still tries! Precious little thing!" His spittle rained upon the face of the young woman as he gripped her jaw. "I was born for importance, and I hate waiting, so I will take what I can when I can."

Releasing her chin, he brought up a hand as his knight tossed a small parcel of fabric to him. Shaking it open, he masked Edda's head with a sack, the drawstrings tied with a knot. He chuckled to himself, glancing around, hoping to draw smiles from his audience. The knight's smile was dull and dry as he held steady the dying boy at his side. Camille examined her hands, rough and dirtied, the king tapping his foot in impatience.

Frustration crept across his face as he peered beyond those in sight, a small thing scuttling in the grass, little white pearls looking back at him. Chuckling, he stepped back, his boyishness ever apparent as he played adult and commander. From under his robe, he produced a dagger and a short sword. The former landed in front of the blindfolded girl, the grass billowing aside, wishing not to touch it.

Twirling the sword, Alastair, marveling at how the air whooshed about, positioned his feet into that of an experienced fencer. His right foot pointed forward, his left pointing to its namesake.

Edda remained in place, unmoved since Camille let her go.

Alastair sighed, exaggerated for everyone to hear, even those out of sight, "Come on now, I'll give you a chance to come at me – you obviously hate me and my family. Even my precious religion that has helped *so* many has drawn your hate!" With the tip of his blade, he edged the elongated knife towards Edda, the hilt now touching her knees. "Come on now, land a blow, best you can!"

She hesitated, her hand gliding forward, padding the hilt with bloodied fingertips until she decided to hold it rather loosely. The gentle heft reminded her of the key to the front door, the comfort she felt holding it before it was whisked away.

Yet she remained on the ground, motionless. The prince began to poke at her with his sword, making little cuts in her torn shift, never drawing an ounce of blood, impatience and hunger making him ravenous.

"Do *something*!"

"My boy, maybe she needs different motivation," Huxley motioned to his knight who reached to Lowell's leg, twisting the protrusion that was billeted into the boy's flesh. He wailed and Edda jittered, her grasp on the knife tightening, knuckles white as stone, no hint of the red of her skin.

"Ahh, I see. Camille was right when it comes to what makes you quake. Martin, come watch from the best seats in the land!" Edda sucked in breath as Camille whirled around to where the prince pointed, a small shape pushing up through the tall grass. Martin carefully made his way over, avoiding the little flowers his friend enjoyed so much. His face was downcast, ashamed of his sneakiness failing him as he took his spot next to his matron.

"Again!"

Lowell groaned, sucking in his tears, breath hissing through the gaps of his teeth as blood trickled down his legs. He was paling.

Martin's face contorted in pain, sharing the experience with his friend in a way he knew no one would ever understand or come close to. He glared at Edda, wanting Alastair to run her through, to end her. Locking eyes with the prince, he gestured at the evil demon before him, vulnerable and ready to die.

"Martin, you can make it happen - you simply need to speak, and then I will save your friend."

The youngest of them all, glanced at everyone, gulping down his fear. "Edda, you are a liar, and you did this to our - to *my* friend. You are everything bad and hide away behind those eyes of yours, lying to everyone." He fumbled his hands. "Everyone else here is more kind and loving than you will ever be. Even the prince is giving you a chance to do something to him - how just he is! You are a coward."

"Rightly so!" Alastair clapped.

Edda was tightening inside, Martin's voice echoed inside her, calling her for what she was - a coward. Yet, she remained seated, gripping her weapon, choosing not to move. She would not play their game, whether or not that made her courageous or foolish.

"Alastair, tell her about her parents."

The prince whipped his head around to stare at his father, a large, looming smile blossoming to show his top row of teeth, his bottom lip curling over the bottom row. He turned to look at Edda, cackling, "My father told me about your parents, well, how they died! I think you were there for your father, dropped to the ground after an arrow stuck him right through. He was a brute, if I remember the story correctly – which I do! A few more arrows did him in, then!"

Edda stirred as her parents tried to hum to her, tried to soothe her deaf heart.

"Your mother took you, far and away in minutes it seemed. You two stayed hidden for quite some time. A few months?" He poked her sacked forehead, unbothered by the dagger in her hand. "It's no matter, for when they did find you and your clever mother, you were ripped from her fingers and a blade met her throat. Why, I can almost see it!" He waved his hands in excitement.

Martin watched Lowell fading, his body limping, his mouth whispering silent things when he wasn't drooling. Time was of the essence and the prince was caught up in his longwinded play. Motioning his head, Martin caught Alastair's eye, the latter glancing as Lowell kept on his feet despite all odds.

He rolled his eyes and continued, "You are your mother's daughter – nothing pierced her skin, as nothing but crushing sullies yours!" He swung at her neck, the blade ricocheting, the high-pitched tinging making Camille and Martin wince.

Edda's head was crooked as she straightened up, lifting her head to face her assailant, unable to truly see the malice on his face, feeling it with her body instead.

"You must already know this! A natural demon, a demon of nature, all of you. A blessing the teachings are, saving us from your folly. However, I digress. Stones could not break her, so, we tried to think of something else and a certain *someone* came up with a simple solution: drown her! That worked splendidly, right father? Down, deeper and deeper she sank with her own weight – pop, pop, pop the bubbles did go, until no more came up."

Alastair shuddered in elation upon telling her the truth, wishing to see her face – he winked at his cousin instead, motioning for her to continue his tale.

She abided, placing her hands on Martin's shoulders, holding him in an effort to comfort herself through him. "I took you then, Marion, named you and gave you a home. A purpose." Her voice was regretful, even doubtful as she looked at her young cousin, her prince and the kingdom's future.

Alastair cupped his hand to his ear, leaning close to Edda, before springing back midsentence, "What purpose you ask? To lure in your kind for us to handle in whatever way we see fit! Oh, how many will die, or, *have* died because of you. Ones you didn't even know about! How I wish to be like you when I grow up! Although, I would like to have a bit more fun with them than you."

Her head looped his story into something she could see, making sense of her recollections, the burdens she would wake with, an unintelligible knowledge her body held that her mind could not know.

She took the knife in both hands as the prince hooted, taking stance, and plunged it into her stomach, into that pit, wishing to swallow her every day since she first gave punishment – perhaps further than that.

It glided along her center, violently scraping to the side as though one were to stab a boulder, tearing through her gown, revealing her tinted skin.

The prince howled, whistling as Martin trembled, the king, his knight and Camille watched, and Lowell slowly died. The youngest screamed, frustrated, "Killer!"

And Edda burst forward, a vice grip on her weapon, held upside down so that she could slash, and that she did.

The prince staggered on his feet in surprise, laughing off his embarrassment as he scuttled to a proper posture, bringing his sword up in time to block a blow made in fury. He sidestepped her, creating distance as she continued to swing in front of her.

Huxley clapped. "It's about time. Try and teach my son a lesson – he's happy to oblige."

Knife angled, ready for a downward blow, Edda's head turned to the voice, ready to take them all to their Hell. She took hesitant steps, trying to remember the direction the King's voice came from, blood pounding and roaring in her ears.

She spun around, swinging as something long and pointed tapped her low back. She bellowed, low and deep, "Do not touch me, vile thing!"

"But, dear Marion, you need to focus. Your challenger is me!" He swung, slicing the shoulder of her dress as she responded with a lunge, plunging into the air beside Alastair's head.

"Boy, pay attention and quit your play!"

Alastair backstepped in shock, holding his breath, twirling his sword before cutting the space between them, striking down at her after his flair.

She deflected, "I am no killer! I am no demon!" She pounced, connecting with the ground, making it quake, her full force at play.

Camille stumbled and gasped, wrapping her arms around Martin, trying to pull him into her, their assailant at their feet, her voice a trembling scream when she shouted, "Away, you foul beast!"

"Camille, why would you allow such atrocities? 'Ow could you merely standby?" Edda's voice was quaking, anger so ferocious, tears accompanied, gushing from her, spittle wetting the sack over her face.

Martin broke free from Camille's arms, standing sturdy between them, arms out at his sides. "D-do not touch her!"

Edda's mind blanked as she reached out, touching the boy's quivering chest, feeling his heart little less than leaping from his chest - she could almost see the ire and fear in his face. He begged her, "If you do not play with him, Lowell will die. Please, I need him."

Lowell's smile flashed in her mind, full then broken and bloodied. Something cracked in her chest, remnants being swallowed by the whirlpool in her. A foreign pain and her mind reached through her wrath, whispering, "*I need 'im too.*"

"It is true!" Alastair sang the words, letting the words carry on the wind from behind her. He watched as she rose to her feet, facing him while reaching for the coarse linen about her head. He chastised her, "Do that and that game is lost!"

"When will it end, then?" she sputtered, remembering the last she saw Lowell, denying the truth desiring her to crumble, the wish to lay her heart bare to him.

"When I say it ends!" Flicking her hand with his blade, the two danced around each other, the wolf playing with the impervious, blind ram. The ridiculous game rushed the prince, making his innards sing in bliss and adrenaline - he wished for it to never end.

He spun her about in circles, redirecting her with his voice as she faced where he once stood - a jester to him. Long days spent with his knights training, practicing, feeling in his element, only to be told of his mediocrity. This was good practice for him, landing blows aplenty.

For Edda, it was endless. She could no longer recall which way she faced, the grass beneath her trampled flat. Following his voice was like following the sun with one's eyes. She pushed forward, growing tired as the boy skipped about, stumbling when she gave a lazy swing.

Fabric ripped along with flesh as a small wound blossomed crimson upon Alastair's chest. King Huxley screamed to his knight as Edda swung once more, sticking the blade deep, falling atop her victim, Martin's screams filling her ears.

Twelve

"It's done, then," Huxley sighed, wrapping his boy in his oversized robe, his child laughing and growling at his slip up, at Edda. Martin wailed as Edda reached for the burlap sack and tore it off her head, ready to faint at the sight before her.

Lowell lay beneath her, sputtering, blood leaking from his pale lips as his hand reached out to her. She quaked forward and back, settling on one side of him and taking his hand as he guided it to his own cheek. He coughed, peppering her face with crimson spittle that matched her panicked eyes, open wide in shock and horror.

With guilt.

"I-I am so sorry! I d-did not mean to, I thought you—" her words were barely audible as Martin shrieked in pain and anger. Camille held him place while he cursed the girl, her figure blocking his sight from his friend, blocking his entire view of the scene as it unfolded, only seeing the prince off to the side and another wounded in his place.

In his eyes, Lowell sacrificed himself for Alastair.

Edda held Lowell's cheeks, his warmth ebbing out and through her as she stared into the fading embers of his eyes. He smiled at her, the remainder of his teeth stained red as he regarded her the same as he always did. Reaching out, he ran his finger along the side of her face, finding the slope of her jaw and following it down before his weak hand dropped to his side.

Her hands found the hilt of the plunged knife, wanting to pull it out and undo her careless mistake, wanting to take it all back, wanting to plunge it in herself to escape this nightmare that lulled her into a complacency. It made her a coward, how she was so easy to manipulate - how quickly she could have freed herself as she began to know more of herself. A fool.

She allowed all of it to come to pass - she deserved to be under the ground, impaled and dying, only she deserved no tears shed, no one to watch her go. She merited only a lonesome and isolated death. The wall in her heart beginning to close in on itself, suffocating her heart as Lowell winced beside her, struggling to move.

"P-please d-do not move! Please..." Her words were whimpers as her lips quivered, steeling herself for what was to come.

He smiled at her through his pains and brought his hand to hers upon his cheek, an object solid between their skin. His mouth moved, words quiet, asking her to close the gap. She swooped her ear to his lips as his words rang through, clear as the blue sky and shining like a full moon, "This is yours, Edda. You'd best 'ide it away before a crow takes it again. I went lookin' for it, I did."

The shape became familiar to her on the back of her hand, jewelry she hadn't even recognized as lost. How unimportant it seemed now as her friend, her kinsman, died before her very eyes, by her very hands, from beginning to end.

Orchestrated to perfection.

With all his might, he gripped her hand, letting his whispers flow unending into her, "Keep it safe. Family is important, this trinket too. Wasn't your fault, Edda. Listen to me, if not now, then later, but 'old onto my words, yeah?"

She held herself still over him, a hand finding its way to the back of Lowell's head. His voice was only for her to hear between Martin's screams and Alastair's increasing laughter, doubling over at the scene before him.

"Lowell, d-do not leave me, please, I beg you."

"I will miss you, but I will see you again."

"W-what?"

His voice was full of hope, "When we go 'ome, Edda."

Lowell's hand began to fall away as she quickly wrapped hers around it, taking her mother's armlet into her palm before cradling his hand, snapping her head to face him, look him in the eyes as they began to close. "N-no, no Lowell, no!"

And he pecked her nose, his cold lips parting as he exhaled, and Edda placed hers over his in a kiss, taking his last breath into her. She cradled him there, not wishing to part, hearing the rattle of his lungs empty into her being.

"Enough with the dramatics, now! To think I would need to say such a thing!" Alastair wiped at his eyes, hysterical, as only Martin's sobs were left to fill the silence.

Then Edda let go, blood lining her lips as she laid Lowell's head back into a bed of flowers, crowning him with pinks, purples, blues, and some the color of agates. His lips were closed but spread in a grin, his eyes half-lidded where they remained fixed on her. She whispered goodbye between broken breaths as she closed them, watching the sparks burn out.

"Alastair, you promised! You said you would save him!" Martin's voice cracked as his voice was ran ragged, fighting Camille as tears ran down her pallid face.

"Martin, my boy, call me highness or majesty! Besides, your friend simply decided to *save* me. How honorable." He glared back before turning to his father, smiling.

"How right you are, my son. Does he have a trophy to take, or do the women tend to carry?"

"They give the trinkets to the women, father. His mother or sister should have it – another to add when we find them."

The King nodded as he began to stride towards the Orphanage once more, his hand gesturing to his knight who used his metaled foot to push at Edda. She remained fixed.

"Come now, lovesick girl, we must bury the body! Lest someone catch wind of this." Alastair crouched just out of her reach, dragging out his words, "Edda."

She snarled at him, scowling as she snapped her head up, still holding Lowell's hand.

"Must we drug you once more? Oh, wait now..." His face lit up as he called out to his father, his King.

"Yes?"

"I see a trophy I would like."

King Huxley waved him off, to do what he liked as he continued on. The boy motioned for his loyal servant to restrain the girl, telling him to hold back her head. She gave little struggle as Camille called to him, "Leave her, enough has been dealt to her today. Please, I need her..."

"Be not a heretic, Camille!" he taunted, taking the knight's dagger from its sheath and giggling before plunging the blade under Edda's eye, watching it pop from its home and into his hand, heavy and solid. Little blood trickled from her empty socket as he gazed in curiosity at her unaltered visage, his face quick to turn to disgust. "A demon indeed..."

She held his gaze with one eye and an empty hole before dropping her gaze again, tears rolling down her face as she began to rock, attempting to wipe the blood from Lowell's face, some his, some hers, smearing it further along.

"Oh now, you're just making it worse," he mumbled before holding up his new trinket, watching the sun shine off it in splendid ways, tossing it up and catching it in his palm, marveling at what seemed to be a stone. He stared into the blackness of the middle and cooed in amusement, "Well, then, grant us eyes, I say."

Camille place a hand over Martin's gaze, hoping to spare him, but he fought her off as Camille swallowed back bile, struggling to stand.

Alastair noticed and smirked as he hopped by, grabbing Martin's arm, tugging him away from the woman. "You'll come back to the castle with me. I think you have so much potential!"

Martin glanced at him, not yet sated. "Kill her, please! You can drown her, you did her mother that way. Do her, she deserves it!"

Alastair gave him a large smile, dragging the boy along as he stared back, still crying tears of sadness and hate.

Camille shuffled forward, leaning down and placing a hand on Edda's shoulder before pulling back. "Ma—" she cleared her throat. "Edda, please listen to him. They'll give him a proper send off."

Pivoting, Edda glared at Camille, her stare half empty, seeing the regret and guilt spilling from the woman's face. She saw an evil instigator and a hint of envy, fading, but there all the same.

She stumbled as Lowell's body was pulled from under her, hefted into the arms of the knight, unperturbed as he strode away before Edda could react. Her hand shot out at the body's foot, then the knight's, before her arm fell to the ground. She was too heavy to move, sinking in place, unable to watch him disappear, to watch him go once again.

Her eye socket was wide and gaping at the ground as she braced herself, blood coating the bent grass beneath her. Dirt forced its way under her nails as she dug into it and all her tears began to pour from her, an endless well as she began to keen, her violent sobs ripping through her throat with such intensity that all around her quieted, her mind subdued with her breaking.

Camille let her hand rest upon the girl's back, her heart spasming, her mind shot through as she cried along with the young girl.

Edda watered the blossoms beneath her, grateful for what they could receive. The walls inside her rebuilt themselves, shutting her apart from all else as her lungs seemed to burst and she let out a scream so piercing, so painful that it rang out silent and nothing stirred.

Not the breeze, not a dove, not the river, not a crow.

THIRTEEN

pproaching the Orphanage, Martin was gone once again, along with King Huxley and his party. Camille carried a catatonic Edda in her arms, her figure deceptive of her heft, threatening to break the matron's arms as she shambled forward. It was a weight she was not happy to bear, but she knew it was hers alone. The prince was a monster, and next to him, the demons she was raised to hate and fear were saints. Her head ached with conflict, with an attempt to rationalize her life as it shattered before her.

Up the stairs, the door opened wide before them, the remaining children standing in wait and creating a path for their saint. Camille's stomach twisted as she glanced at them, her legs quaking as she took steps that made the floor boards screech, moaning even if she dragged her feet. The stairs were next as she stood at the bottom, looking up to the second floor as little feet lined up behind her.

Their voices were small, and if different children spoke, she couldn't tell, forgetting how many were even left – less than a handful now.

"Lady Camille, where are Martin and his friend?"

"Gone."

Uncertain feet glided along the floor. "What happened to Marion?"

"Edda is under the greatest duress one could imagine."

"Edda?"

"Her name is Edda." Her voice was curt, firm and cold, the only way she could keep herself from collapsing as she began her slow ascent, the steps seeming to bow beneath her.

"Why do you care? Is she not a demon?"

She paused, sniffing back the waters that raged at her flimsy dam, focusing on each step. Below her, the children waited, patient, for her reply. Sweat broke along her brow, trickling down her high cheek bones and her slim neck as she made it to the top, holding back a smile over her little victory.

The question was repeated, "Is she not a demon, Lady Camille?"

"No, she is no demon. She is just a girl, a child like you all." She stepped forward, toward her own room.

"But, in the basement..."

"She was controlled, my dears," she hesitated, biting her lip as her tears seeped out. She fumbled the knob and the room opened before her, sun streaming in the windows before her, lighting up her beloved tapestries and welcoming her and one of her orphan daughters.

The children began to follow, baby ducklings they were, knowing not what to do without proper direction. "By who?"

She made it to the bed, laying a silent Edda over her soft woolen blankets, gasping for air whilst doubling over the girl, her legs wobbling violently from the trip and the events of the day, the weeks. Camille sucked in air, knowing she could not rest yet, straightening her back. A steady exhale helped her compose herself as she turned to the children.

"Now, then, there is bread from morning as well as cheese and butter you can use. You will need to feed yourselves for tonight and put yourselves to bed when the sun sets. Understood?"

They nodded, save for one who nibbled at his thumb, stepping forward to fill Camille's doorway, shaking off another child's hand attempting to pull him away. A string of drool connected him to his finger as he opened his mouth. "Who made her? Was it a demon?"

"It was no demon, not like the teachings, but it was evil nonetheless." Striding to the threshold, she waved them off, sinking with her back to the door after closing it, tucking her head into her chest and whispering to herself, "It was me."

She sobbed until the sun began to dip outside, painting her walls in colors that reminded her of Edda's eyes, eyes that remained unsodden, clear and warm the entire time she knew her. If the girl was to feel anger, sadness or pain, these emotions played on the outer intricacies of the girl's gaze, never sullying the love she always carried. It was a beauty that Edda was made not to believe and trust, by Camille's own hand.

But her entire childhood, her devout following of the teachings—could it all have been a lie? Perhaps it was a twisted truth, misconstrued. Yet the blessed child of their king had played with tortured souls and when his folly would have cost him, another took his place. The prince, when Lowell's punishments began, was changed from over a year prior, and Camille had shamed herself over her blooming doubt that began when she saw his eyes. "He could still change," she muttered. "It all could still be true. The two were not of evil, but Alastair is still young. Yes, there are exceptions, still."

Yet he laughed heartily, his belly full of joy at the sight of wretched acts.

Taking tight fistfuls of her loose gown, she twisted the fabric, holding back her tears as she rationalized the past month, the past decade. She stole glances at the girl in her bed, eyes wide and staring at the ceiling, blood covering the front of her gown and dotting her face – brown, dried, and flaking. Camille forced herself to look at Edda's arms, at the snaking red scars that bit her deep.

That was Camille's part. She devised such a room, such a chamber for a girl of only six. Then there was her mother, bubbling to the bottom of a stream, deep and alone.

Again, her stomach flipped and twisted as she held back bile, seeing everything her hands committed as she tapped her head against the thick door behind her, thumping it harder and harder still, fixed on denial, fixed on how she was raised.

The dying light caught the radiant thread of the tapestries around her room, setting them aglow, as though the weaved suns were setting as well. She once loved this at dawn and dusk when the rising sun motif caught its mimics, her room cast in brilliance, dazzling her and deepening her faith.

Letting it wash over her, the light lifted her heart as heresy seemed to leave her. The beauty, the splendor – she did what she had to, and the fitting of her stomach, of it settling itself only reaffirmed this, her path, her truth. Eyes wandering over all the tapestries, she found herself smiling, releasing her gown and rising up to bathe in it.

A new light caught her eyes, a new reflection in her room that seemed to glow brighter and more intense than her precious hangings, her lovely sunrises and sunsets. It shone a deep crimson that seemed to twist and breathe, alive and wriggling, pulsating.

She was drawn toward it, her feet moving of their own accord as well as her hand, reaching forth to grasp the overpowering light, to hold it fully and completely. The purest light of the room.

It was smooth as stone, and cool. The light separated into strands that wrapped in familiar patterns, taking the descending sun's light as their own and making it ever more than it could be alone. The spaces between them were smooth as well, but black to her eyes. She was taken, overcome—

—until the shining under her fingers shifted, the flesh they marred hidden behind her trance. Camille struggled to process it, wrapping her hands about the lights as best she could, attempting to hold it, to contain it and have it on her own.

She craved to possess it for the same reason she lined her walls with tapestries that captured the light of the sun.

A perfect benevolence. Her life's mission, the forefront of her mind, her consciousness. She gripped the writhing light as it pulsed beneath her fingers, palms, warming from her hands. She fell to her knees. Surely His Royalty had blessed her with this, bestowing it onto her for her determination, her persistence, the pains and torments she struggled with in performing her duties.

Something dark raised up towards her. She felt it move the air before her face, coils of splendor following it as she welcomed it, her gift, letting her eyes close and open anew. This bundle of light, coiled and moved in a circle, the center of which remained black. Of this there was only one, and it washed her in waves of love and kindness.

You need me repeated in her mind as she began to cry once more, wishing to hold a brilliance that did not belong to her, shame taking over where her doubt once bloomed. Fingers traced along her cheek as Edda's single eye captured Camille's sight, the blackness of the room fading into the light of the coming moon.

"Why, Camille?"

"B-because it was what I was meant to do."

"By whose decree?"

The matron gestured to the tapestries surrounding them, unable to speak, unable to break away from the girl in her bed.

"Did they use wires and metal trinkets on you?"

Camille shook her head, eyes wide.

"Then it was by you, was it not?"

She blubbered like a brat whose world was ripped away. The only goodness she had ever given was at the expense of another, and another, and another. His Royalty's light did not shine on her, not now and not again after she'd seen the light within Edda, under her own skin – that which she had to render and twist, to crack and break to finally realize.

Her blindness struck her through, stabbed as she released herself from the girl, made her way across the bed, slow and heavy — lighting the fire. Edda's eye followed her back, boring a hole in Camille as the matron began to gag, horrendous and ugly. The pit within her ached as she sank into the indignation of her own actions. Catching her breath, she turned to meet the young woman who now sat amongst her blankets and pillows.

"You are a coward, Camille, like me." Edda dug deep into her pocket to produce golden jewelry cradling an agate, lined with intricacies that appeared unnatural.

"You looked through my belongings? How dare you overstep your boundaries – I instructed you to be better behaved!"

"One to talk, are you? It was mine to begin with, my mother's first. Lowell found it – I 'ad not noticed it was missin'." Edda caressed the armlet between thumb and index finger, letting her finger glide along the stone before pocketing it, her eye never leaving Camille. "You are a crow, a thief wishin' for all it could not 'ave – 'ow many lives 'as it cost, so that you could remain envious?"

Tremors rippled throughout Camille as she listened, the newfound hole in her soul wishing to all but swallow her.

"Was the love of H-His *Royalty* worth the traumas you've inflicted on innocents?"

"You are not kind, nor loving, child! Are such words of love?"

"Yes, for love and kindness are not of deception, but of truth." Edda's legs swung over the edge of the bed, feet connecting with the floor as her body followed her gaze of one gorgeous eye, and one hollow, vacuous socket. "Was torture, murder, and thievin' of love and kindness?"

"Y-yes. It was necessary!"

"Lies, Camille, you still fight what you need to accept."

"I-I cannot. Please spare me, Edda, please, I beg."

"I cannot spare you, for it is not my absolution you need, nor some royal creature in a castle of the past and future. I do not inflict pain. You made me do so – I was a coward, unwillin' to fight it."

Edda came closer to Camille as she collapsed and shrunk into herself, scuttling near the fire, flames threatening her. "I did nothing that was in my own control!"

Bringing a finger to her tongue, Edda then moistened the dried blood about her limbs, letting it color her fingertips before she bent down and smeared red streaks under Camille's eyes, covering the dark circles that had grown from exhaustion and denial. "You cannot sleep and many are dead — you cannot rest. Why?"

"I am afraid. Afraid of you."

"And?" Edda continued to draw lines on Camille, parallel to her tear streaks. The bloody artist began to cry herself.

Camille battled herself, trying to overcome her emotions with her mind, attempting to quell the brewing storm. The room was quiet as Edda continued to leave streaks down Camille's neck, retracting her hand to gather more of her medium before drawing twisting streaks on the woman's arms. Edda sunk before her as she fought her own guilt, little sobs escaping her lips.

"I was always wrong," Camille gasped. "I only see it now."

Breaking from her own trance, continuing her painting, Edda chuckled, closing her seeing eye to cast a haunting stare at Camille with the empty pit in her skull. "H-h-'ow blind you are. And now, a-a-and now," Edda sucked in a breath, "Lowell is dead, a-and mama, and papa, and many more." From Edda's throat came a low droning, a soft howl as she expelled her pains as slow as she could, into her matron before her.

Camille reached out to the broken child, pulling back as she took in the twisted and smeared blood on her arms, matching the marks of Edda's to perfection. She wiped her arm against her dress once, then twice, more and more. Her skin was stained with Lowell's blood.

Camille screamed with fright and pain as the marks became more vivid and she cursed feverishly at the world. She scrambled to her feet and stared at that which once comforted her and scorned it all along with herself, "I served you and you damned me! I did everything for you and you leave me to suffer!" Frustration dripped from her as she descended upon her tapestries, scratching and tearing them from her walls and feeding them to the forever hungry fire.

Naked walls surrounded them in minutes, as Camille wrapped her arms around Edda, scratching at the surface of her own forgiveness.

Fourteen

All there was to do now was maintain the day to day. Edda and Camille maintained a silent agreement of sorts as the children were cared for and adopted out. The king's letters were few and far between. Camille reported less to him, and her hours spent teaching scriptures and passages crawled to near nothing.

Both the caretakers wore long sleeves now, Camille just managing to cover the faint bloodstain tears Edda had painted on her. She accepted the marks over time, hoping they would fade as she persisted in penitence.

Edda wore a black cloth over the missing eye, sometimes pausing to tap at the taut fabric, to feel the flimsy hollow skin bend beneath it. It had become a curiosity, replacing any need to mourn her missing piece. Lamentation was practiced for what transpired months ago in a method most painful: she spoke little to nothing, her eyes downcast and averted from others' looks, a wall erected within – the dullness in her eyes apparent to all she allowed to see.

She would not leave the orphanage for any means, keeping herself within the stone structure, no desire for anything. She was hollow, and with it, she was complacent.

Every time the two occupied a room, Camille would watch Edda with guilty eyes, her faith waning more every day. The children would awaken her from wandering her own mind, only for her to turn the same gaze unto them; these children stared blankly in response to her telling the orphans 'to run in the fields and make imaginary plays' — the children she subjected to torment by Marion's hand – a demon of her own making.

How foolish.

At night, she stole away to Edda's old room, bequeathing her vast room to Edda in an attempt to quell the vacuum that occupied her soul – she lived in a limbo she created by accident, never knowing the Hell she would allow to exist.

The basement was locked to all but Camille as she stole away to it, standing atop her perch where she practiced her manipulations before finding herself an occupant of the more sullied portions of the chamber. She dirtied her gowns and chemises as she knelt where her Marion was hung by the head, holding her arms aloft in an attempt to imagine through the eyes of another.

She would close the metal cage about her head and neck, attempting to let herself hang as a child of six first did. The wires she occasionally wrapped about her arms and pulled as tightly as she could muster, stopping to cry once she winced and felt the skin beneath begin to flex, stopping just before popping under the stress.

The fixing for the eyes she could not manage to hold before herself, the horror freezing her in place.

Then she would sit across from the spot of the marionette, back against a pole, feeling it dig into her spine as she twisted her arms behind her. Dried blood, Lowell's blood, would sully her dress each time she did this, yet the spot always remained as dark as the first day his blood spilled.

She would sit here for hours after the children had gone to bed, candles lit and flickering in the mirrors, giving the illusion of tens of hundreds of candles as they reflected and played in the darkness that filled the spaces in between. Before her, dangling from wires and a cage, she imagined glowing eyes of love and kindness, ever watchful as the abuse was committed. How had she twisted something so beautiful?

The markings on her arms burned as she tried to experience it, knowing full well her guilt would never match a fraction of what all those she touched would live with day to day.

She let her head rhythmically bounce off the pole behind her, coalescing into a resounding pound that echoed about her until the spot grew numb, pivoting to numb a different portion of herself as she continued to stare into the void before her.

She abandoned her post when the shadows danced about her, her reflection sprouting imaginary black feathers and a robust, willowing beak.

Headache in tow, she would snuff out the candles, exiting the basement to meet the back of Edda, staring out the window at the top of the stairs. She wondered if the girl saw anything outside as she locked the door behind her.

Once the latch was turned, Edda's heavy footfalls would begin their march upstairs, Camille bidden to follow as they walked together to her new bedroom. Once entering, she could hear Edda turnabout, making her way to her own room.

Camille felt akin to a child brought to bed.

A fresh chemise next to a basin and glass of water awaited her atop the vanity, old and leaning to one side. She would change, wash, and drink before kneeling at her bedside, clasping her hands in prayer, struggling to find the words she believed she needed to speak.

To whom she prayed, she did not know, sometimes to her old god, sometimes to the air, and sometimes to those she tortured and allowed to die. Edda's mother and father were ideas in her mind, whereas the variety of children who left as broken beings flitted about. Edda and Lowell crossed by often as she worked to let go of her life's work and teachings.

She whispered pleas and apologies, genuine, but conflicted at times, for His Royalty still grasped at her, pulling the hatred away from herself and directing it towards those who had always received it.

No one could tell her how to free herself of her sins, no one could provide answers now, and knowing this, she would retire her mind to a shallow sleep, waking to repeat the cycle the next day.

Only one night, pulled into a deep slumber, she dreamed of one who was blind.

Within an infinite gray vacancy that went on as far as one could see, the woman's features shifted endlessly as though she were made of smoke, some bits disappearing from existence then reforming from the woman's center. Her edges were white, fading into the color of the surrounding world – her eyes were without a pupil or iris.

Camille staggered towards the woman, every step a leap of faith as she toddled forward on one foot, three toed and scaled, and another of human flesh. She struggled to keep her head held high as her nose dragged her head down, heavy, black, and curved – her neck too thin and weak to maintain such features for long.

She was tired as she sat next to the woman, feeling the coolness of her wisps against her naked arm.

Neither spoke as they watched a horizon of nothing, allowing it to fill them both. It took an eternity for her world to sink in, causing Camille to break down into sobs as the blind woman took her hand and held it.

Following a strong urge, Camille looked below her as black feathers spun in a tight spiral underneath until distance was gathered and they fluttered away. Her head was growing lighter as she turned to look at the one holding her hand, the one comforting her. She met milky eyes that saw nothing and everything, constantly shifting, constantly plagued by what they saw.

"Guide me, please."

The figure shook her head, her eggshell gaze turning to mist for a moment, perhaps a blink. Camille's clawed foot twitched as she begged once more.

The void answered her, as her being vibrated, her heart shaking. A woman's voice spoke, "Guidance is not when one is told all of what they must do. It is the direction they are shown. Endless guidance prevents one from growing, from living."

"I am lost. I do not know which direction to face."

"That is what I show you now."

"I see nothing!"

"Then go to it."

"I cannot, I do not understand."

The empty figure paused in thought before speaking again, "Tomorrow, what will you do?"

"I will wake Edda, then we will fetch the children..." she listed her daily tasks, ending with her visit to the basement before her being led to bed.

"So you see the way it will go?"

Camille nodded, beginning to understand. "Go to nothing."

The smoky figure nodded, a maternal love ebbing from her. "That is all I can tell you, Camille."

Standing upon two feet, ten toes in all, Camille stepped forward, turning around to see the blind woman was gone. Twirling about, she lost direction, seeing absence everywhere she turned. She called out, "Who are you?"

No one answered, but she felt the space about her warm in a smile.

* * *

Camille felt more renewed today, better able to face the inkling of what she believed she was meant to. She stood before Edda's door later than usual, having already sat the children down to eat. Feeling half-surprised and half-thankful that Edda had not come out of her room, she rapped at the door.

After a minute of silence and continued knocking, she twisted the glass knob and entered. Edda stood opposite the door, gazing out of an open window, her hands resting atop one another on the sill.

Gathering courage, Camille crossed the room to join her, looking down to see that the morning dew of spring had brought a creeping fog along with it. Together, they watched it seep between trees and blades of grass before Camille swallowed her hesitation and placed a hand atop Edda's. "I have much to show you today, Edda. The children are set to enjoy their day – I believe the younger are teaching the older how to play again." Camille paused, wincing at what her words hinted. Standing straighter, she curled her fingers around Edda's, a feeling that seemed to warm her when it once would have repulsed her.

A blind eye met Camille before Edda's fogged eye did, reluctance disguising the love that lived there. Tucking away the brown waves of Edda's hair, Camille let herself be taken by a wish and laid a gentle kiss on the girl's cheek. The edges of Edda's lips quivered as she let herself be led without question to a room new to her.

Camille's classroom was dotted with desks, each with little books turned upside down. At the front was a desk backed by a large white, smooth wall with lumps of charcoal resting on the windowsill adjacent, like a large piece of paper with quill nearby. The room was musty, a fine layer of dust covering all but Camille's area, where she wrote letters to prospective adopters and other important tasks.

Pulling out paper, ink, and a quill, Camille instructed Edda to write, watching the budding woman scratch along the surface of the paper.

Camille once more held her pupil's hand and taught her to copy her own handwriting and the finer aspects of running an orphanage.

She could not help but feel a smile grow on her face as her pain began to melt at the joy of what she imagined a mother would feel.

Fifteen

Edda had grown used to her new vision after a few days, seeing through one eye at a single perspective. She vaguely remembered reading a story or two about a warrior who lost vision in an eye and needing to relearn how to use their blade, reteaching themselves to recognize depth.

Perhaps it was easier for Edda since she did the same services as any other day and these deeds required no quickness. The hollow hole in her skull was an oddity that the children stared at, even if it was covered day and night. Edda took to brushing her closed eyelid – a few times she caught herself staring at it in a mirror, a finger reaching over the edge of her face and into the red vacancy, only to find a smooth surface behind.

There was much more she struggled to acclimate to, to accept fully.

Camille had been quite kind of late and allowed her more time to fulfill her duties – something she found appreciation for while remaining cautious. The woman's look of ire had disappeared, or at least had lessened. Her matron took to watching the girl with eyes of sadness and remorse, any anger or hate replaced by doubt, pain, and sympathy. Edda tried to maintain distance with her but when Camille began to spend hours in the basement, she found herself wishing to comfort her. She chastised herself for such a feeling, but still she succumbed to it several times in little ways.

Despite the torture she had to endure for over a decade by Camille's hands, it was difficult to hate her.

After all, Lowell was dead, her hand having driven the knife through his stomach. He might've been saved if it hadn't been for his stint in the basement – *that*, she blamed on Camille. Edda knew it was also her fault, both victims of manipulation, one more twisted than the other.

In the end, she dealt him his death, the abrupt blow meant for Alastair until the mercenary pushed Lowell in his place. Camille tried to soothe Edda's mind by telling her so, but it didn't change anything.

Lowell was to die one way or another that day.

Edda still heard him whispering to her around corners and behind doors. Her parents would join him at times, speaking inaudibly only to disappear once she followed the voices. She wished she could hear them, understand them, but she found herself glad to not know. After all, what could they possibly tell her that was not filled with hate and contempt for the young woman?

Now, she was learning to write, a task she had practiced in secret, her old lettering scratched and shaky like a chicken trying to compose pretty letters with its sharp claws. Tracing Camille's spiraling scripts aided in the process, as well as learning the proper way to hold a quill. Once more she felt thankful towards the woman, an odd sensation.

Due to this tutoring, the children were more often left to their own devices, regaining, to some degree, their own sense of whimsy.

They played a little louder than they ever had before, pretending the sofas and chairs of the parlor were little boats at times while others took to hiding about the Orphanage in closets, tucked in corners, and inside cedar chests that took at least two little ones to open. They were careful not to make messes of any sort regardless of the changes rippling through their temporary home, the older children remembering their beatings. The orphans still regarded Edda with caution, flocking to Camille more — the ideas planted in their minds by hours of teachings were not easily plucked by the roots.

Camille and Edda never spoke of the basement, nor the teachings, letting the structure of the Orphanage unravel however it may.

"Edda, no, your writing must appear the same as mine. Trace again." Camille's tone was warmer, but her firmness was ever present.

The young woman readjusted herself, following the bends of Camille's written words as she did her best to commit each swirl to muscle memory. Although it was not as thrilling as it was in the beginning, it was still more pleasant than much of her time had been. Moving to write on fresh paper, she mirrored Camille's handwriting.

"Nicely done, Edda. You took to the quill quickly."

Edda's mouth twinged at the corner as her stomach pitched. Her voice was quiet. A struggle, it had been, to speak since everything transpired, since everything changed so abruptly – save for Lowell's stargazing setup in the room upstairs. "Why did you not teach me sooner?"

Camille gathered some papers, straightening the edges against the desk. She began to tidy up their lesson for the day and sighed, "For the same reason I did not let you sit for the teachings: it was unnecessary for you to learn such skills, especially when it was not among your duties."

"Is it now?"

Her matron paused, rubbing her eyes and clearing her throat. "It is a good skill to know and I feel it is what I must do – to do right, or at least, better by you." Edda nodded and tried her own flourish once more, only for Camille to point at the error. "Look at how I slant mine. Is it the same?"

Edda shook her head, her single eye peering at her teacher's face before finding the paper once more. "Why do I need to match yours?"

"So that in the instance you must write a letter for me, no living soul would be able to tell the difference. What if I am ill and King Huxley or Alastair writes, what then?"

The quill fell from Edda's hand, fresh ink dripping onto the paper. The girl rubbed her hands along her sides. Camille stole a glance at the girl, biting back irritation as she cleaned the metal nib against a cloth and dabbed at the drop of black ink that began to spread like veins along the paper.

"W-will they ever return h-h-here?"

"We can do all we can to prevent them from doing so, but the royal family does what it wishes in the end."

Edda's hand snapped up to graze her bandaged eye as Lowell's voice danced near her ear. She shook her head, refusing to listen. "Will you allow me to learn the teachings? As a favor to me as well?"

Camille grabbed Edda's arm, pulling her outside the room, turning abruptly to lock the door behind them. Her voice was guarded – protecting something that had once belonged to her, something so precious and sacred, and that could only do further damage to her pupil. Camille's gut twisted as her mind was forced to ideas she struggled to kill.

"Is it because I-I am a demon?" Edda's question was cold and firm.

Camille snarled at herself, failing to keep it from Edda. "Of course not! It is not meant for you, not ever!" Camille froze as Edda looked away, beginning towards the parlor. The matron placed a hand over her mouth, the other hovering over her midst as her heels clacked rapid against the floor. Edda's hand was ice cold when Camille grasped it, colder than it felt of late. Planting herself in front of her ward, she placed the other hand on Edda's cheek. "Edda, I apologize, but it is for your benefit – I did not mean to be so snippy. I merely have *conflicting* thoughts concerning the teachings and you."

Edda blinked, the hollow eye twitching beneath the cloth, her hand slipping from Camille's. Lowell used to speak ill of the lessons, and there was no doubt that being called a demon was the friendliest way her kin were spoken of. Maybe it was for the best. Perhaps Camille was right, even if her delivery was strained. "Yes, Lady Camille. I will h-head to the kitchen. Soon, it will be dinner."

Edda left Camille in the parlor, the children off elsewhere rediscovering their youth. She rubbed her arms, reminding herself of what else occurred for *her* own good as her heavy footfalls made the wood groan in some weaker spaces. Through the dining room and into the cozy kitchen, she began to chop potatoes and herbs before she fetched water to boil.

There was a damp cool by the well as she lowered the bucket, turning a wheel to control the pulley. The crows barely squawked these past days, but the mourning doves were ritualistic in delivering their cries every morning and night. At those times, Edda allowed herself to grieve for her parents, Lowell, the children, and Martin. There were times she cried for herself, although these were brief and she would steel herself from such selfish acts, trying to be less than the beast she'd come to know. Her stutter still held, steadfast in anchoring her in old, unwanted ways.

The sun was still shining through the trees that left small pockets of sky visible, but the rays could only pierce so deep through the fog that had been crawling along the ground for the past month or so. Sometimes the miasma climbed the air and hung high, but whatever it did on any day, it remained present. Edda enjoyed it, the light gray haze that only let her see so far out windows and made the grass look like a wisping sea, tickling her toes if she chose to be barefoot for a time.

The children appeared afraid at first, not having seen such a fog before, but they took to it given time, cupping it in their hands and watching it spill over from their little fingers before being tossed in the air like ghostly water. Camille watched it, unconcerned.

Pulling the bucket free from its restraints, Edda dragged her feet through misty hands grazing her ankles, taking all the time she could to get back to cooking.

"A gift..."

Her steps faltered as she tried to listen to what sounded like her father. She strained, trying to hear, but nothing more came from him. Looking behind her, she searched high and low, only seeing the well and flowers erupted from the blanket of fog.

She continued inside, setting everything in place, striking a match, lighting a fire, and making a meal for the children inside. Absentminded, she cooked and stared out the window, watching the light, thick mist dance in little spirals as though someone unseen stepped in it.

* * *

"Edda, why do the other kids call you tattered-tongue?"

"Child, such a thing is impolite."

"But I do not understand."

Edda's hand found her pocket and she rubbed a red stone tucked inside. "Because some words I cannot say correctly, like h-h-happy."

"Oh."

The dinner table grew silent, clouded with a tense, awkward air, the little girl embarrassed over not understanding her peers and older idols. She took a mouthful of stew, chewing a little as she stirred her wooden spoon about the bowl. Camille glared at the children who snickered as they attempted to hush themselves. They stopped when Edda's warm eye fell upon them.

"Does it hurt?"

Edda let a chuckle escape her, "No it does not."

"Why do you do it?"

"Stutter?" The little girl glanced at the others around her before nodding. "Because I speak differently than most and I wish to change."

"Why?"

Now Edda looked around her, holding Camille's gaze the longest before answering, "Because h-how I speak does not belong where we live."

"Why?"

Chortling spread among the children as the girl stared at Edda, her eyes curious, genuine and innocent.

"Because she is a demon – an evil creature that should only serve us," a voice answered.

Camille's mouth hung slack as she stood, slamming her hands on the table she glared at the ten-year-old girl who had answered the question. "You are to show respect to your elders! Edda is no demon, no more than you or I, and you *will* treat her as you treat *me!*" Anger flashed through the matron as the girl shrunk, taken aback. Camille's rage was a new sight to them all, and in defense of Edda, no less. "You will apologize at once!"

"Edda, I am sorry..." The girl looked down at her food, her shoulders hunching as she curled into herself.

"Lady Camille, you taught us that she is so! And what she did to us for such small transgressions!"

Camille looked between the nine-year-old boy and the motionless Edda, hands folded in her lap as she listened to things she already heard, already knew. A shiver ran down Camille's spine as her figure buckled, her voice quieting. "I was wrong, child. The teachings... were wrong. Edda's actions were not her own."

"Then why teach us lies?"

"Because I believed them too. I was blind and taught you all to be as I am – as I *was*. It was all I knew."

The children were quiet now, sullenly casting confused and skeptical glances at one another before an eleven-year-old girl spoke up, "Whose actions were they?" Her voice faltered as her sense of enemy turned into a new and frightening question. From her seat, Edda could see the young girl rubbing her arm. Edda remembered there was a thick scar there from when she scratched the terrified girl several months prior.

Camille was frozen, leaning over her stew. All eyes were upon her now as her legs quaked beneath her, the shame and guilt threatening to break her being. She shook under all the pressure, and then breathed out, regaining her calm, her voice wavering, "Something far worse. An ideology and a devoted follower." An ironic smirk dashed her face before dissipating, her brows knitting together.

"I am scared," one child whimpered.

"I do not understand," spoke another.

They all looked between Camille and Edda, the latter keeping her gaze on the table but lifting her head. "You needn't be afraid, for h-harm will no longer come to you in this Orphanage. And, some questions, you find the answers to when you grow older. With time, you will understand Lady Camille's words." Edda stood, gathering up some of the empty dishes and utensils, placing them upon her wooden cart.

"Mar – I mean, Edda?"

Giving a tender smile, Edda let her eye fall upon one of the quieter children. "Yes?"

"Why did you not fight the creature that controlled you?"

Edda's head rocked back and forth, her vision bouncing around the room, lips pursing when she found Camille, a thick brown lock of hair falling from behind the matron's ear. She decided to look out the window, the sky darkening as the sun brought them twilight for dinner. The fog was taller and peeked inside through the thick glass. "I was afraid, too. If I was to act, it would h-have gotten worse. Or so I believed."

Edda left the room, pushing the dishes she had gathered along for cleaning. A child behind her began to speak again, his voice directed at Camille, who stood motionless over lukewarm soup, "Camille, when will someone come to adopt me? I want to leave."

"Soon, my dear, soon."

Sixteen

Edda's penmanship differed little from Camille's as they moved onto prose and communicative letters – mostly concerning adoption and enticing the rich to take in the rejected, abandoned, and many times forgotten children.

The wording of the initial letters differed little, names and dates having been changed from one to the next. It was writing correspondence and answering questions in proceeding letters that proved strenuous for Edda. She was rigid in more ways than her body and skin as she struggled answering her teacher's prompts eloquently and attractively.

She was asked how many children there were, and what features they had, if there was a disparity in intelligence within the selections, if any were at a proper age for understanding and being able to learn the tasks and responsibilities that they would face upon becoming adolescents without breaking under the pressure, if there were children who possessed an aptitude for horse-riding, and so on. Camille insisted these were questions she'd had to address before, more than once, even.

Answers needed a little flourish, a hint of honesty, and variation so no two letter were quite alike, save for initial outreach. Every Monday and Thursday, one of the royal carriers would arrive just for the Orphanage—an expense the King was happy to indulge in, granted his will be done and the children follow the teachings.

Huxley's letters were a different matter entirely, filled with empty platitudes and updates on the children's progression within the religion and their behavior, notably Edda's. Within his letters, old and recent, she was still referred to as Marion. To Edda's relief, his letters were few and sparse; to Camille's concern, they were few and sparse. Practice was difficult when the King's varied letters arrived farther apart and requested a variety of information.

"H-he asks if any creatures arrived of late in this letter. Do 'creatures' mean my people?"

Camille pinched the bridge of her nose after smoothing the sides of her fastened hair and nodded. "Yes. If we answer there are, he sends for scouts and others to capture them..." Camille sighed, staring at the floor.

"H-ha-how did you know?"

"They did not hide the best, sensing that you were here. You also took to the windows when they were near as well, searching the tree lines with an absent look about you."

"I did not realize I did such a thing."

Camille turned to Edda, who rested her arms on the desk in front of her, eyes fixed on the opposite door. She tucked the girl's hair behind her ear. "You cannot forego all your intuition tells you, no matter how much you push it down. It creeps up in a multitude of ways."

Edda shifted and began reading a new letter, one from a future adopter. She could not remember a word written in the parcel. "Terrible, is it not?"

"We seek others like us. Is that not how families are born?"

"H-how did you come across my family?"

"Luck, I would say. One of the eldest children was playing in the field and glanced a little girl being plucked out of the sun, into the wood."

The young woman squirmed and repeated, "Terrible." Her tears dampened the cloth over her empty socket, the other eye letting a trickle down her cheek. Camille moved to wipe the girl's face, but she turned away.

Camille bit back her sigh. "Truly, but it was because of the actions of others, not some little girl who hardly understood the world and its horrors."

Outside, a bird passed by the window, its shadow dancing on the wall.

"When my parents died, was it quick?"

Swallowing, Camille steeled herself to answer, trying to balance between her calm, collected self and her newfound sympathy. "Your father, yes. Your mother... I am sorry."

"Why did you not drown me?"

"Children are more disconnected from the last battle, the one that made you all scatter." She walked towards the window, to the left of the white drawing-wall. "Children are also malleable, making them easier to control. You could serve a purpose, but your parents could not."

"Terrible."

"Come along now, we must get through more letters before the day is at an end."

"Why are you to leave?"

At this, Camille was awestruck, having failed once more to notice the wit Edda possessed. She did not answer, taking to staring out at the fogged grass outside. She shuffled her feet.

"You abandon me after all you've wrought?" Edda muttered in a small voice, standing so her chair groaned along the floor as it moved back. She walked to stand behind Camille, wishing for comfort, for something other than the fearsome twist of her gut. "I cannot do this, all you've taught me. I am no good at it!"

Turning away from the window, Camille was met with a warm eye staring into her dark ones. The beautiful hues of red and yellows, twistings of black lines glossed over with more tears as they ebbed with compassion. Camille hushed the voices in the back of her mind, locking them away as they screamed warnings of manipulation from the one before her, a demon in front of her.

She wrapped her arms around Edda, gently swaying, the voices subsiding as guilt won over, that and a loving feeling only maternity could bring. "I must make penance, Edda, and here I cannot. I am no good for the children."

Through little gasps upon Camille's shoulder, Edda spoke, "You are actin' a coward."

Once more she swallowed her emotions, her frustration and wanting to strike out at the vulnerable young woman before her. She clenched Edda's gown, scrunching her eyes shut, regaining control – she wanted to change, needed to. It was taking more effort than she believed. Her exhale was shaky as the baby hairs on Edda's head tickled her nose. "I may be a coward, but at least I am no longer a crow. At least, I try not to be."

"Less than before ..."

To her surprise and delight, Camille found herself smiling, leaving a light kiss on the girl's forehead. "I no longer wish to be one. I cannot do that here."

"Because of me?" Edda pulled back, her thin, red lips stretching into a taut line, dark brows furrowed as she began to step away.

Camille met her stare, fixed and firm. "Because of how *I* am about you and the others. You were born of a nature you cannot be rid of – for you, that is wonderful. I was conditioned, made to be how I am. I need to break free of it, and I do not believe I can do so here. You are more capable than you realize, you simply need more practice.”

“When do you leave?”

“When you feel ready, and you *will* feel ready.”

Edda looked to the floor and traced the scars beneath her sleeves. She contemplated before giving a slow nod. Camille raised her chin and wiped her cheeks with her sleeves, giving a small smile before motioning to the desk once more. The younger woman looked over Camille’s shoulder and out the window for a spell before turning back to her work.

Camille puckered her lips before falling into step behind the girl, pushing her chair in.

Whilst memorizing the variations of answers, Edda paused. “Do you think they will come again?”

“We will do our best to give them reason not to,” Camille smirked before drawing her lips into a slight frown, careful not to let it affect her tutoring. Edda seemed to accept the answer, whispering Camille’s written words in an attempt to commit them to memory.

Camille watched, periodically glancing out the window at the fog, her mind awash with uncertainty as it grasped for proper direction.

Whatever that may be.

Within weeks of writing, two children, the eldest of the lot, were adopted. It was all done through the workings of Edda, with the oversight of her matron, of course. There hadn't been need of much back and forth, for the couples were older and without heirs.

Camille kept an impressive log of the wealthier families throughout the land, along with how many children and the age of the wives. These families were the only ones capable of taking in an orphan. Edda once felt mournful that she was never an option, but inside, she knew home was not when she was chosen – she had to be returned home. This feeling was embedded in her being, further confirmed by her parents' whisperings as she slept, and the last words Lowell had uttered to her.

When repopulating the Orphanage came into play, the children were brought by an outsider or appeared on the stoop, sad and alone, as though drawn by the hope of love and kindness. The Orphanage was a beacon of sorts to those lost, alone, and with nothing. The blood running through them mattered not, for the whim of their brokenness called for much the same.

Huxley had written to Camille, requesting an update and reporting on Alastair's developments in fulfilling his foretold destiny. His pride shone through the letter detailing how the child had learned to hold back on his theatrics and play the long game: to make everyone love him while he did his work in the shadows.

Camille shuddered, remembering the doubt that the boy had planted in her. Something in him more horrible than that which she outright feared and was taught to hate. Edda took to paper, writing a response without input, letting herself be taken by the majority of her life observing the perfection that is, or was, her matron. It was placation without a hint of Edda on the page.

When the reply arrived, all the tutoring, all the time at the desk and letting the children come back to themselves, paid off.

Camille cried when she realized what was to come next, her tears cascading down her cheeks as Edda turned to her, a soft look about her. "Camille, I believe I am ready."

Since Lowell's death, they embarked on a path to change, perhaps the easiest part on their journeys to perdition, to absolution. Much was left to overcome as Edda kept away from the children, offering smiles as she rubbed her arms, remembering the brevity of kinship she experienced, of what befell by her hand.

Camille, anxious as she packed what she needed, decided to travel and experience the lives of those robbed, wanting no resemblance of the envious, ireful, perfect creature she was.

Gathering the children for farewell, she hugged each one, squeezing as though attempting to take back what she'd done. With Edda, she embraced with a grip so tight, she believed her arms were to break. Edda draped her arms around the woman's thin back, rocking side to side. The elder began to weep in the loving hold, gratitude spilling through her as she forced herself away from the girl with the red-tinted skin and warm soul. Cupping Edda's cheeks, she touched their foreheads together, her thumbs rubbing the new matron's face.

Sucking back breath and sob, she whispered to Edda, "You are beautiful, and I love you."

Edda's mouth fell before she smiled, and she stood on her toes to kiss Camille's forehead. Her insides lightened, relief and contentment momentarily filling her. Her teacher's words filled a hole she never realized existed. There was still blame and guilt, but nothing could overshadow their brief exchange.

Gathering around the door, all the residents of the Orphanage watched as Camille stepped into a cart she hired outside of the royals' knowledge, the top open with a single man and horse to take her away. Fog covered the ground, wooden wheels of the poor man's wagon obscured, along with the hooves of the horse's feet, the creature licking at the mist that floated up to pet its head.

"Bit foggy. Where shall I be taking ye?"

"Take me far for now, far and away."

The coachmen paused in thought before flicking the reins, the horse turning away from its playful occupation and pulling them forward. Camille waved as she disappeared into the rising gray, praying to the blind woman of her dreams as she turned to face the nothingness before her.

Edda hovered at the door as the children stepped away, gathering themselves around the evening fire. There were only a few young ones now, two never knowing discipline, the third having known. The young boy turned his back to the fire. "Lady Edda, what will we do now?"

The young matron shivered, shutting the door, and after the lock slid into position, she placed the iron key in her pocket, feeling it clink against one of her many agates. The heft of it not as comforting as it once was, now more foreign and driving home her responsibilities. Her thoughts rattled and repeated: *I do not know, I do not know what to do.*

Closing her eyes, she leaned against the entrance, willing the spinning fear to quell and the wall around her heart to maintain its purpose. Exhaling, her mother's voice entered the back of her mind, soft and urging, "Go and be lovin' and kind. Teach them of forgiveness, my sweetin'." Swallowing, she paced, her heavy feet disquieting, her innards shaking until she took a seat amongst her newfound wards. She held out a hand to the boy she once raised it to.

Looking between the outstretched palm and Edda's face, the boy's brows creased in apprehension before he placed his hand in hers. Her fingers curled around his, as tender as her words, "First, let us play a game."

He smiled, as did the other two. Within, her heart's barricade quaked.

Seventeen

"Edda, I finished practicing."

"You do better by the day," Edda remarked at the oldest boy's, Geoffrey's, handwriting, how it was more legible and controlled. Next to her, an eight-year-old boy threw his quill down in frustration and cried. Edda crouched in front of him, her hand hovering towards the young David before she raised his chin. "Look at me."

David kept his eyes down, sucking in breaths. "I am no good, and no one will want me!"

The youngest girl stood undisturbed at the front of the classroom, using charcoal on the white wall to draw. Geoffrey twisted his lips and regarded his own parchment.

"Such a thing is not true. We must practice to improve but are still enjoyed regardless."

"Matron Camille said we needed to be *perfect*."

"Camille left because she did not wish to be perfect."

Looking up out of surprise, the boy fell into Edda's gaze and softened. With a shy smile, he picked up his quill, rubbing clean the wooden desk's surface with the back of his hand, and began again. Edda let herself smile back before turning to see the girl had gone to look out the window before running back to leave scores of black charcoal marks that waved and lowered like ripplings in a stream.

Watching with her head, Edda stood behind the desk, once a podium of sermons. "What is it you draw?"

"Ed-da, Ed-da! Outside, the fog is going up and down!" Little Abigail bounced with her arms outstretched before continuing her art piece.

Edda walked to the window, watching the mist rise and fall as though it breathed. It had been a few days since Camille departed, the remaining children being taught skills Edda found meaningful – writing, reading, cooking, cleaning, methods of independence and self-care. None complained at their new and daily structures, of the lack of religious dribble once forced into their minds.

Staring out, she leaned forward, her head resting against the pane as she let her thoughts take her, lulled into a gentle hypnotism as one boy began to tutor the other, the girl using a small wash bucket to erase her oscillating errors and a towel to wipe it clean.

She thought of His Royalty, the religion of Royals, a self-encapsulating title under which most practiced, having owed their lives and livelihoods to the Huxley lineage as far back as she knew in all of Wyrd, farther back to those who arrived from across the ocean. History barely existed before then, bits and pieces remembered orally, passed to children too young to remember: tales of jealous crows and adapting warriors, stories of families who looked nothing alike but were of the same make.

That was where her knowledge tapered off, that and the disgust she felt at the name Wyrd.

As far as she could see, all was a gray ocean as she rested her fingers on the glass. It called to her, gentle and calming, her thoughts racing through what she must do, her obligations. Would the children be able to exist without knowing the religion of the land? Her eyes darted to a dusty bookshelf pressed alone against the far wall where the leather bound holy books sat neglected.

Attempting to leave the window proved fruitless as her feet remained fixed and she relented to gazing outside once more. The time of day escaped her, the sound of the orphans fading out, their instructions and their giddy chatter. They were happier here than all the children were in Camille's time, and the laughs washed over her superficially as she restrained herself from growing attached. They would be gone soon enough, and more would replace them. No one would stay long.

The thick glass at her fingertips groaned as she lightly pushed and leaned further. She could almost hear the glass begin to crack.

"Ed-da, is it supper yet?"

She pulled her hands away and kneeled before the girl, her hands dirtied with soot. "Yes I suppose it is. We must tidy first, mustn't we?" A short nod and playful smile danced over the little one's face as she spun about to wash up her black smudges, her drawing one of a dark sea with reaching tendrils. The boys gathered their parchments and dried the wall where the girl had used a wet rag. It all happened in a blink before the little artist tugged on Edda's hand, pulling her to the door and out to the kitchen.

The three stood opposite her and waited with expectation.

In a daze, she shook her head, "What to eat?"

"Fish and barley?" The oldest boy suggested.

"Please fetch us water, the two of you lads. And you will huh-help me cut the fish. Wait h-here now." At the corner of the kitchen floor sat the tiny cellar door, the ground beneath cool and away from pests. The bedrock was near the surface of the earth throughout the land—one needn't dig deep to reach it. The stones kept salted meats well preserved. Edda descended into the shallow hollow and pressed her hands to the walls, the coolness of it passing through her skin.

She used to hide here soon after the disciplines started, being so young and finding comfort only in a dark hole, the stones cradling her in safety before the light was allowed in. She hesitated to leave, even now, her hand outstretched towards the lifeless fish, their glazed-over eyes fixed on the ceiling, her other hand planted on the wall, fastened to it.

"Edda, I'd like to eat, yeah? I'm so 'ungry!"

The words drifted down from the kitchen and played at her hair. She looked up to see the children waiting. She snatched the fish and climbed out, sniffing back tears. "Put the fire on, boys. I trust you."

They struck a few matches and set water to boil, pouring in barley, and watching the grain bulge. The little girl sat propped on Edda's knee as she held the child's hand and guided little knife strokes and wondered how Lowell would look if he were still alive.

* * *

"Ed-da, what happened to your eye?"

The boys ate diligently, ignoring the question that echoed in the sparse room. Unfortunately, if Edda did the same, it would be rude. "It was damaged, so it needs time to h-heal."

"Can I see it?"

Edda's hand hovered over the bandage before she forced it away. She could spare the younger two of her own atrocities. "No, not today, dear. Take along your dishes when you're done and ready yourselves for bed. Perhaps there will be a story tonight." She beamed at the children before standing up to do the washing.

It didn't take long for the other three sets to arrive and disappear. They were not picky eaters, doing most of the cleaning themselves. For this, Edda was thankful she only needed to soak everything in hot water and wipe up the cooking area.

The last remaining light was bidding her goodnight when she realized the water was lukewarm, her hands redder than normal from having soaked in the heat. She had been staring outside again, an uncontrollable focus overtaking her when she saw the fog toppling over the stone wall, filling the backyard even more than before. She finished up, leaving the water to sit overnight, an urge calling her to the front door.

Her feet thudded on the wood, sending vibrations all around her as she unlocked and swung open the entryway. Nothing but the dark woods and mist awaited her.

"Time for a story, now?"

Disappointed, Edda shut out the external world, turning around, shaking away her blank expression she grinned at the children sitting aglow in the flickering warmth. "Do any of you h-have a story?"

Raising his hand, little David was met with a blown raspberry and tongue wagging in the air. "You tell bad stories! You make them up!"

"Most stories are made up! You do not know anything!"

Abigail pouted, her eyes round and pleading.

"Some stories are true, but some of the best are not real. Why not give h-," Edda paused, swallowing. "Go on, give it a go."

Excited, the boy raised his hands, his mouth wide before pulling everything back in. "I cannot think of anything ..."

"Ed-da, I can't like it!"

Chuckling, Edda took Camille's old chair, turning it to face her audience. "You what now?"

"I can't like it!" the girl exclaimed, wrapping her arms about her, a blanket clutched in her tiny fists. The oldest boy traced the grains of the wood floor with a finger, his head propped atop an open palm.

Leaning back, Edda tried to think of a story herself, prying open her memories. She rubbed at her arms and glanced about the three who waited, eager for her tale. Her head grew light and her hair fell away from her ear, concealing most of the wrapping about her head. Whisperings gathered around her, audible to only her as cool air filled her lungs. "It is short, so listen close and listen well."

"A woman, so blind, yet all she could see.

Eyes white as snow, others say blessed was she;

For what would occur never passed 'er wakin' gaze nor dreams

They called 'er seer,

'Er kin did so,

Ever wishin' to relieve what grieved 'er.

Yet doomed she was, she understood,

To live long a life pained and woeful.

'Ard pressed, she was to see the beauty, covered in all 'er despair,

Tried and failed, many did, actin' as soothsayer.

Struggled she did, to find 'er balance,

Takin' 'er many years.

Tragedy and 'orrors she kept to 'erself,

'Ome seemin' to fade into nothin'

Their words, now memories, filled 'er up,

Showin' 'er the truth of 'er blessin'."

Edda blinked away the voices, wondering what she spoke of. The children shifted on their haunches, confusion marring their faces. "What does it mean?"

"What was the truth of her blessing, Edda?"

She shook her head. "I am not sure. It is as if another spoke for me."

Again, the kids readjusted themselves. "That is how I feel when I tell my stories! When I really enjoy what I say, it feels like it begins to tell itself! Edda, I understand!"

She was surprised, to say the least, but rewarded the beaming David with a smile of her own, feeling his kindness pulling at the stone wall in her.

"Unfortunate, your tales are so poor!" Abigail teased.

David looked at the floor beneath him and began to trace circles with his finger. He bit his lip in dejection.

"Come now, we do our best. Mine was not terribly well done either. Little one, you made h-h-him sad. Perhaps an apology?" Little Abigail crossed her arms and shook her head in protest. Lowering herself from the chair, Edda crouched in front of the girl and took her hands, squeezing them. Looking up, the girl stared into the beautiful red iris before her. "We can express ourselves in a more kindly manner, but I believe an apology would be best for now. Don't you?"

Understanding as best she could, the little girl turned to the boy and cupped his face in her hands, asking for forgiveness. Geoffrey stood nearby and rubbed his arms, mumbling to himself. Edda took her place in front of him as he turned away. She opened her arms only for him to reject her, sniffling. He spoke a little louder, for Edda's ears, "You hurt me and speak of apologies?"

It stung, as it should.

She pulled him into her arms. Despite ignoring her gestures before, he fell into her, painful tears running from his eyes. Edda joined him and rocked. The boy was older than Martin: she wondered if he could be freed from the anger. She whispered confessions and asked for his pardon, yet he only cried.

It did not come across as sincere as she meant. Although she was heavy and hurting, something stopped him from feeling the impact of her in this time, cradling him instead.

She lifted her face to the ceiling and rolled up a sleeve, placing his hand over the valleys that scarred her. His breath hitched as she pushed through her resistance. "I will never live a day without the pain I h-have brought you. From the pit of my soul, I am most sorry for the agony I made you carry." She squeezed him and he leaned into her, turning to face her, his bottom lip jutting as his nose ran and his eyes spoke of acceptance.

Within, the guilt in her gut stirred, swallowing one of her heart's bricks. She ignored the discomfort rearing its head and wiped the boy's face with a handkerchief.

"Icky!" The girl laughed, her and the boy having made up. Ashamed, the eldest wiped at his eyes and sucked in hard through his nose. Edda pet his hair in comfort as the fire flicked behind them.

A chill ran through the Orphanage as everyone looked toward the closed windows. The light dimmed in the room. Geoffrey turned to tend to the fire, David and Abigail gripping each other. Edda rose and stepped to the window.

There was only darkness outside now, the fog barely a visible wisp as the room relit with the boy's added fuel. Edda leaned closer to the pane, the new brightness surrounding them, illuminating a small palm print in the glass.

Upon placing her hand in the same spot, there was a gentle knock at the door.

Glancing toward her wards, Edda dashed for the door, twisting the heavy iron key and jerking the door open without thought.

There stood a small girl, five or six at the most, with eyes large as saucers and a silvery gray. Her hair was long and blonde, reaching her waist. She stared up at Edda, unblinking, and smiled most beautifully at the matron, following Edda's gesturing to enter. The door locked solid behind as she gazed over the others opposite the room from her. They all stared, baffled.

"What is your name?" the young Abigail called out, relinquishing the boy from their fearful huddling.

The quiet girl shook her head, looking up to Edda. Her skin almost seemed to glow in the flame's light as her lips parted, her voice quiet, like a whisper in the wind, "What is my name, Edda?"

Without missing a beat, Edda crouched, staring deep into the girl's eyes, seeing more of her own reflection. The girl was familiar, as though she had been around them longer than any of them knew. "You h-have no name?"

Her head shook as she regarded Edda expectantly, placing a small, cooling hand over the woman's arm.

Edda smiled as ebbings of love flowed through her, "Let us call you Maisie."

Eighteen

Maisie seemed to glide through the Orphanage, little concern over what others did or thought. She was akin to a ghost, yet, Edda knew, she was more kindred to her than the other occupants.

She was one needing of protection.

Watching the others go about their days, she began to shadow Edda until she eventually began doing tasks before her matron could, and so well at that. As days passed, Edda began to realize that the girl was older than one might believe, beyond the physical.

In writing and reading, Maisie was voracious, exceeding even the oldest boy's abilities with a quill. Aside from the girl drawing upon walls, the boys grew jealous, discouragement taking hold. Maisie would walk to them and place her small hand over their larger ones, telling them it was okay before grabbing Edda's hand and smiling at her, motioning with her head to take over whilst she flitted to the window, seeming to float in the air in between bounds.

Her feet totted at varying paces while she watched the world outside, giggling to herself as Abigail joined her to watch everything and nothing.

"She is strange, is she not?"

"Yes. When I looked at her, I feel worse about myself. Is that how it is meant to be?"

"Is she a demon?" The eldest boy's voice was nonchalant, though he spoke of facts.

Maisie watched the boys over her shoulder as they conversed.

"Do *not* speak of another in such a way!" Edda snapped, firmer than they'd known. They flinched and Maisie turned back to observe the world, her feet slowed to a stop. "Do not compare yourselves to another."

"She is too young to know the word *demon*, and I do not compare! She makes me feel so, when I look at her eyes."

"Children at any age may understand your tone. That word is never meant to be used h-h-here! And, perhaps confidence is what you lack, dear, and you are meant to see it."

The boys grumbled as they continued their work, casting skeptical glances at the newcomer.

They maintained distance throughout the days, remaining unconvinced of anyone's words, fixing on the emotions Maisie evoked inside them with a mere look. However, Abigail took a shining to Maisie, having another girl to play with. Maisie reciprocated here and there, the two of them giggling as they spoke of what lay beyond the windows. They even shared a bunk.

Come supper, the children all contributed and sat with their plates piled high and low with food. Edda felt comfortable with what she had now, despite how much she stopped herself from truly enjoying it.

The boys shoveled greens and starches into them while the rest watched in amusement. Even Maisie smiled.

"Where are your parents, Maisie?"

Edda opened her mouth to scold, defensive, when the young girl spoke for herself, "I haven't any."

The younger boy, David, continued, unperturbed, "Me neither, they fell ill. Yours?"

Edda glanced at Maisie in a panic as the child cocked her head in thought and shook it slowly, repeating herself in a voice barely discernable over the others' chewing, "I haven't any."

Geoffrey pitched in, "Where are you from?" His eyes darted to his fellow lad, returning to squint at Maisie a moment later.

The girl smiled, dropping her utensils, lifting her fingers to create waves in the air and little spirals. Her lips parted, her little teeth shone bright, delighted as she recalled her origins.

The youngest girl chuckled, "The fog, like what I drew? I have not heard of a town like that!"

"There is no place called *Fog* in Wyrd. I would know, I have read all the books we have!" The eldest clenched his drink, mouthing *demon* to his friend. The latter chortled before his face fell in apprehension.

Edda was none the wiser as she was fixed on Maisie who faced the former, her smile bright on her face and her eyes dancing with love.

When tidying up, Maisie tugged on Edda's sleeve and pulled it up. With little fingers, she wrapped her hands around Edda's arm, enveloping the red wounds as best she could and beaming at her matron. A coolness of gray seemed to flow from the child's fingertips as it danced in the grooves. "It is alright," she whispered, gentle and sweet.

Kin she was, Edda knew, but different from her and Lowell.

Little incidents continued amongst the boys, much to Edda's frustration, and more to Maisie's silence. The punishments of old would never resurface, but Edda's patience was pressed.

Some gifts were stronger than others, especially so if one were missing part of themselves.

Fall was coming to an end as Edda wrote and received no interest in return, the children seemingly unwanted. Maisie's quiet ebbed and flowed but she took to shying away when the boys came about to whisper. The other girl followed Maisie like a pet, wishing to comfort. They both took to staring out windows, watching leaves fall and barren branches scratch one another in autumnal breezes.

"Ed-da?" A tug upon the matron's dress. "Ed-da, Maisie stopped talking to me. Does she not like me?"

Shaking her head, Edda followed Abigail, to find Maisie leaning against the window overlooking the cobbled path. The front door was left open as the boys went out to play, gathering branches and doing what boys believed men were to do, as much as boys without fathers knew.

"Maisie? Are you alright?" Silence.

"Ed-da? Why does she not like us?"

"Shhh, Abigail, I am sure it is not you or I. Let me sit with Maisie and you fetch some bread to nibble." The small girl glanced and a smile bloomed as she turned about to bring along food for the rest. Edda continued, letting her fingers run through Maisie's platinum hair. The girl stepped back from the window, remaining fixed on the mist that crept out of the wood and flowed along the grass, rising up the trunks of trees, hanging from branches.

"Maisie?"

The small girl cried, mumbling, incoherent, rubbing her face. Maisie placed her hands on the glass, quaking.

"What do you see?"

"He will hurt me ..." She cooed, her hands tracing over the edges of her ribs, fingers lining each one, her lips pulled back in a grimace as she watched the miasma give her a vision only she could observe. "He hurts my sister too! Save her!"

"Your sister? Who h-hurts you?"

"Later, I will see her later, and so will the man who lies and plays. He likes games, but we do not like his games!" Her hands slapped the thick pane. Spittle sprayed from her mouth. Edda crouched and embraced her little body, trying to pull her away.

"There is no one there, Maisie!"

Her shaking stopped as she gasped in awe, her brows unknitting and her mouth parting into relief. She pointed out the window and giggled, snot rimming her upper lip. She sniffed.

"Is h-he gone?"

"There is a boy, Edda, he will save us – I see him, small and afraid but growing big, big and strong!"

"What is his name?"

Her large, gray eyes sparkled with love as she beamed, her tearful fit lost. "He has brown hair and eyes like the deep, dark ground beneath all of us. He will take us home! Edda, we will go home and see everyone again!"

Edda's heart lurched, pounding against the fraying stone wall encapsulating it. The child's words gave her hope, the whirlpool beginning to rear in her stomach as it gurgled words of discouragement and sin, guilt and of demons. "When?"

Maisie's face fell as she muttered for the two of them, "Long time, so long."

With an aching heart, Edda dabbed her eyes with a sleeve, choking back reprieve. She raised her eyes to the wooden ceiling, following the lines created by the beams, coughing, "Maisie, I cannot wait much longer. We need to go h-huh-ho-home ..." A low moan escaped her lips as she wished to join her mother and father.

Tiny hands covered her eyes then travelled to her cheeks; small thumbs resting at the edge of her lips. Edda stared into Maisie's mirrors and fought the innate love and kindness there, some from herself and the rest from the child before her. She did not deserve it, she deserved none of it – she would hide herself away to avoid all the pain, closing away the goodness that came with it.

After Lowell, none of it was worthwhile. A fleeting dream falling way to a waking nightmare.

"Maisie, I h-hu-hurt, what I ha-have done cannot be forgiven. I deserve nothin'-nothing. Can I go h-home faster?"

Resolute, Maisie shook her head as Edda began to sob, the thumping of her chest and the churning in her midst threatening to end her.

"It is alright, Edda, you will sleep!"

"Sleep?"

Fervently, the child nodded, her tears dried into trails on her pale cheeks. "They all forgive you, the boy too."

"The boy?"

Removing her hand from Edda's face, she made little tappings in the air with her fingers, smiling, "The boy with twinkly eyes! He wishes you heard him now, but you will again! I promise!" Maisie tilted her head to the side, listening to voices, her smile falling away to lips parted in curiosity, gently mouthing silent words. Her eyes danced back and forth before Maisie pushed her thumbs into Edda's mouth, tugging at her matron's lips and pulling her tongue out of her mouth, wagging it back and forth.

It was what Edda did in the mirror to herself.

The look in Maisie's face was both playful and serious. "No, no, Edda." Her silvery eyes flashed sparkling embers, familiar and mischievous, unconventional – as though another channeled through her. Edda's tongue was released, sliding home as she blinked.

"Is 'e 'appy?"

Maisie totted her feet in excitement, squeezing Edda's face between palms so tiny, a squeal escaping her as she leaned forward and kissed the tip of Edda's nose. Maisie's smile looked old and practiced as she chuckled, turning to face the window before she spun away and pranced towards the kitchen, calling for the other girl.

Edda sat in shock as a gentle trickle flowed down her cheek, curving about her thin lips. She tasted the saltiness of it as warmth creeped throughout her being. She grinned and glanced outside, the fog having dissipated, as though it never was.

Carrying a plethora of sticks, some bulky, some twiggy, the boys walked up the cobblestone path as someone tugged on Edda's skirt. She turned to be handed a piece of bread, squished by tiny hands but presented with shameless smile.

As it should be.

With a grateful chuckle, she knelt to receive the gift, wiping her nose and wetness from her face.

"Ed-da, why are you crying? Maisie is okay now! Do not cry."

Another laugh escaped her before she smiled at the girl before her, the child's grin beginning to mirror the warmth she felt herself.

Without thought, Edda leaned forward and laid a loving kiss upon the girl's forehead. Pulling back, Edda was now met with Abigail beaming ever so sweet, the child leaping upon her, thanking her with a squeeze.

Nineteen

"Little freak!"

These names, this feeling, felt familiar to Maisie, as though she had experienced it before. Part of her knew she had, remembering different iterations of the terrible moniker, the same connotations negative and hurtful. All of it caused a familiar twinge inside that she wished to pluck out.

"Do you do anything more than stare?"

"Why do you say such mean things to my friend?" Abigail defended Maisie in place of Edda, doing the best she could.

"Look at her! She sends chills down my spine and his!" Jabbing a finger in the younger boy's direction, Geoffrey shuddered. Maisie shivered at the theatrics, portents playing at the edge of her fading visions.

The longer she spent in this Orphanage, in Wyrd - a name so utterly strange to her - the more she felt her senses diminished and herself shrinking to fit something all too small for her liking and her entirety.

"No! She is fun and nice, unlike you two dolts!"

David stepped forward, grabbing the back-talking girl by the shoulders and shaking her in revenge. Barely a squeak left her lips as Edda ripped the boy away, her entrance silenced by the chaos. The victimized girl let out a whimper. Maisie reached out to pet her hair, a subtle comfort.

"Why are you two so insistent on pesterin' Maisie?" Edda's voice was stern, pained and full of reproach.

The boy in her hands shook his head with shame, the older one crossed his arms vehemently, refusing to meet her gaze.

A jolt ran through Maisie's mind. "I will be off, soon." The agitator smirked, victorious. "Edda, they will come soon – who is coming?"

Edda released the boy, the allies regrouping. Maisie's friend started to whimper in protest, wishing her friend would never leave. Edda's face was quizzical, the newcomer full of surprises she could never quite get used to. "'Ow is it you know?"

Maisie blinked rapid in response and continued to run fingers through the crying Abigail's hair. She was unsure herself now, brows knitting in confusion, searching for an answer that began to lock itself away.

"Hellspawn," the elder boy hissed as Edda whipped around. The boy flinched and let out a sad whine.

"Shoo! Leave us, now!"

Maisie gripped Edda's arm now, mumbling calming words as they continued on, the boys running out the front door to play with sticks and expend their energies. Wrapping her arms around Maisie's waist, Abigail gripped her tight, sniffling into her back. "Am I wrong, Edda?"

"In a few days, one will come from a manor from the Northeast – Brindley Manor. That is all I know now."

Maisie nodded in recognition, a small smile on her face as she grabbed her friend's hands and ran up the stairs, the slaps of their feet full of excitement. Edda watched them run along as she crossed the floor to the entryway, peering at the boys tossing broken bits of cobble at one another.

She called for the younger and he obeyed without question.

"Why is it you say such cruel things to the new one?"

He shuffled his feet, unsure how to answer, glancing outside at his waiting friend who gathered more munitions.

"Look at me, look me in the eye, and give me an 'onest answer now. There is no need to fear speakin' the truth heh—" Edda swallowed, fighting an old pinch in her tongue and willing herself to let go. "Do not fear speakin' the truth 'ere."

"He says she is bad and she says some strange things. Sometimes, I feel like she is better than me, but I think I work hard at what I do, like my writing." He shrugged, his face downcast as embarrassment spread through his cheeks, a darkening pink.

"We all say and do oddities, do we not? Even I am peculiar at times, but am I so bad to deserve name callin'?" His head shook in the crook of her neck as he settled into the embrace. "As for your studies, I believe you are doin' very well. Some are quicker studies than others, and some subjects are more appealin' than others. There is no shame there. You are where you need to be, and if that is at the beginnin', that is just fine, too."

"What did you struggle with, Edda?"

Tensing for a moment, Edda steeled herself to dive back into dismal memories full of scrutiny and punishments she wished to never face again. Her heart skipped, sucking in on itself as she settled on a simple, silly truth. "Cookin', bakin', all things in the kitchen, my dear."

The boy pulled back, studying Edda's face to find the lie, only to see her giggling at him.

"I like your food!"

"For that, I am glad! It took me so long to learn." Her smile stayed, forced, as Camille flitted through her mind, her demonstrations and lessons filled with frustration and anger towards Edda's younger self. She inhaled, "Let us be nicer to Maisie, hmm? Now run along and send your opponent in, It'll give you chance to gather your own resources."

With a wink David was off to gather pebbles and stones as the older boy trudged inside. He wasn't much shorter than Edda, destined to one day dwarf the matron. She lifted his chin and asked him much the same as the other boy.

He tore away, closing himself off. "Because she is very much a freak and a demon. No good will come from her, and that is just how it is."

Anger loomed over the boy, threatening to spread over Edda. "She 'as done nothin' to you. Why do you not like 'er?"

"I hate her."

"Why?"

Searching his mind, Geoffrey's lips trembled, his hands raised to clutch opposite shoulders and he began to curl into himself, trying to protect all he believed himself to be, his opinions, his feelings. He bit his lower lip, letting no words slip by.

"Sweetin', you are safe to tell me."

"I just do not like her!" He lashed out, forced into a corner of his own mind.

"Even so, it is not right to pain 'er."

To this, Edda was met with a glare before her ward stormed out, unfurling his arms as he marched to his battle station. The younger boy squealed, exclaiming to no one in particular how he hadn't as much time to prepare; how it was unfair.

Blame seeped into Edda – how she made him behave so.

Throat tightening, Edda jerked the door, leaving it ajar to where a handful of light could enter. Rushing towards the basement, she rattled the knob, reaffirming it was locked tight. Her breath heaved, distress drenching her in sweat and panic.

The words tripped over themselves while she calmed herself, "Camille is gone, there is no punishment. She is gone, and 'is stormin' about will not make it 'appen again." Her exhales rattled out her lungs, slowing to a gentle cry as she let her head slide down the door and slumped to the ground.

* * *

"Are they really here for Maisie?"

"I am not entirely sure. They never asked for h-her, specifically, but Maisie seems to think so."

"Are you sad, like me?"

"I am always sad when one of you leaves."

"Promise?"

"Promise." Edda pinched the little girl's cheek, wondering if she could feel upset at a child moving on and relieved at the same time, whether it be Maisie, or the remaining few who were chosen. Life became a little easier being more alone. Edda had never known freedom while living at the Orphanage, instead having a deep sense of obligation that meshed with attachment and enjoyment of most of the children – as best as she could understand.

With Maisie around, the other girl took to her, making Edda's heart thrum inside her breast, wishing to break free while also trying to tuck itself away and hide. The unease and ire swirled like a beast in her midst waiting to suck the joy out of her experiences.

Little efforts from Maisie and her Abigail almost broke Edda, coaxing her heart to be laid bare, but with persistence, the boys' behavior, and fear, she held steadfast, the images of a living and dead Lowell fixing her resolve in stone.

"Sit, Ed-da! I want to make your hair nice."

So she did, the child fanning out her dark brown locks and running it through with a wooden comb. The gentle raking against her scalp reminded her of her mother's comb, except that was made intricately of whittled bone.

Maisie was off somewhere, taking to exploring the recesses of their home, expressing her wish to find shiny things and repeating her fruitless quest each day. When Edda showed her the armlet, the girl studied it, rubbing the agate and holding it before Edda's bandage before returning it to Edda's hand. The precious metal was not the correct sheen for Maisie's liking.

Little hands worked Edda's hair, thick and coarse, into strands that began to weave together, snaking into a tight plait. The child had a knack.

"'Ow did you learn to do it so well?"

"I remember my mama taught me, and Maisie lets me practice too. Your hair is a bit easier, it stays where I put it!" She squeaked in triumph before letting out an exaggerated, "Oh!"

"What is it?"

"I think it needs a little more." A brief pause followed small, delicate claps as the girl continued, "Thank you, Maisie!"

Like a ghost, there was Maisie, back from her journey and in Edda's periphery, not a sound announcing her entry.

"What is it you needed?"

"You will see when it comes out! No peeking!"

Running her hand over the voluminous braid, Edda just about reached the bottom when the artist pulled at her hand. She tsk'ed her matron before a light tickling ensued.

One of the boys entered the classroom, alerting them to a knock at the door. Promptly, Edda rose, the children falling in line and keeping their distance. Maisie's protector stood in front, wishing to hide her best friend without making it too obvious. Maisie played along, grateful yet eager.

At the door, Edda paused between each lock, taking her time to undo them. She understood what the littlest Abigail was playing at, for she felt much the same.

She had an obligation that sat deep in her being, which Maisie had foretold in hints, both grand and miniscule.

The door pulled free, groaning with heft and letting an autumn breeze stir up the den. In the sunlight of the stoop stood an old woman with hair white as snow tied into a loose bun. They greeted one another, the guest entering with a hunched back and eyes narrowed into just discernable slits. The children gathered in front of the fireplace feigning play and storytelling, eavesdropping on the adults' discussion.

Edda excused them to occupy themselves elsewhere as the adults took opposite seats, much like Camille did with all her guests, a tea set betwixt them.

"Thank you for comin' all this way. Camille is who wrote you, but I am afraid she is out for now. I am Edda, and I will aid you through the process."

Reaching to pour herself tea, the old woman gave a knowing smile, her thin, pale lips pulling up, plumping her cheeks. "I am Mergo, dearest Edda. No worries on Camille, I knew she would be out." She sipped at the tea, a potent peppermint that Edda had begun to grow in the front yard once she gained more freedom. "I am delighted to know you've kept your accent. The wee one must've really reached you."

"My accent?"

Mergo leaned forward, elongating as though her horrid back didn't pain her. "Your accent matches your eyes."

"Who are you?"

"I am Mergo, my dear."

Shifting in place and squeezing her skirt, Edda swallowed, continuing on, "There are a few preliminary questions before you observe the children and take your pick."

"I wish not to waste your time. I am 'ere for Maisie, though I believe she told you I was comin'."

Without seeing Mergo's eyes, her accent sent Edda into a brief stupor. Questions flooded her and she struggled to get a single word out at the grinning woman. After several attempts, she strangled out a query, "You are from where my parents 'ail. Where do we come from?"

A gentle nod, Mergo's face glowed, her mind dancing with old memories. "That I am. We are where we come from, child, only our names 'ave changed."

"Where is 'ome? We looked for it everywhere, wanderin'."

Setting down the cup, Mergo leaned back, sighing, "Once, all was 'ome, yet time 'as changed our land. Where it is now is blocked, a place called Fyren stands to guard it. 'Ome was where we first called it so, and last as well. Tosach, North on the tip of a crescent moon, protected by swamps, feared by many."

"Why is it feared, Mergo?"

"Because we are feared, Edda, though I believe you 'ave come to see that in your wakin' life."

Camille came to Edda's mind, her raptures and teachings. She was a demon, according to the teachings, and those teachings came from the monastery where all religious articles find their origin. Her crimson speckled eyes widened and she whispered, "The 'ate and fear runs deep, like poison."

"It does, but yet, we live."

"Not well, I am afraid." Edda rubbed at her arms, squeezing when the image of Lowell and her parents flashed through her mind.

"Maisie told you of a boy yet to be born, did she not?" Edda nodded in response. Mergo continued, "We will be returned 'ome. Not much is to be done besides to tell our stories when 'e comes to collect us."

"'Ow do you know this? 'Ow does little Maisie?"

"Maisie will soon forget. She is still new to this time and place. Each day 'er knowledge tucks itself away, especially without her trinket."

"Trinket?"

"Bring your golden armlet 'ere, Edda." Mergo's wrinkled finger raised to point upstairs, before all her fingers wriggled at Edda in a wave; the young woman raced upstairs, the steps and wood moaning under her hastened pace, up then down. "Give it 'ere, dear."

The touch of Mergo's fingers were warm, seeping through Edda's body as though a spark had caught tinder laced throughout her being. It was delightful. The armlet was appraised carefully, Mergo tracing each edge with gentle touches, admiring it before she closed her hands around the stone in the center. She brought her narrow gaze to meet Edda's, though her eyes still remained unseen.

"What of my 'eirloom?"

"Good, you know what it is then. We all 'ave one, passed through the women since we are better connected to the land, more in tune. If women are born to a family that is, and if the women remain." She brought her clasped hands in front of her head as a gentle *ting* echoed in the closed space. "These connect us better, our strength comin' from those before us, our ancestors and family. Most of us are born the same, and all are born with a gift."

"Love and kindness?"

"That is yours, Edda."

Looking down at her hands, Edda raised one to her wrapped eye, brushing fingertips along the cloth, wishing to puncture it, to find an eye beneath, to not feel so broken. She spoke of Lowell and crows, of her parents and Camille – Mergo's words cleared doubt she could not push through by herself. In between breaths, she thought of Maisie and Lowell then made her wonderings known, "What were Lowell's gifts, and what of Maisie's?"

"She is a tricky one, Edda. Think of fog: transient, all encompassin', and to some, terrifyin'. Think of gray: empty, between black and white – in the middle. Think of silver: reflective, coolin', gentle, and needin' of care."

"She is like a mirror, but she knows little secrets."

"Our people thought of mist as a great nothin' where all answers could come to you, or none, depending on 'ow stubborn you were. Intuition is another way to define it: you resist what you are told, or you embrace it and act accordingly."

"And Lowell?"

At mention of his name, Mergo smiled. "Dear, think of what 'e did and 'ow 'e made you feel."

Steeling herself, Edda thought back to the first time she met Lowell, his sparkling eyes evoking exploration, inquisitiveness, and an impish curiosity. She giggled, struggling to find the words to define him.

"Some are 'arder to name, for some are gifted with the more abstract."

"And you? What is your story, Mergo?"

She squeezed the armlet, knuckles paling, her tone remaining steady and calm. "That is a story for another day. Come to me, child, and take off your bandage." Edda did not hesitate, moving to Mergo's side and kneeling on the floor as though it was natural to bend the knee in front of one such as the old woman before her. Mergo was like her, she knew, but she was more. The cloth wrappings fell from her head as she looked up to the woman, as though begging for a blessing.

Mergo brushed her knuckles over Edda's present eye, closing it, then she raised her hand to open the vacant space in Edda's skull, the skin loose with missing purpose.

Darkness gave way to tricklings of light that fluttered into the windows. A pressure and weight found its home in Edda as a missing piece laid into her with a light *tick*. She could see Mergo's pruned hands pull away, a golden armlet in her open palm, the inset missing the stone.

She blinked, once then twice. She rubbed at her eyes, her *eyes*. Gazing at her hands before her, tears poured out as she laughed in exuberance and disbelief. She touched her sagging eyelid, feeling the solid mass behind it. Edda swung her arms around the old woman and squeezed, pouring out all her gratefulness, all the appreciation she could muster. She felt like she was warming up after being cold for ages.

Mergo laughed before tucking the golden heirloom into Edda's pocket. "That, you keep. It will be important to another later."

There were no questions in Edda's mind now, her grin so large that near all her teeth showed – this woman had given her more than she realized she knew, her words to be trusted in this life and the next. She nodded with glee, gripping Mergo's hands, sharing in each other's warmth.

"I must be goin' now, Edda. Can you bring me Maisie?"

Edda's heart sank as reality in its marvelousness came with its caveat. She couldn't help but ask, "Where will she go?"

"Why, Brindley Manor. There is another there, a fiery girl just a little older than 'er. Maisie's gifts are to ebb away until she is a bit older and they both need to grow together. To reawaken together. That is their story, Edda."

"May I come too?"

Mergo shook her head. "Your place is 'ere. 'Ere is where you will waken."

Edda furrowed her brow as she stood up. "I am already awake. I know what I am."

Tapping at her own heart, Mergo's lips puckered before she smiled. "Reclaim, then. That may prove more difficult than findin' out what you are." Edda clasped her hands, trying to focus on the calloused piece in her chest, at the crumbling but intact wall she had built. Mergo reached out and pulled the young woman's hands apart, patting them. "It will come with time, and you will 'ave 'elp. Do not force it, dear. Now, please fetch little Maisie for me?"

Edda's footsteps were dense as she inched to the classroom, Maisie hugging her crying friend inside and the boys looking through old books Camille treasured, scratching out and writing in their own words. The eldest boy caught sight of her first, his companion following suit as they gaped at their matron.

Although awash with emotion, she was luminous to them, both her eyes vibrant, one more than the other, but working in unison to evoke a penetrating heat like no other. It was Geoffrey who ran up to her and hugged her first, followed by David, then the crying Abigail. Joy bubbled up as she wrapped her arms around them.

Just as they came, each one broke off and ran to Maisie, squeezing her in turn. The boys cried, profusely apologizing, their hearts having changed to expressing themselves in earnest as opposed to hiding behind childish cruelties.

The children cleared as Maisie stepped forward, Edda squatting to meet her face to face, the young girl placing her small hands over Edda's reddish-tinged cheeks and gliding her thumbs just below Edda's eyes. "You are beautiful. I wish to be so too, one day." They took one another's hands as Edda replied with a smile, leading Maisie into the parlor.

Mergo opened her arms to Maisie once they passed into the next room, the child releasing Edda's grasp as she leapt into the elder's embrace. There was a cold prick in Edda's heart while she watched; bittersweet washing through her.

"I 'ave waited for you, little Maisie, longer than you know."

With a giggle, Maisie replied, "I know! Although I know I will forget, soon. That is alright, it has to be."

"It comes with age, my little doll."

Nimble on her toes, Maisie turned to face her sorrowful matron, beaming despite the tears dripping down her chin and neck. Maisie ran to her and patted Edda's arms before she tugged on her dress, pulling her down to her level once more.

"Yes? What is it you would like to say before you are off?" Edda tucked fine locks of hair behind the girl's ears.

Maisie's lips twisted, straining to grasp the wisps in her mind, "Edda, you will get help. Someone will come soon, but you need to visit where she drowned."

"Who? My mother?"

Maisie lifted her hand to the side of her head, making fluid movements with tiny fingers. "It is all wishy washy now, it goes away – but I know your father is there too, a bit differently, but he is. They miss you." Edda's face fell at the memories resurfacing, at their voices she hushed until they all but ceased. On her tiptoes, Maisie kissed Edda's nose, "It will be alright, I promise."

On a silent cue, the child skipped to Mergo's side, her feet bare against the ground. She never liked to wear shoes nor stockings. Edda followed them to the door and watched them walk down the stairs, Maisie running ahead to the large speckled mare that awaited her two riders.

Mergo pivoted at the base of the stoop, lifting her head to meet the one with new eyes. Edda bowed her head and curtsied as Mergo followed suit. "I will see you again, dear. We all will.

Chin up, eyes open. Lowell wanted you to explore, unafraid."
She smiled, broad and knowing whilst thrumming fingers over
her heart. Giving a wink, she let Edda glimpse her own eyes.

Lifting Maisie onto the horse's back, Mergo followed. The
children gathered at Edda's sides to watch the swaying of the
creature's tail until it was too far to see.

"Ed-da?"

"Yes?"

"I will miss her."

"Yes, as will I."

"Ed-da? Your eye?"

Wiping at the dew on her face, Edda crouched to face the
girl, the boys standing behind and gazing at the unbandaged
woman. "What do you think?"

"You are pretty like a bird."

"What kind of bird? A crow?"

The child shook her head, her lips a gentle parting as she
traced a finger along Edda's curved nose. "A different bird, but
a nice one."

"Thank you. Now run along, we must get you all something
to eat. It is difficult each time one of you leaves."

The youngest two children scattered, leaving the oldest
behind. He bent down to pick up a flower, colored red, yellow,

and black. Handing it to Edda, Geoffrey could not help himself as he stared. "My mother grew flowers like these. She said these ones were special. Some think they are diseased, but they are simply more difficult to come by so people think them strange. It fell from your hair."

"Will you put it back for me?"

He did so with a brisk nod and quick fingers before running after the others.

Edda closed the door and made her way to the kitchen after her three wards, pausing to glance out the window, hoping to see any trace of fog lingering.

Nothing floated in the sunlight nor between the trees.

And yet she was happy, for the old woman with eyes white as snow had given her more than she ever expected, and there was still more to come.

TWENTY

It did not take long for only Edda and the oldest boy to remain – at most two months since Mergo had taken Maisie along with her. The oddity was that no other children came to their door. Although, if one looked at the woods and not simply the trees, it might've been a good sign of the world outside.

If only it was a definitive omen.

After Maisie, Abigail spoke fond and tender words in memory of her friend, asking Edda if she'd received word of what Maisie was up to and how she was. To everyone's chagrin, once the children left the Orphanage, they were never heard from again, and Maisie was no exception; an unwritten rule. It seemed to be that new families would keep to themselves while the old were left behind.

Being the next to go, the young Abigail admitted to missing everyone already as she left, even the boys. She was off to the Northwest, a small village whose lord wished for a little princess to pamper and his sons to learn how to protect a woman. Edda admired that widowed man, hoping for all the best.

David was next, split between leaving and staying, wishing to take his friend along but wanting to break free from the role he played. As a subordinate, lackey, kid brother, he hadn't a say, or rather, did not allow himself to have one out of respect and an odd reverence for the older lad.

When the prospective parents came to choose, both overlooked the eldest boy without a second thought, as though he were a spirit caught just out of sight.

Each time someone left, Geoffrey cried, even when Maisie did – he hid himself away in the back garden, pretending to sniff flowers when he was really attempting to clear his nose. Each time, his tears more bitter until he was left alone with Edda.

He was resistant to her, not in a poor behavioral manner, but rather, he disengaged, giving bland and short answers. It stung her, seeing him so afflicted with a pain he could not vocalize – being left behind and feeling unwanted, somehow broken.

The boy continued reading and writing, improving vastly when he had nothing more to do. He would head to the nearby stream to bring back fresh fish, collect firewood, and whatever else he could do to occupy himself and provide. Edda let him, knowing it was important to him.

Late at night, she could hear his wanderings about the Orphanage. There were creaks down the stairs and about the ground floor. Sometimes he went outside, and she wondered if he would leave. He always returned after a spell, taking to standing at a single door in particular and rattling the knob. The sound of it made Edda's gut turn over, wishing to purge all of its contents. She would never forget the sound of it, for even in death would the basement door haunt her.

It had to, for she deserved no forgiveness, no matter what Camille, Maisie, Mergo, Lowell, or any other had told her. She wanted to be plagued by it, for she believed it was the path of the penitent. The love she felt renewed in her became a more fierce battlefield, and at times, she was tempted to remove her new eye and to wallow.

The last child in her care was one who bore the effects of his whippings by her marionette hands, reinforcing her pain.

Every morning the boy greeted her, aided in chores, and honed his skills while she wrote letters, sending them to the far reaches of Wyrd, hoping for a response. The royal courier began to arrive once a week now, his deliveries shrinking in size.

Edda was appreciative, however, in the lack of correspondence from King Huxley and his brood. The last letter she received told of Alastair's accomplishments in manipulation. He *rivaled* the pagans in his abilities, surpassing whatever natural gifts they had.

He was a prodigy.

Martin was written of little and all Edda knew was that the boy who despised her with all his heart was growing rapidly, and that he was most loyal to his prince, his new favorite person.

These letters were ones she burned.

"Perhaps winter arrivin' is why no one is lookin' to adopt and why no children come to our door, now. Even the birds 'ave stopped singin'. They've all flown away."

In response, Geoffrey glanced at Edda, continuing in eating his stew as they sat across from one another. Every time he met her eyes, his mouth would twist, remorseful and melancholic, before tearing himself away. He nodded, but she wished he would speak.

Exhaling, she scooped more hearty food into her mouth. She observed Geoffrey, wishing she could reach him. Every day, she told herself that given time, he would. Months passed and she repeated such phrases morning and night, trying to keep a semblance of hope alive.

Clattering her spoon along the rim of her bowl, Edda sighed, "At least there are no more crows about the forest."

"Camille reminded me of a crow."

She could not help but smile at this, pleased he answered, and that he thought of something similar. "As did I. Please, continue."

"Isn't much to say beside that." He paused, letting food fall from his spoon, making low splashes and thick ripples in his bowl. "Why do you hate crows so much?"

"I did not say anythin' about h-hatin' them."

"You do not need to say so for me to know. When you were able to see again and the little one said you were akin to a bird, you asked if it were a crow. You were so hopeful it wouldn't be, I could see it in your face. That, and you wear a little scowl when they chatter or are within view."

"I did not realize—"

"We have spent much time together, time alone and in small company. You smiled at the mourning doves, albeit a sullen smile. Those were the birds that pained me more than crows."

Lowell's words regarding crows burned in her memory, reminding her to be wary of the things that stole, the jealous creatures of black wings. "Why do you dislike the doves?"

"I asked you first, Lady Edda."

The corner of her mouth twitched. "They steal what does not belong to them and show no remorse doin' so."

"Do they take when you are looking or when your back is turned?"

"Lookin' or not, they will commit thievin'."

"I believe they take what we miss after we realize it is gone. Like it's too little, too late – is that how the saying goes?"

Wheels turned in her skull, anger churned, and her heart buckled against its enclosure. Lowell said they were something to be wary of. Were these *birds* not something to utterly loathe? Would everything stolen from her still exist with her if she had held on more boisterously, more attentively? Edda was younger, then, and did not realize all she had, and could not have known she was taking her gifts, her family, and her Lowell for granted.

Despite how she resented his words, the young man had a point, and she struggled to reconcile with it.

"Mourning doves are too sad for me, and I do not wish to be sad anymore, Edda. They exist, making their sorrowful coos and going about surviving. Although, they do show us to cry and go about our days, so they teach us too." He shoved more food in his mouth, letting Edda take in his words as he chewed.

They sat in silence until Edda's soup grew cold and the boy's dish sat empty.

He cleared his throat. "People are not birds, I think, because they have the capacity to change. In the end, it is just a thought."

Edda wondered if Lowell and the boy's words could both be true. With enough silence, she began to believe so.

Then the boy began to cry; soft, at first, then jarring warbles came from his throat as his breath became laborious. Before Edda could stand, to offer any kind of comfort, he evaded her gaze and excused himself, bolting from the dining room and upstairs.

Inside, she twisted, counting her inhales and exhales, steadying her trembling limbs. She questioned why he had broken down in such a way. She wondered, too, if it had been because of something she had done.

Or even, simply, what she had not done.

* * *

Scarce was the boy and bored was Edda, wondering when she should take the trip to the river, if it was something to do in a moment of clarity, or during a push of knowing it is what must be done.

She chose the former.

Meandering through the Orphanage, she had become a creature of habit, one who only knew how to take care of others, lost when on her own. The boy had gone on in the frosty morning and had not yet returned. Edda felt a little ill at the thought of him now caring for her. She tapped her eye, feeling its warmth, and continued her plodding over creaking wood.

She missed having purpose.

The only duty she could bring herself to do was write letters, advertising the boy who remained, to those who hadn't adopted and those who had. For now, and for the season, it seemed, all avenues had dried up—a well without water, one you would look into for hope of salvation, only to find dust settled at the bottom.

So she walked, now confined to the classroom, to a heavy bookshelf she refused to clean, refused to acknowledge, and pulled out a neglected book. It was one of several, double rowed with pages well turned and practiced.

They were the lessons of His Royalty, naming her as an affront to His being.

Taking it to her desk, she flipped open the tome, seeing words but not reading them. The hardened leather cracked beneath her stoic fingertips as the pages tried to nick her hands. If ever her hands were plump and moist, surely the book would have succeeded.

She closed the book, thrumming fingers against it before opening it again, flipping through before slamming it shut, hands quivering with her squeezing, trapping words and ideas from escaping their rightful prison.

Making her way to a window, she gazed at her reflection as it drew near to her. It was cloudy outside, not that there was anything to see now besides barren trees and crisp leaves. Edda hooked a finger in her cheek and tugged it aside, pulling her tongue out without speaking. The habit had died, but reliving it was a semblance of old. She was uncomfortable without the structure, with being alone.

Wiping the spittle from her jaw, she looked into the eyes that stared back at her, one a lovely whorl of reds and yellows, the other a brilliance like no other. Perhaps her gift had made her need people, perhaps which was all she was needed for - for others. A disgusting comfort loomed in her belly, bubbling through her gut. She knew where she would find the answer, and she found every reason not to go.

Clarity be damned, for she would remain and squander, waiting for her purpose to find her – for if she only existed for others, what was she without them?

A deep sadness urged her to rip out her heart before she turned and smacked the thick book from her desk, watching it careen into a wall near the door. It slapped the floor, opening to a page near the beginning, just as the boy walked in.

Geoffrey picked it up with a distorted reverence, tracing a finger over words he once knew verbatim. He, dragged his feet to Edda, holding up the tome and pointing to a section. "I believe you need to read this."

The pagans of the land may have come before us, claiming to know and claiming to own, but within them lies a truth most horrid.

Around them, you are made to forget your truth and to adhere to them in a blind fashion – their wills all powerful, their wills that bend man, women, and children.

For what they claim is their blessing is our curse. They manipulate, lie, cheat and steal that which is not theirs.

Minds and livelihoods have been lost to such deception.

It is one of the many duties, perhaps one of higher values than most, of those who follow His Royalty to wipe this scourge of creatures from the face of our land, stripping them of all they own, within and without of their physical being.

They may seem like us, crying, screaming, smiling and dying, but they are the utmost wicked of demons that should ever plague humanity.

"Why?"

"To know what we were taught to believe, without question. This passage was read to us time and time again. This is how we were taught to think of you."

"And now?"

"I should think many still harbor it within themselves – especially those who were punished by your hands. Regardless of who controlled you."

"And you?"

The boy paused, Edda counted her heartbeats as they pounded against her ribs. She swore she could hear them cracking.

Before her, once more, the boy began to weep. She reached for him, feeling the tremble of his shoulders before he pulled away, keeping his head down. "I do not know how to feel. I am torn – for you have shown me such love and kindness of late, but the vision of you, your glowing eyes as you struck me again, and again and again. The passage I have engraved in my mind. It was you who made me realize how I treated Maisie, and how I was wrong for it – yet I still feel wronged by you and it is as though you have forgotten of it. You are both warm and cold at the same time, and it hurts terribly." The boy crumbled to the floor, his hands rubbing up and down the length of his arms as his sobs grew more violent.

Taking her place beside him, she wrapped herself around him, willing warmth to fill his smaller frame. His words were sinking in, penetrating her heart as she realized the gravity of her shutting away what happened, keeping it locked below them. As tormented as she felt, with the utter stoppage of punishment, she had neglected the one who remained.

And here he was, a mess in her arms.

When she finally spoke, her voice cracked as her tears dampened his hair, "For the pain I 'ave caused you and for 'ow I ignored your plight, I am ever sorry, dear Geoffrey. It was never somethin' one should experience, never somethin' anyone should endure. Regardless of who or what, it was by my 'and you suffered and forever I will carry that pain. One day, although selfish, I 'ope for absolution as I look back and pay penance."

He shuddered against her clavicle, expelling deep groans no child should be capable of. She joined him, letting her heart rattle loose as she let the pain in and out of her.

In no time, the sun had set, leaving them huddled in a dark and cold room, filled with poison books and empty seats. There was a freedom in that darkness, a freedom and a suffocating aura that only meant to push them out and forward.

Edda stood first, raising the child to his feet. They walked to the parlor in darkness, to where a dying fire whimpered to them. The boy fed it.

"Lady Edda?" He sniffled, his eyes swollen and cheeks salty.

She kneeled before him, and this time, he met her sight. "Yes?"

"With time, I think I will understand more. I think, too, that I forgive you – not completely, but it is there. Who you have shown me to be is becoming more than what I believed you to be."

Her sight blurred as she leaned in to kiss his nose. Pulling back, he smiled, and she hoped some of his pains were quelled, even if it would only be for a short time, like before.

Both agreeing to forego dinner, Edda took to the stairs first, looking behind to see the boy stopped halfway, looking over the sitting area as the flickering light diminished before their eyes. He rested his eyes at a point behind the seating area before continuing his journey up.

Leading him to his door, she hugged him goodnight and retired to Camille's old room. Pulling the crushing blankets over her, she watched the darkness mingle with the moonlight, holding back sleep until she heard footsteps descend the stairs and the familiar twisting of a knob.

TWENTY-ONE

The moment she heard him hesitate on the stairs, Edda knew what to expect come morning. The main entrance was unlocked and swung wide open, the early chill frosting the main room.

Even though she knew he had left, she checked every room, every corner, every inch, twice to be certain. He left a short note, folded neatly on his bed that read 'Thank you' in a beautiful cursive. Pocketing it, she stood before the open door, stepping on the stoop and let the silence wash over her. The icy wind howled in her ears.

Barefoot, she ventured, leaving the Orphanage unattended, and scoured the lands, to the fields and through the woods. Just before reaching the river, she turned back.

Geoffrey was long gone, but she left the door unlocked in case he should return.

He had been spending longer and longer amounts of time exploring, and she knew he had planned it, waiting for the last of what he needed: a final apology, and for him to release some of his deep plague and, what he could, of forgiveness.

Wind battered the exterior as the rattling echoed through empty halls instead of happy feet, instead of the voices of children. The vacancy was chilling, and Edda took a seat on the sofa, letting the emptiness fill her.

For now, she truly was alone.

And it haunted her.

Motionless she sat, feeling no hunger, no pain, not even the chill that drifted in through the open door.

The emptiness and the blankness pushed her from within and from outside, contorting her body in her mind – she pictured herself twisted, bloating and deflating in tandem as the Orphanage made her ears ring with a high-pitched scream.

It came from the basement.

She still held onto the key though she hardly used it, reluctant to even release the lock on the torture chamber. Edda's breathing quickened, sharp and brutal as the latch came undone with a *click* that permeated her childhood and adolescence. The edges of her vision grew dark as she let the door swing open.

She stared into the black void, and it stared back. It called to her as it tried to rip her mind and heart from her. She sucked in a breath, swallowed her tears and lit a nearby candle without turning away from the blackness.

Each step, it seemed, wanted to knock her down and drag her where she never wished to go. The air oppressed as it reached for her throat – hands hidden in the shadows, hands made of wires and metal, wanting to put her back in the shackles that bound her entirety.

The red ribbon scars pulsed over her skin, the sensation delving deeper into her bones making them burn as though they could burst, splintering, able to rip through her.

Yet they did no such thing.

A candle lit here, a candle there, enough to keep away the suffocation.

She stood in the center and stared at the pole the children were shackled to, then down to the dirt soaked in Lowell's blood. Her heart was frozen as she stepped to where she hung, looking up to see the metal cage that used to hold her head aloft, the wires connected by webs hung limp nearby. Before the apparatus was a heavy curtain, and behind was a wooden set of stairs that led to where Camille use to control Marion, her puppet.

Edda could still feel Marion shriveled and groaning within her when she stood in the basement and when she ascended the stairs. What used to hold her eyes open sat next to the cross-braces that dictated her every move, whether she remembered it or not, awake or not.

Absent-mindedly, she stuck out a finger and pushed at the wooden controls, watching them tumble over, careening downwards, the metallic strings slicing through the air as they used to do to Edda's limbs, their sounds of thunder.

Her hand grasped for what was left behind and she walked to where everything fell and whispered, curious, "Marion?" She knew she would never get a response but called another, "Camille?" Nothing still.

The tiny flames scattered about reflected in the large mirrors that captured and held every pain ever committed in this space – every scream, cry, whimper, curse, laugh, and sigh. It captured Edda, too, as she stared at her reflection, seeing how her eyes glowed here, realizing what all the children had seen before.

In her, the old her, Marion stirred, moving to fill in Edda's limbs.

"Edda?" Her voice was hoarse when she called for herself. After all, there was no Marion, only her. Only Edda.

The wires snaked below her feet. Her heart pounded as she picked up one of the crosses and cradling it like Camille once did, her hands and fingers dancing as though she played a pretty song on the piano.

Boom

The sound echoed in her ears.

Boom

It came from within her.

Boom

Tears streaked her face as she scowled.

Boom

Then the dam broke and the whirlpool in her gut grew angry, spiteful, hateful teeth, and her heart rattled in its cage, ripping through the barrier that encased it. Edda screamed, big and broad, a warrior in battle, a bear who lost its cub, a child who lost its parent, and a person who had lost their life.

She whipped about, flinging the puppeteer's tool into a mirror, watching it shatter.

She jumped to grip the lofted cage, and with her unnatural heft, she tore down Camille's structure, stepping aside as it clattered in a grand heap where she once stood, where she was made into a demon.

The metal eye-holder in her hand was cold, much too cold to bear, and she put all her strength into it, letting it crash into a horrid mirror, her image breaking into a hundred pieces before splitting into fragments on the ground.

The pole was next.

She stood in the center of the old blood, let it seep through her skin. It was Lowell's and it was that of many before him. She gripped the rod and tugged, tugged, and tugged again. Rage fueled her, her mind awash with the thought of her parents and those she never knew that died in search of her - in search of kin. She thought of Lowell's parents and sister, of where she had come from, at why she survived whilst others were murdered, wasting away in unknown graves, nameless and forgotten.

She roared, her voice cracking as she ripped her challenge free from the ground that stained her feet red.

She ran to each mirror and struck them until she laughed. They screamed and cried as they were broken, releasing all they kept inside, letting it fill the wretched room upon their freedom, though they were spirits or ghosts. The pain could not be contained in anything or anyone - it only led to the poison that perpetuated the Orphanage, those who lived there, and those who committed the vilest acts imaginable.

Her feet were left unscathed whilst she sauntered through the glass to complete her destruction, leaving the smallest sparkles to twinkle in her trailing.

Even when everything lay broken and dashed across the ground, the wooden beam in her hands pricking her with invisible, stinging splinters aplenty, she felt unsatisfied.

Perhaps that is what Camille felt at times, only she was more heinous then, before her heart shifted and she left everything, abandoning those in her wake.

She knocked every candle down, extinguishing their flames with her swings as they met with the dirt below. She found the shackles that bound the children and cast them into a far corner, crushing broken glass on impact.

The darkness was all that was there now, but it was no longer devious. It mourned.

Dragging the wooden weapon behind her, it thunked on every step on route to the parlor, leaving the basement open for the phantoms to finally be free. She brought the beam to the fireplace where it clattered in two, her ireful episode having split it. Edda tossed it, piece by piece, into the maw of the stone structure, casting a match inside.

Once it caught, she walked to the classroom, making several trips, almost drowning the growing flame with leather bound books, dried and cracking.

The pages took to burning brilliantly, offsetting the shriveling, shrinking leather that refused to catch, taking to charring and bearing the ashes of its contents. The smell was that of hair in a candle, the leather crinkling in its purification, as did one's nose in repulsion.

Soon enough, no books could be read, their venom no longer viable.

Then she swayed and hummed something her parents used to sing – the words lost on her little mind. The glorious heat blew back her dark hair, illuminating the reddish pigment of her skin and her light-sanguine eyes. She began to dance, back and forth in celebration, allowing the joy to run through her as she lifted her arms high, the shadows on the wall showing others with Edda, unknown and unseeable to her.

The hate in her was a little less, now, and she could feel her heart a little less bogged down. She turned to the open door and ran out into the frosting evening.

She had to go to the river.

****

Impossibly, the gentle flow of the wide and righteous waterway was frozen over. Not even the well was iced by this time.

Edda dared herself and stepped forward, feeling little crackles beneath her. Part of her wanted it to break, despite Mergo's and Maisie's foretelling that she had longer to go.

The cold on her feet was nice against her newfound heat, and she walked until the chilled layer beneath her was so thick that nothing could break it. She was a bit surprised she had even made it this far. Laying down on her stomach, she spread out her limbs, wishing to dissolve into the ice.

She waited for something, and she received nothing.

Propping herself up on her hands, she stared through the ice, wishing to see the bodies of those cast beneath it, wanting to see the bodies of her parents, floating to greet her on the other side of the barrier. The dark water beneath glared at her until she only saw herself reflected back.

She pounded her fists and screamed, "Mama! Papa! Mergo told me to come 'ere and for what? No one is 'ere, no one will be! It is simply a deep river and it will not even take me!" The ice would not crack now, and she beat it until exhaustion overtook her.

She curled up and winced with despair, with loneliness, sputtering and wailing until she fell asleep.

A deep sleep it was and long had it waited for her, for her heart to open just enough to let them in.

"Edda, my sweetin'?"

Edda stirred in the hollow of her mind, in her dreams, the grandest void of gray, of possibilities.

"Child, do you hear us?" A deeper voice now, familiar and warm.

Edda mumbled in response as she remained balled up, curled into herself. She felt hands below her and arms lift her into the cool air, holding her close against a warm barrel-chested man. It was her father. She recognized his smell after all this time – piney, wooden, and *him*.

Fingers ran through her dark hair, wrapping it about a lean finger, then two, then a hand before the spiral was released to bounce back into its original place. A sweetness wafted to her, and she knew it was her mother, who exuded an aura of love and kindness so potent that only the most devoid soul could oppose her.

Eyelids aflutter, she gradually unfurled to look about her, her hands curled into small fists, gripping the tunic so close to her. Her feet swayed in the air. She was different.

Once again, she was a child of five, and now she was afraid.

"Look at us, please, my sweet girl?"

Edda shook her head, screwing her eyes shut – what would she see? Would they be alive or dead? Would it be them or creatures wearing their faces as grotesque masks? Could it be Alastair, cracking a smile most wicked behind a kind façade?

"My little Edda, 'ave a look-see! You needn't be afraid, not 'ere!" His jovial bellows followed her being lifted high up above heads and land.

Carefully, one eye pulled itself open, followed by the other. As she was held, arisen, below her were her parents, beaming at her, her father grinning, her mother holding back tears.

As was her body, her voice, too, was small again, "Mama! Papa!"

They pulled her in tight, holding her so that she might burst at the seams if she weren't built to withstand their embrace.

Long, thin fingers held her face, squishing her cheeks as she was directed toward her mother. A thumb ran over each eye as her mama sighed in relief and joy, "You can 'ear us now, sweetin'. We missed you forever and a day."

"'Ow could I not 'ear you before?" She cooed.

A tickle under her chin and a squeeze at her side came before her father's voice chuckled out, "You were so closed off to us, to everythin'! That little wall around your 'eart 'elps no one."

Edda's body began to elongate as she spoke, "I 'ad to. I did 'orrid things, and I could not be close to those I wished. Can I come with you both? I beg you, I cannot be alone. I do not wish to be! There is nothin' more to distract me from the pain I feel, and I see no escape from my nightmares!" Her feet were on the ground now as she began to sob.

With all the compassion only an angel could muster and a sparkling in her eyes, her mother spoke, "Yet you overcame, did you not? You will again. We 'ave seen it pass, as did Mergo and Maisie."

"'Ow? What else is there? I... I cannot forgive myself."

"For?"

Edda sucked in the damp and chill air of her dream, letting it fill her lungs, plumping them full of the gray miasma that was transparent enough it might as well not have been.

She coughed and choked on the words as they spilled, "I 'ave beaten children. I 'ave gotten our kin killed. I killed Lowell, and 'e only meant the best for me."

"And?" her father inserted himself, his tone a question most oblique.

"And? What do you mean 'and'? My actions are that of a demon, of a creature not born but spawned. I was never meant to be of this world!"

"Yet you are, and the world is a picky one."

"The world made a demon."

Her mother's voice cut in, serene, "Would you forgive a child?"

"I... Yes?"

"Let yourself be free, Edda, because you were and still are that child."

"I am an adult now! I am the 'ead of the Orphanage, I am no child!"

"In body and responsibility, you may be but 'ere," her father reached out and tapped at her temple, then her heart, then her abdomen in turn, "'Ere you are still our little girl, 'urt and alone, afraid. You could not be what you were and the punishments furthered that. Your mind put up that wall, and others as well as you created the seething pit that eats you from inside."

"But what do I *do* about it?" Edda wailed, lost, dribble spilling from her curled lips.

"You let it be, yeah?"

This voice was different, not her mother's or father's. She cranked her head to look around. A younger man stood behind her, his eyes sparkling with curiosity, with life's wonders. He stepped towards her and reached out a hand, each step making him grow into a handsome man. He reached out both hands now.

She wished for joy but the bitterness inside her caused her to collapse, falling in a heap of scattered pieces.

Lowell knelt beside her and lifted her chin, not caring about how damp it was, not caring for the pitiful look on her face. He leaned in and kissed her nose. "I told you I would see you again."

"I-is this 'ome?"

"Not quite, that is still a ways off, but it is close to it."

She reached for him, tucking her arms under his, afraid to feel warm blood seep from him, afraid he'd go limp under her arms, limp and then stiff, like the body she left him as.

This he never did, so she listened to his heartbeat, rich and alive.

"Let it be, Edda."

"'Ow? What can be done about it now?"

"Exactly."

"What?"

"What can be done about it now? You were manipulated, made to be what you were not from when you were just a baby. Your authenticity stripped away to 'elp you survive. You 'ave proven such actions were not yours, and you work to repent every day. You need to forgive yourself, to free yourself, and let what 'appened simply be that - what 'appened. Yeah?"

Lowell looked behind Edda, towards her parents, and although she could not see them, she knew they nodded. She felt the warmth of their hands come down on her shoulders. The scars on her arms heated up in a way most pleasant.

His smile was wide, all his teeth showing as he chuckled, "My Edda, look at 'ow you glow."

She needn't see it to feel it, from deep in her, out of her, and through her eyes.

"'E's right, sweetin'. We told you time and time again what you are and you know what that is. It does not matter 'ow deep you shove it or deny it. No one could ever rip it from you." Her mother was right, as she always was.

Kissed atop her head, she felt the strength of her father over her, sheltering her, showering her with love and kindness.

That is what it was, and that is what she was told she deserved most – that is what she denied herself most.

Flashes ran through her mind, of her tearing at her tongue, of her withholding care and affections from needy children, of the crimson trails grooved into her arms growing more complicated with time. Of her head, caged, her eyes fastened open and her arms moving against her will.

An empty socket.

A deep, pained groan pushed itself from her heart as most of the wall came toppling down, the creature in her gut shrinking even though it had more to get to, more to eat, more to ravage and rip from her. She leaned into Lowell, her Lowell, and willed the whirlpool to leave her, understanding that it was of her making and she no longer needed it, wanted it.

It did not dissipate, only shrunk.

"Edda," her father called to her. She sucked in a breath and listened. "It will take time, but through it, you will come to the other side. It will not be easy, and some days, it will be just as 'ard as the first, but you will feel all the better, love."

Different memories whispered to her now, rapid but not fleeting. Playing in the water as a little girl, her face smeared with berry juice. Her father tossing her high in the air, her mother spinning her. Martin when he was little, using a wooden spoon to tap at her until she played with him. Lowell following her about, teasing her and pushing her. Maisie playing with the children, staring out windows and speaking from the depth of her being, from a pool of knowledge only briefly accessible. Mergo giving her sight and speaking of things immemorial, wisdom old and promises set in the fabrics of time. Of the boy forgiving her, showing her where she did do wrong and allowing her to grow from it. Of the chamber she had destroyed and the books she burned.

All the way to now, to this place in her dreams, to where she could finally be reached.

Their arms pulled away, the love remaining.

They called to her to open her eyes.

As she did, before her stood a mirror, but not one made of backed glass, but a simple reflection staring back at her, made out of the silver ocean that floated in the spaces between. It reminded her of Maisie, and she leaned close.

Staring back at her, was herself, Edda. Reaching out, her finger touched something smooth and solid, heat transferring between her and her echo. Gazing over the outline of herself, she saw the red-tinge of her skin, the deep grooves that lay beneath her fallen sleeves. She witnessed her broad chest and shoulders, her dark brown hair, beaked nose, and thin lips.

Then her eyes, glowing. They were the same as the stone that beset her golden armlet but doubled. She could trace the white lines that emerged from her pupil over the solid matter before her. The same white lines curved like the wings of a regal raptor, lines descending from those wings like rain. The closer she looked, the more the lines seemed to move as though alive, swaying as though it were a gentle shower.

She sat back and let everything come through her, from her.

She wept , allowing herself to take in what she had so long denied, all without looking away, and she smiled, laughing with release, a promised reprieve that she could finally let fill her.

At least for this moment in time, for her father was right.

Yet, this precious instant was one of the most beautiful she'd ever known.

Then it was gone.

And she did still smile.

"Sweetin', you can go back now." Her mother was at her side now, her father opposite, Lowell before her, holding her hands and rubbing the backs of them.

"Alright." She did not want to, but she knew she had to, and that all would go as Maisie and Mergo said – that all would be fine, all would be well. She had believed she'd feel bittersweet, but only sweetness filled her, her heart beating with exuberance like that of a little child.

In turn, they said goodbye. Her father, despite how big she'd grown, lifted her above his head before letting her fall into his arms, laying a kiss upon her cheek. Her mother took her hand and danced with her, spinning her about, then holding her close, kissing her forehead.

Then Lowell, the last one with her in the now warm void, embraced her, a hand at the back of her head, the other across her shoulders. She cried in his arms, longing for him even now. He pulled back and kissed each of her eyes, then her nose. He smiled, big and gracious, his bottom teeth crooked but charming – something she had never noticed – and he winked and laid a tender kiss on her lips.

Then he was gone.

The ice was solid beneath her as she awoke. It had never budged, cracked or wavered while she slept, and she had slept for longer than she could ever know.

She stood, feeling the smooth, slick surface beneath her, and stepped onto the frosty riverbank. Behind her, the ice split, separating into tiny pieces, and the river flowed once more.

It seemed nature had given her the chance to heal, and she was glad she took it.

Journeying back to the open, empty Orphanage, she no longer felt hollow, only more and more full. The fireplace had died, not an ember to be seen as cold, shining crystals crawled in through the entryway.

Each day would be a practice now, of being better, doing better.

She set about cleaning, forgetting something else she was promised.

Forgetting that one last gift was on its way.

Twenty-Two

Winter was a dash in time as spring arrived on the night of a full moon, a soft rain melting what remained of the snow.

The whirlpool in Edda's stomach was little to nothing now as she released much of the blame on herself, forgiving, letting it be. She could walk past the basement now, door open or closed, and not feel a thing about it – all the ghosts having escaped. Those passed had even stopped speaking their whispered words having been said and heard.

It was a time of rest and healing, rebirth.

She spent the time managing the structure and herself, no longer sending letters, no longer receiving, and the Orphanage became her domicile. Yet, she would be lying if she said she did not miss the totting footfalls of children. She enjoyed the moments she could, and let herself feel anguish, pain, and sadness as it flooded her in waves that abated more and more quickly.

The wall around her heart nearly diminished, but it remained stubborn still. Edda knew it would give, it only needed little more, and she would do her best to give that little more, however much it took.

She wrote the names down of all the children that were under Camille's charge and under hers, remembering each face and thanking them, and apologizing to them. Camille's name was also on that list as she did the same for her.

She wondered how her old matron was, where she had gone, and if she had found absolution. Edda found herself wishing to speak with her again, to share her own process of healing, wondering if Camille's was similar. Through the winter, she noticed they were more similar than different.

The crows began to caw outside once more, along with the mourning doves who came much later. Both made her smile now, realizing that both were simply living things, different parts of life's varying experience. She remembered Lowell's words and Geoffrey's, how different perspectives changed entire paintings, neither fully correct nor fully false.

She enjoyed their singing as she would walk at all times about the property, far away and close by. The flowers in the field had begun to bloom: red, yellows and blues, and the ones that were rare that she once believed were diseased.

No, they were simply different.

She sparingly picked them, caressing their soft petals and careful in holding their fragile, green stems, dew dripping from the morning sky. These flowers, she brought back and put in a variety of vases that she had found scattered about the Orphanage.

Edda had come across dresses left behind and began to sport them. They were sleeveless, and the marks on her arms had changed in her mind, the shame having fizzled away. Now they were reminders of her growth and how she needn't stay trapped in a cage she may not have created, but one she fostered.

The world grew louder outside as her inner peace and love filled the wooden rooms with the more joyous memories.

She dared say she was happy now, better some days than others, but overall, she was content.

Sometimes, a melancholy creeped at her when she wished to share it with another, yet she knew that she already did, in a more ethereal sense.

She played with the flavors of tea much of the time indoors, writing recipes and singing songs that entered her mind, knowing some were from her mother and father, some of her own.

One evening, the fire flickered, crackling against blackened stone as she experimented, added some tiny, dried flowers to the steeping brew. She hummed until notes spilled from her low and wordless, sounds held that raised and lowered as they reverberated through the structure, making her frame vibrate in the most pleasant fashion.

It felt like bliss.

Knock knock

She paused, looking over her shoulder at the front door, unlocked, waiting for the sound once again.

Knock knock

She stood, brushing off her dress as the floor creaked beneath her weight, and she stepped, excited and a little nervous, toward the entryway.

Opening it, no one stood before her, only the swishing of trees making sound now. Peering beyond the edges before noticing the new, mewling thing at her feet, swaddled in a blanket and waiting for her on the stoop.

It was a baby with light brown wisps of hair, eyes closed as it suckled at the air. Something in her breast swelled as she slid her hands beneath the tiny babe, lifting it close to her bosom before turning back and shutting the door behind her.

Sitting near the fire, she brushed at the child's hair, knowing it was a boy without needing to see. The tiniest hands grasped at the air, chubby fingers curling and releasing before they found Edda's dress.

His eyes opened, one a deep dark brown, like that of the ground from which all grew and all would be returned to and,

and the other a sparkling blue, like the sky. She was as overcome with awe as she was with her present that she hadn't expected.

A name came to her, sudden and purposeful, and she whispered, "Cian."

He smiled at her, little dimples pecked his cheeks as he pulled at her.

What little remained of the shelter her heart resided in turned to dust as she cooed at the baby. Unbuttoning her top, she felt she knew Camille had always wished to feel, the love, care and kindness spilling from her in the most joyous of tears.

She was a mother.

Twenty-Three

Time was splendid with the boy of eyes blue and brown. One of note, the other, not. Yet, special he was, all the same. He followed his mother eagerly as he grew, from crawling to a teetering walk, to running along in her footsteps.

They had no interruptions for an odd number of years, until another orphan showed up on their steps - was showered in unconditional love and happiness, their future appearing bright as they stepped out into the new world, into the arms of new parents.

No one stayed long, and that was alright, as Maisie had once said. The Orphanage was a waypoint for many, and now, it was no longer one filled with agony.

As the flowers of the field and back garden bloomed, so did light fill the home - it's original purpose lost as it was made anew from within.

Words were the little Cian's favorite now, as were questions as he tracked each of his mother's heavy steps, bombarding her with sounds, muddled and sweet. How he loved stories, too, stories of heroes, villains, friends, and grandparents.

Other than Cian and Edda's happiness, her personal withholdings no longer a hindrance, all was quiet year round – not a dove's cry nor a crow's caw.

"Mama! Mama!" The toddler would grab at her heels as she cooked, resorting to slapping as high as his little arms could reach.

"It's almost ready, sweetin'."

Up his arms went, and so did he, high up and giggling so delightedly, he warbled as spittle bubbled on his lip before bursting. Edda laughed along with him. She remembered little Martin then, a passive thought, years ago.

She had thought of him before, recalling tales for bedtime.

Only telling of fondness, for Cian had allowed her freedom from her invisible shackles. Forward and onward, chin up, too. That was life now, and as it came, she would make amends, but as for what was, nothing more was to be done but learn.

She was grateful.

Spinning him about, she let him collapse against her, his head cradled by the nook between shoulder and neck. His small hand traced the red lines that snaked over her arms. She would never hide a thing from him if he were to ask – these scars caused by 'mean monsters that thought they were doin' right but were truly doin' wrong.' Afterwards, he liked to touch them, calling them pretty and warm – just like her.

And now, in the summertimes and warmer days, she could wear the sleeveless dresses left behind by Camille.

Dipping her finger into the stew, the boiling warmed her. She blew upon her finger and let the small boy have a taste. He grinned, and the night blurred by until he was tucked in next to his Edda.

"Tell me stowy, please."

"One in mind?"

Lower lip puckered, he thought as she rattled off notions of dolls, hunters, fog, and lovely, enchanting moons. He shook his head and pulled the blankets to his eyes in thought. Edda walked to the dancing, trilling fire, and stoked it, the flames reigniting.

"Ah! The twinkly man!"

"The what?"

She watched the boy jump up, lifting his fingers and making them dance, as though he were poking through parchment above his head. With a flourish, he whipped his hand to point out the window.

The stars. He wanted to hear about Lowell.

Pulling him down to lay under the plush and heavy blankets, she laid beside him, cradling him in her embrace. Kissing his head, she told the story of a young adolescent who grew within her mind to be a man, dependable and curious, challenging, prodding, and loving. How he loved the stars and collected them within his eyes to share the wonders with others, willing or unwilling.

That was how they worked, their kind, and that was alright.

Cian pointed to his own eyes, his blue eye pretty to behold, his brown eye making one feel connected, both to him and to the land about them.

"Love, you are special, too. Like Lowell, like Mama and the rest."

"Is he Papa?"

"No, but 'ad 'e been 'ere, 'e would be. Lowell would 'ave loved you so, just as I do."

"Later, see him, Mama?"

She paused, remembering promises of returning, cautious in her response, "I do not know when, nor 'ow, but someday, yes. You will meet 'im and many others."

"Where go?"

A bitter truth ran through her, nicking her heart on the way. A small pain now, time would care for it. "I do not know, but for now, 'e is safe."

"Mmm." He gabbed little more, his breath slowing and deepening. He tossed and turned out of Edda's arms, curling around a lump of red, soft bedcoverings he gathered each night. She waited little longer before attempting to tiptoe out of the room, the creaky floor doing nothing to hide her steps. She was glad the boy was a heavy sleeper.

Slipping into the old, empty room where the orphans used to stay, she approached the far window, a bed pushed up against it, a blanket draped over it. All this, she kept clean in honor of Lowell. Lifting the blanket, she crawled onto the small bed, sitting crossed-legged and letting the light of the moon fill her, bathe her. Speckled about the sky were dashes of constellations, like salt spilled over a blackened surface.

She visited here from time to time, and each time, she cried. Longing, remembrances, little and larger joys rippled in her tears. The man she saw in her dreams, the Lowell that was not allowed to be of this world, would be proud of her.

The wish to reach him loomed over her, and in this small pocket of magick, she knew they were closest.

Closing her eyes, she imagined him kissing her cheeks and holding her shoulders – the bitterness falling away as the sweetness filled her. For a moment, she swore she felt him do as she pictured.

Reality blurred as she wiped her face, smiling as she whispered *goodnights*, followed by *until next times*.

The dark hallway connecting every room on the second floor welcomed her as she plodded to her bed. Once she felt alien to this place, now a semblance of belonging. The salty remains on her cheeks cracked at her grinning. She felt a fool, being so happy. Joining little Cian under the covers once again, Edda thought of Camille and hoped she had found what she looked for, what she left for.

Just as any day, Edda and Cian slept, the moon gradually giving way to a burning, joyful sun.

* * *

Cian's hair was a lustering brown as he grew, his blue eye a sparkle, pretty to see, his darker one binding you to the world and all its natural beauties. Whenever children left, they stared at his darker orb the longest, sighing deep before hugging him goodbye, then Edda.

He was ten, now.

"Mama, why does no one speak like you?"

"'Ave I not told you before in stories aplenty?" Edda looked no different than a decade before, her face bearing no signs of age. Without wrinkles and lines, she was a carved statue, the only weathering on her arms.

"I know they are only stories. I just wonder, I have wondered since I found that book in the study."

They walked through the field as they spoke, avoiding the bountiful flowers that blossomed more each year since Cian's arrival. Edda's gait faltered as the boy turned to face her, letting himself fall amongst the tall grass. "Cian, what book?"

He held up his hands and made his fingers walk the air, "When you enter the room, the shelf that sits on the far wall." He brought his fingers to his mouth, mimicking the teeth of rodents. "I believed I had seen a mouse peeking from under the furniture and when I looked, there was a book there, dried, shriveling, old."

"You read it?" Crouching alongside Cian, she plucked a few flowers then decorated the boy's head as though his hair were the earth they grew from. He always liked it. From the first time she did so, he was happy.

Sitting in silence, Cian let himself be adorned, lifting his hands up to then let them fall to his thighs as his lips twisted.

"I will 'ide no secrets from you, sweetin'."

"It spoke of demons and a rising sun that would purge and enslave those that still stood." His hands covered his dark iris. "It said demons bore mani-pu-lative abil-i-ties."

Restraining a smile and praise, she kept at her craft, listening.

"Is that us? Is that you? Why you speak different?"

Switching places, Cian busied his hands with his mother's floral jewelry as she answered, "My parents spoke as I do. The older of our people do – unlike most, I believe we are more of the land. We are imbued with it."

"Are we better than the others?"

"What would be your answer?"

Without hesitation, he tucked a mottled red flower behind Edda's ear. "No, just different."

"Yet some call us demons, monsters, and creatures."

"Why?" He sat in front of his mother, planting the flats of his bare feet together, leaning back and digging his fingers into the dirt.

"They fear us."

"But why?"

A gentle breeze picked up, the petals of their gildings tickling their faces, the quiet clinging like a tacky film. Minutes ticked past as Cian patiently waited for the answer, not allowing himself to think of one of his own.

"They each 'ave reasons, Cian. Some be envious, lookin' to take what belongs to another in any way they can. Some are afraid of what they do not understand. Some simply 'ate us."

"Why?"

"Some people are born so, some are made to do so."

"How?"

Edda shrugged, letting her breath slip out to catch the wind, coalescing into a single element. She padded the ground beneath her before gazing at the boy she had been raising for a decade – she believed she'd done well. He was curious, but grounded, patient, kind, and loving. To him, all were friends and family, for there was no room for ire. At times, the thought crossed her mind – what if he had arrived at the Orphanage earlier, or if another had reared him? What if both eyes were brown?

A long, slow blink ushered away the idle ideas, and when she looked to him again, he was looking back.

"My dear, do you dream?"

He nodded, surprised by the question but delighted, too.

"What do you dream of?"

He giggled, letting his feet tap the ground, left foot, then right, left, right. *Tap tap tap tap.*

A burgeoning smile flashed into a full grin, lighting up his face and crinkling the corners of his eyes as he dashed to his feet, small pebbles of dirt falling from his fingertips. "Mother! I dream I am a knight! I fight monsters with large horns and even bigger claws!" His fingers crooked as he snarled, attempting a menacing façade. Edda giggled at his retellings. "I dream of protecting you and our home, letting all who gather inside for solitude. I dream of family!" His hands were raised, faltering when his smile did, then everything fell.

Edda kneeled in front of him, cupping his cheeks in her red porcelain hands. "My child, what is it?"

He struggled to meet her gaze. "For a long time, I have had a dream that comes back, again and again. Do dreams have meanings?"

"Some do, some do not, I 'ave come to know."

"I dream I look in the mirror, and both eyes are brown, but it is not me. It is someone who looks very much like me but is not me."

"Are you frightened?"

"No, I wish to meet him."

We will meet again, when we go home.

Standing before Cian, she gathered his hands in hers. She was unsure whose voice whispered to her, but she'd come to know it no longer mattered. "I believe you will, if you wish it and you make it so."

Cian huffed with delight, chuffing with an unknown triumph before breaking away from Edda's grip in a single motion. Turning to see, she was met with a snapped stem poking the corner of her mouth. Another of his favorite things: to stick a single flower in his mother's mouth, as though a thing to chew – she should have expected it.

The only difference this time being he sported one too.

He cackled, silly and boisterous and nibbled his greenery. "It tastes strange, but I enjoy it all the same!"

* * *

Long and thin Cian grew to be in a few short years as his hair met his shoulders, tucking behind his ears, and he watched the world outside his window with fondness.

His bedroom was that of an old storage room his mother helped him clean and assemble, just across from the room the orphans would sleep in during their stays, short and long. It had been some time since someone had slept there.

Some nights he would sneak in and gather them into Lowell's bed and talk about the stars and the world around them. He would rehash stories Edda spoke of, adding his own twists that came to him in daydreaming moments and sleep-filled nights. If no one was to join him in his musings, he would collect his mother, and they would sit in silence, a myriad of emotions flowing through them.

Edda would always cry.

As much as it hurt to see, Cian understood it and let her mourn uninterrupted.

Sometimes, it felt as if others joined – one or more, the amount he could never quite say.

One day, when the sun he loved casted morning shadows, he stood in his entryway and stared at the closed door before him. No one, no abandoned child had graced their home in what felt like years. In that same time, birds and other critters alike had stopped making songs.

Cian felt full living here with his adopted mother, but he was lonely too. He felt that there was more waiting for him and yearned to find just what it was.

Seeing him again helped nothing – the boy in the mirror, in his dreams, covered in filth and bending over letters that flitted through the sky like fowls. How much Cian wished he could reach out and help the boy say those words he scrunched his nose at, frustrated and discouraged, alone near a cold stone wall.

Down the stairs and out the door for his morning walk, alone and before his mother had awakened, he trotted. Sometimes the rush of the wind spurned him to run. Other times he would climb a fine sturdy tree and wait for the fauna to gather.

The river called him today, fresh and flowing, rapid in some parts, serene in others.

It never took him long to go where he needed to, as though the ground beneath him helped usher him along. Here, where he chose to sit and dip his feet, here, it was calm.

Covering half his face, he watched his reflection shift as he did – blue to brown, blue and brown, blackness. He focused on the sun's warmth instead, opting not to see.

Edda never really liked the sun, or, at least, she had conflicting emotions regarding it. She wanted to like it, but she was fettered by the unseen. That old tome Cian once found bore a faint resemblance to a rising sun on its cover, the book's contents speaking ill of others. Of his mother.

Half of him.

His hands fell as he laid back, shifting himself along the banks and letting his fingers play with the water's surface before plunging his hands in. His trousers were getting soaked, but that did not matter, never did. Here was bliss.

Missing the songs that used to accompany him, he began to whistle like a songbird, then flapped his hands in the water and gave a small caw though he were a crow before he resumed the pretty tunes.

Closing his eyes, the leaves of the trees tickled one another while they danced – whistling was difficult when one smiled.

So he stopped, listened, and wondered.

He wished he knew how his mother and father looked. Edda did not birth him, this he knew very young, and it did not bother him. He was grateful and he loved her so – he could have two mothers and that was alright by him.

It was curiosity that piqued his mind, not just of their looks but who they were, what they did, if they still lived and why they gave him up.

It used to sting at him when he thought of it, but he gave them the benefit of the doubt. Their reasons were theirs, and he was in no horrid place now. This place could only be paradise – one to share with any and all if given the chance.

Standing, he waded through the water, droplets falling from his fingers back to their source.

The water was to his waist now, yet deeper still the river ran, the current calm and inviting. Soaked clothing could not sink him for he was in control in this space.

The water seemed to still about his chest as he leaned his head back, wetting it whilst closing his eyes. Cian listened like he had so many times before.

Tears gathered in his eyes as he found his footing, the silt of the river weaving between his toes, grazing his flesh, the water lovingly nudging him. The wind puffed, whimsical, at the dark hairs that wandered from his head, not following the path of the rest. Silence permeated, blanketing the subtle sounds of nature, covering the beating of his heart, the blood pulsing within his ears.

In love with life, this moment, he wept, adding some of himself to the flow of water, to this passageway for much visible and invisible.

He smiled at the thought of sharing such a bliss with another – Edda, and someday, a sibling, a love. The hope was a small notion, for nothing could rob him of his experiences and his growth through the years, under his mother's loving eyes.

At that, a brief melody dashed through the air, and through his bleary vision, a bright, little bird was in view, then not.

There, and gone.

"*Beauteous*," he whispered.

The sun gathered higher now. He had to be going to greet his mother with fresh flowers; such a thing was not only a gift for her, but also him. The sand released him with relative ease, his slow, shallow steps casting small clouds about his underwater footfalls - the water so clear and crisp that one could see all from the bank.

Up and aloft, sopping with the river, he let himself drip as he playfully kicked his feet to let go of any stubborn debris sticking to him. He stood tall, squeezing his shirt and trousers, wringing them out while they hung about him.

Tapping the back of his head, Cian decided that could dry on its own, giggling as water trickled down the back of his neck.

Blissful, he marched towards home, to the Orphanage. Grass stuck to his feet as he swung his arms forwards and back, a quick spin here and there as he imagined the dancing in the books and stories he'd heard.

Before long, flowers pebbled his way and he plucked, some blues, some yellows, purples, and pinks. Of course, he topped off the bouquet with the special flowers, the ones that resembled his mother's striated eyes, red, yellow, and black - full of a deep richness that was palpable and engaging.

Onwards again, his pace was more at a saunter as he skittered with excitement, the cobblestone pathway becoming more and more overgrown with ivy and other greens, the trees greeting him same as every splendid morning.

"Good morning, my trees!" A coo.

"Good morning, boy."

Cian stopped, a disquieting burning in his gut coming to life. He'd never known this feeling, this anxiety, this gentle *anger*. "Who speaks to me?"

Stoic, firm, resonating, it replied, "I wish for you to deliver this letter."

Glancing between trees, no one was around him. Leaning to peer around gave no soul away as well. The ground beneath him belied a shadowing presence. Cian spun about, looking up at a well-built man – one he could never protect his mother from. His heart travelled to his throat as his body grew more rigid.

The blonde man leaned over, his eyes twitching when they met with the young boy's, the former's darkened color too difficult to discern. He held out paper folded into a parcel. Shaking, Cian held out a hand to take it, glancing between the looming figure and the note.

"Give it to your mother, now. Do not stray – I wish for her to know what comes."

"W-w-who are you?"

With trembling lips that quickly scowled then became neutral in a blink, he answered, "She will know. Do *not* dally, for I will know." He raised his hand and flicked towards Cian, motioning him to scurry away.

And he did, shame hot on his heels as unfamiliar tears began spilling from him. He burst through the front door, the quick steps across the pavement vacated from his mind as if a bird had carried him home.

Edda, her hair pinned back and her short-sleeved dress a pretty dark green, had just made it to the foot of the stairs. She was puzzled, then worried as she rushed to her beloved boy.

"Cian, sweetin', what 'appened? Why do you cry?" Her voice carried warmth as the tension of Cian's body began to melt away, her hands lifting his chin so he'd face her. He handed her the letter, quick to retract his hand.

Staring at the parchment, she remained still as a statue.

"M-mother? Will you read it?"

With a passing glance over him as his mother unfolded her surprise, her attention focused, scanning the writing before her. It was only a few short lines, yet they were enough to make Edda flush, her eyes widening.

"What is it?"

"It is the past, comin' to straighten itself out."

"I do not understand."

With her arms wrapped around him, the flowers in his hand hung limp as he lost all sense of composure among his confusion.

"I love you, my Cian. I 'ave one more story to tell you."

Peering over her shoulder, he read the short letter in its entirety: *Camille returned to the castle, Marion. I will see you soon.*

Twenty-Four

The basement never bothered Cian, or at least it never picked at his mind like it did after Edda told him the story behind the broken glass and twisted metal that lay in the underbelly of his home.

When it did disturb him, it was only for a little bit.

The twisting marks along her forearms helped him recenter himself.

If he could not stand up to the man who delivered the letter, how would a child defend herself against a crow-like woman who stood rigid, strong, proud, and full of unmitigated spite?

Edda's story only lasted minutes as his stomach gurgled, twisting and bubbling, then settling as he reached out to trace the lines of his mother's arms. The front of her gown was dampened from all the pained tears she let run.

If he was to fear her, if he was to believe the few words of an angry religion from a crumpled book, then he would have to believe the same of himself. Half of him or not, blue, or brown, it did not matter – for both made him whole.

His mother was the one who had suffered, not himself. He never knew her to be the manipulative demon she was purported to be, by book, word, or action. Not anymore than he knew himself to be.

Then she spoke of Lowell and the blindfolded swordfight that ended with her running through her greatest friend, and the one she would forever yearn for.

Here, they both sobbed bitterly, guts wrenching from the turmoil and trauma. Cian needn't have been alive for it, for he could feel the space around his mother change, heavy and unrelenting.

He wondered how she could have lived so long carrying these wounds, this knowledge, how she possibly went on, how she could withstand waking up in the morning and greeting children, to see the sun, to smile and take care of everything before her.

Then he saw it.

She wiped at her eyes, then the sun struck them at such an angle that her agates, one a perfect gem, the other having been bestowed by her own parents, glimmered and shined, standing out from her red, swollen eyelids and cheeks.

Cian found himself rising from his spot across from her and falling to his knees as he wrapped his arms about Edda, squeezing her tight and feeling the love and kindness of her very being radiate through her tattered, healing soul.

He spoke in between gasping, shuddered breaths. He spoke of love, of saving, of growth. He spoke of her light and life.

Then when their ragged gasps pittered out and a gentle air came about them, he smiled, pulling away and fixing his vision squarely on hers, placing his hands upon her cheeks, letting the sunlight cast her in a luminous glow, "Be free of it, I absolve you. Be free of it, I forgive you."

What Edda saw in her son astounded her, his blue and brown eyes both alight with the compassion she had always wished to see in her own reflection.

Like a blessing, he kissed her forehead, overcome with the will of the world about him, with the will of two entities, of two beings, of two races.

Relief and release.

The Orphanage breathed deep, into its depths then exhaled through the basement, purging itself completely.

* * *

The door remained unlocked for whenever that man decided to reappear. From the frame hung the flowers Cian picked, a long, woolen string connecting one stem to the next – it had been a few days now, yet each flower was as brilliant as it was the day it was plucked.

Edda told Cian it was Magick, and he knew it to be true. He had experienced it every day, in the fields and in the trees, in the river the most.

The windows were open, too, the curtains and drapes drawn to let in the light, for there was nothing left to hide.

"Who was the blonde man, Mother?"

"Martin."

"Lowell's friend?"

"Yes. Martin may 'ave once called this Orphanage 'is 'ome, but 'e was raised in Alastair's cruel castle instead."

"Do tall stone walls surround the castle? The Kingdom of Draeden, too?"

Edda shrugged as they took trimmings of the back garden's herbs. "I 'ave never seen or known it. Why is it you ask?"

"Remember the boy in my dreams?"

"Yes."

"I see him scouring about, looking for pages at the base of a stone wall that goes so high it touches the clouds."

With hesitation, Edda's hands paused, trying to recall something little Maisie told her over a decade ago about a boy. She wondered what Maisie looked like now, in her early twenties. "I 'ope you find 'im someday. Or that 'e finds you, sweetin'."

A smile plumped Cian's cheeks before they fell at a scuttling in the woods.

A crow sang its hoarse song far away, leaving behind sour notes.

"Is it a jest? A joke? Will Martin ever show?"

Edda's hands slowed as she thought of the boy. He was now a man, raised alongside Alastair - hatred likely being his center. "Perhaps. 'E may be a coward now."

Cian was boisterous in his laughter, letting it fade with creeping fear. The man who gave him the letter was imposing, carrying malice on his back. To believe him once a boy seemed surreal; to think he had giggled and laughed as he was spun about in his mother's arms as Cian himself was, seemed a lie.

Although he knew Edda to be near impervious, he could not push away the dread that began calling his gut home.

"It will be alright, child. Days 'ave passed, as will many more."

The waiting kept them awake, Cian in his bed and Edda in the parlor, sitting next to the prancing flames of the fireplace, waiting for Martin's return home.

Cian peeked at his mother most nights, watching her from between the stairwell balusters. Neither could sleep after the letter. As time ebbed without any visit, they could find some shuteye here and there, but nothing terribly substantial as their shared fear grew. The young boy figured his mother knew he stood watch from above as she did below.

Tonight was cold, however. It felt different.

"Cian, love, come sit with me. The sun will rise soon enough."

The stairs creaked under his steps, weakened by his mother's heavy plodding. A long, knitted blanket was draped about his shoulders and dragged behind him like a king's robes as he descended. Maneuvering about the fire, he pulled up close, the bursting embers and flames knowingly retracting.

He sat.

"Tell me somethin' on my Cian's mind? A bother or a little thought."

Wrapping the blanket around himself as he retracted his legs, he smacked his lips as he sorted through his thoughts. He patted at his thighs under his coverings. "Why have there been no visitors for some time now?"

There was silence as Edda leaned on the arm of her chair, her palm cupping the slope of her cheek.

"Where have all the birds and creatures gone?"

The air stilled as Edda stood, walking towards the front threshold, the door cracked open. Her voice was firm and full of a tender kindness, "I believe Martin knows."

A slow swing as the entryway creaked open, the large man Cian remembered now filling the frame, a twinkling of dawn coloring the outside world behind him. He stared at the bundled boy dead ahead, the same resonant voice billowing from him, the woodwork reverberating in unsettling ways as he announced, "A black, flaming mist—a scourge is spreading across the land. It drives people from their homes lest they be devoured." Stepping inside, the room appeared to shrink around Martin. He forced himself to face Edda, his face carved with rage and reluctance. "It started from two demons, North of here."

He was met with a smile as Edda cooed back, "Welcome 'ome, Martin."

Twenty-Five

"Why do you return after so long?"

"Time is running short if we are to kill the still living demons. We believe it will stop the spreading plague."

"You 'ave come to kill me, 'ave you?"

"I see your stutter is gone, you beast."

Martin took a step towards Edda, feigning ferocity. His former caretaker took notice. She opened her arms in an embrace and stared into his dark eyes, wrought with some unending torment, "Sweetin', come. You are safe 'ere."

"You are a filthy demon. I cannot stand to live while you breathe."

"Why does your Alastair not accompany you?"

Clenched fists were his response as a vein in his neck began to bulge, his face burning red. "He was maimed by one of *your* kind!" Now his steps were no longer restrained by fear or angst as he bounded towards Edda, gripping her shoulders.

She stood solid, her nerves unmarred, beaming ear to ear. "Maybe 'e was deservin' of it. You believe a child who would push another in front of a sword a 'oly blessin' upon us?"

"*You* killed Lowell! I saw it!"

"And Alastair laughed, did 'e not? I saw the look in your eyes that day, the conflict. You only 'ated me. That is all there ever was."

"You drove it through him in a rage, you monster!"

"Is Lowell not of the same breed as me? Would you 'ave killed 'im to stop the scourge?"

"I would not need to kill him!"

"So it is merely I you seek to kill, not some faceless demons."

Edda's gentle, prodding tone permeated Martin's skin and bones as he squeezed. Cian could see the man's arms bulging beneath his shirt, the pressure so immense he knew his own bones would crack. His mother was unfazed.

Cian shivered.

Martin shoved at Edda, her feet remaining firm and relaxed.

"You cannot 'arm me, little Martin."

He shook his head. "I will crush you, like the wires. I can drown you, like your mother. Perhaps I can burn you."

"To what end?!" Cian hollered from his cocoon, "What if, what if you did? If the scourge did not stop, what would be the point of it?"

Martin faced the young boy, the sun beginning to flood through the windows now, casting Cian aglow. All Martin could see was blue and brown. Blue and brown. He scowled with horror, disgust. "There is no end to this plague."

"There is a choice, sweetin'."

"Do *not* call me such things!" Martin smacked Edda across the face, a cracking echoing through the empty halls. He cradled his swollen hand and turned to Cian screaming, his eyes were bloodshot, his pallid face intermixed with crimson wrath, "Boy, do you *know* of the basement? Do you know of the atrocities of your *mother?*"

The blanket sloughed off Cian's shoulders as he began to stand, something new fueling him. The knowledge? The opportunity to defend his mother? Was this what being a man felt like? "Yes, I do! I forgive her! I understand her and what happened. Do *you?*"

The two men stepped towards one another as Martin continued to boil over, "There is nothing to understand – she does not belong!"

The blanket was left behind once Cian bolstered forward, surging with potential – was this how Lowell felt when he stood his ground in his mother's stories? Is this how his mother felt before Martin now? "Perhaps it is *you* who does not belong!"

Gritting his teeth, Martin growled, before his brows perked up in realization. His laugh was low and guttural, the escalation so rapid that Edda could do nothing. With his long arms and legs, he vaulted the sofa between him and Cian, wrapping his large arms around the young boy, squeezing so tight Cian lost his breath. The door was wide open.

Bolting from the Orphanage, Martin knew the boy would pose no trouble. Edda may have been nigh impervious, but she was not as quick as him.

Besides, Martin knew where the river was, and the deepest depth of it at that.

* * *

Edda screamed as she ran after the thief and her child, the fear and panic in Cian's eyes as he was plucked from where he stood seared into her mind.

She was always heavy and slow, despite how she appeared. The deception of her body was never truly a curse until this very moment. The ground sunk beneath her thudding feet, though damp with a rain that never was.

Through the fields, she could just make out Martin's silhouette as it disappeared into the trees far off. Best she could,

Edda tore through, not seeing the flowers she kicked apart, not witnessing what she trampled, nor the spot where Lowell had died as it passed underfoot.

In her mind was only Cian and how he could not end up like Lowell.

How she may become the demon she was proclaimed to be if anything were to happen.

Panting, thin and thick trunks reached ever above her as she scanned for movements. Gutteral, pained moans left her through gritted teeth as she searched for some hint of direction. Hissing through her lips, she pleaded with frustration, and a rippling whirlpool in her soul ready to devour her and whatever else, "Where is 'e? Martin!"

A gust came from behind her and tore the hair from behind her ears, covering her face. With a ferocious palm, she ripped it away, only to see the grass below darkened with depressions. A trail appeared before her.

Alert, she pushed forward, scrutinizing every bend in every blade of grass. It was taking too long. Martin could have killed her boy by now, but would he? Was there any room to doubt?

In a clearing, the burning sun cast itself down upon her as she spun about, too blinded to know her direction now.

She cursed, turning her head to the sun, its vileness etched in her mind and heart. "Damn it! Foul thing, twisted and rotted. You are more the plague than the darkenin' mist 'e spoke of!

Give me my boy!" The earth welcomed her as she crumpled, her despair gutting her in the familiar clearing. Heaving like a wild boar, spittle hung from her lips as ugly cries spilled from her.

Then a hand hushed her, and silence became her friend.

"'Ush now, you are not far off. Ground yourself, dig your feet deep into the grass and dirt. That's a girl, yeah?" Wide eyed, Edda attempted to turn her head, but it was fixed. "No, no, let me show you." Her jaw pivoted, led by a gentle gliding of her chin until she faced a tree, pocked by a bent, fetid arrow.

"L-Low—"

Then the presence was gone, her drive returned as she pushed off the ground and ran true. She thought of how her mother died, how she was drowned. It was what Martin wished for, whether it was devised before the sun rose or after, when it began to light the sky.

Cian was of the utmost importance. She had to save him, there was nothing more to do. If she had to sink for him to live, so be it.

A brief wonder came to mind, of how such a death would feel, if she might even enjoy it.

A breeze wrapped about her ear, taking such thoughts away as though they never were.

Edda could hear the river now, how it beat the rocks in its way, how it battered around curves, and the sound of something that did not belong.

* * *

"It is too deep!"

"Precisely the idea!"

"Why do you do this, Martin?"

Pulling along the child to the opposite shore, the assailant found footing for himself, a precarious ledge hidden below a steady current. One arm held against the water, helping keep them steady and afloat, the other constricting his hostage.

"I was so afraid to step over the threshold, you see. To step foot in that *place*. To see the woman who not only *beat* me but *murdered* my friend. She terrified me. *Me*! She cannot continue to walk this land! I *had* to make my move – those black, fiery, snaking tendrils grow closer. I see what they do. I cannot see it anymore."

Water pelted their faces, Cian bearing the brunt of it whilst being crushed by Martin's limb and relentlessly left gasping for air. Still, he found enough breath to speak, "Am I to feel s-sorry for you? Feel pity?"

The arm gripped tighter. "Close it, half-breed, or I shall think it wise to push you under!"

Cian could no longer hold back, sobbing now and adding another layer to his struggle to breathe. "I-I am just a child, like you once were."

"But *that* is your mother."

Through the thick droplets covering his dark lashes, Cian could make out Edda bursting through the edge of the trees, running up to the bank of the river. Without hesitation, she stepped down, a single foot at a time. The water rose, travelling up her body, soon to her waist and beyond.

"M-Martin, please, 'e is only an orphan boy I took in. 'E is innocent. I beg you, let 'im go. I am where you wanted – please!" Her words were growing difficult to discern for Cian, water plugging his ears. The place he once found peace now making him fade.

"I will let him go when you are below the waterline! Good and gone!"

"I am sorry, Martin, you know I adored you and Lowell." The sun cast dancing luminosities upon the water, reflecting in Edda's agate eyes. She stepped forward into the raging river.

"Do not speak!" Cian was plunged below for a moment too long. Martin struggled to lift him up. The boy gasped and squealed, struggling against the water and clutching at Martin as though he were a savior. Edda walked on.

Cian could not see Martin's eyes as they gazed back at the woman he was once so fond of, just for it to be ripped away by her own hands, over and over. Alastair had fed him heaping spoonfuls of hatred and anger. Cian could not see the conflict within Martin's clouded vision, his intuition covered by another's ploy. Not even Martin could know his small position on the chessboard.

Yet he played it well, despite his inner turmoil. It seemed the only way.

Edda was to her neck now; her sight focused on the boy she remembered wielding a wooden spoon and acting as her shadow so long ago. He was one of the many she wished to witness grow and flourish into something so beautiful. One of many she had the pain of scratching, of clawing, of whipping and twisting.

Perhaps it was better this way.

"Mother!" The words forced their way from Cian's drowning lungs and filling throat.

Edda's nose dipped below the surface, the strength of the river not enough to push her along, save for her long brown locks that trailed the surface. She continued to stare, her eyes flitting to Cian before being engulfed by the all-encompassing water.

It was when her hair, like the roots of a tree, were swallowed entirely, that both Cian and Martin let out wails for reasons of their own. Then the scrambling to the bank began, just behind them. Martin struggled, his strength having dissipated with the thrashing sprays. They both went under when his foot slipped, bursting forth with Martin heaving the young boy to the dirt edge of the water.

Digging their feet into the soft incline, catching a few rocks on the way, they crawled onto the grass. Martin took exhausted breaths as Cian sunk his fingers and toes into the soft dirt below them. Ripping away what he could, he pelted his tormenter with mounds of dark mud and grass.

Sitting upright, an arm raised to try and defend himself, Martin stared, his blonde hair slicked back, his furrowed brow betraying what one would think a victory. His lip trembled as the accosting continued. He let his shield fall and let it be.

"Mama! Bring back my mama!" Cian screeched. "She was all I had and wanted! All I needed! All she did was love me!"

Martin's face shadowed over.

Cian shouted, "She told me stories about you! All she did was *love* you!"

With dirtied fingers, Martin covered his face, his knees pulling themselves tight to his chest. He moaned with pain, his mind in tatters.

Cian let his hands remain at his sides as shock settled, as anger ebbed over him, strong as the river, and then weakened like a small breeze. Over and over.

He was too young to make sense of it.

He needed his mother.

TWENTY-SIX

Below the surface, all was peaceful. Sinking was not so terrible, although the warbling cries above reminded her of what she was leaving behind.

Yet, the twinkling that shone through, like stars in the daytime, made the descent rather pleasant.

She was no longer necessary. She had played her role. It was not easy but now, she could forget. Cian had given her a blessing, a forgiveness. There were no qualms left. An easy death was at hand.

A welcomed death.

The bottom tickled her weighted feet as they soon fully planted against the smooth riverbed. She continued to watch the hazy light filter through and dance with the ever moving current and smiled, exhaling some of the little breath she had left.

Although heavy, underneath the surface, she felt light and began to glide her feet about. Nimbly, she turned around, smiling as she waited, without an ounce of fear.

She paused when she knocked loose a long, white and hollow thing that began to float up and away. A bone, she surmised.

"You found me, sweetin'"

Clear as day, her mother spoke to her. Fingers and toes curling, Edda shrank within herself, covering her ears.

"I could 'ave gotten back to you, but they bound me so that I could not climb. What is it that keeps you 'ere at the bottom?"

Between fearful, slitted eyes, Edda peeked about only to see the dim darkness surrounding her, the metal fixings in front of her, and the loosely connected skeleton of her mother trapped by the smallest bit of horrid luck.

"'Ave you given up? After all that 'appened?"

Edda shook her head, her brown waves swept up like seaweed. She was at peace, she wanted to hear nothing more. The choice was made – there was nothing more to do.

"The boy needs you. To rob the land of love and kindness is a cruel thing, and to rob your child of it is truly 'eartbreakin'."

The water weighed on Edda now as she searched for the tranquility that graced her moments before.

"To rob yourself of it is another entirely."

With warm hands below the cool water, Edda's ears were freed, without fight, and her hands were guided to the rocks in front of her, a difficult climb, a short but arduous journey to the top, to a life, the one she cherished many times, and to one she condemned plenty others.

The warmth wrapped about her now, rocking her side to side as the unwanted and soothing words of her mother brought about an ultimatum, "'Ere you make your choice. Will you finally forgive yourself, or die believin' you did?"

The cold was left to cradle Edda, her vision beginning to fade as her mother's words echoed in her mind.

She let her hands fall away from the jagged stone surface and shook the shackles that bound her mother, watching the bones float up and away until they became part of the river's constellation above her.

Then, she waited and cried.

* * *

A hiss of wildfire, far away, but creeping close. Wet wood sizzled, the low and piercing sound making its way across the land.

A familiar, tormenting sound broke Martin from his stupor.

It was coming, it was coming for him.

Edda's death did nothing to abate the scourge, only to hasten its pace.

How foolish he felt, how ripped in two.

Yet he would not let it take him, he could not. He deserved to live. He had been through too much, and his life was just beginning. He was meant to return to Alastair, to proclaim his victory, to raise this boy to see the truth of the world.

He shook his head.

He wished to sit in that bunk pressed against the window of the Orphanage and watch the stars with one of the few people he felt he belonged alongside. He wanted to feel as though he belonged once again.

Martin's hands snapped away from his face, slapping the ground below him, Cian giving a glance towards the man as he watched the encroaching black mist. Jolting to his feet, Martin gripped Cian by the arm, pulling him off the ground in one fluid motion.

Cian failed to break free. "Let me go! Murderer!"

Panic marred Martin's features now, his fatigue long gone as he tried to unroot Cian from his spot. "It comes! We must leave!"

"Let it come! I believe it would do us good!"

Martin's face contorted and he began to laugh from deep within his stomach, an uproarious hilarity striking him that he could not understand and never would. "You wish to die?"

"You wish to live?" Cian scoffed, as though he were an adult. As though he had an idea. Ripping up his sleeve, Martin brandished a long running scar down the entirety of his limb. "Boy, you know *nothing*!"

"Then why not allow me to die! I know of the basement, I know of the puppetry, and I know of Marion!" The boy shoved Martin. "I know of my mother too! I know how you forced her to die for me like your beloved prince forced your Lowell to die for him!"

Martin gave another belting laugh that ended in a squelch. "Perhaps I should leave you here, but I feel that would not sit well with me later." Casting a glance at the mist, he saw it was closer now. Martin's hairs stood on end as he ripped Cian from his rootings, shaking the boy before dragging him. The lad scratched at his captor once more.

The river would be quick to cross since his vigor had returned and now that he would not need to fight the current in place, he could—

A solid wall stood before him, one he collided with. It was dripping yet drying rather quick as it radiated a warmth he'd known before.

"I made a decision. Cian, are you proud of your mother?"

Martin fell to his back, his hands and feet working to lift him back up, but they were useless and limp now as he stared at Edda, bones drifting down the river behind her.

Her smile was wide and glowing, her red and yellow eyes sparkling like never before. She crouched before Cian and kissed his forehead, and he grinned widely back at her, sniffling as small rivulets made way down his cheeks. She brushed back his dark, earthen hair before turning to face Martin on the ground, extending a hand. Comfort ebbed from her fingertips as he attempted to reach out

Manipulation.

Alastair's voice echoed in his mind as he scrambled to his feet and pulled a small knife from a hidden sheath within his trousers. He pointed it at Edda and grunted, the only words he could manage in his state being those to keep away.

Edda opened her arms and waited for Martin to come to his senses, to find the child within him that knew what was best. She wished him to find the intuition a young one would gravitate towards. Yet he was an adult now, and he had been lost for too long.

He ran at her, slicing up the length of her soaked dress.

She stood firm, the grooves along her arms luminescent like her eyes, her arms held open for him.

"Stop it!" Cian screamed.

The blade dulled against stone skin with each scrape, eliciting a dash of sparks with every collision.

The love was even in her voice as she let it flow from her, "It is gettin' close, Martin. I can 'elp you. Return with us. You are welcome to."

He knew he did not deserve it and continued his fruitless onslaught, blinded by tears and unresolved, misguided pain.

"Enough!"

Cian jumped between the two of them, his boyish hands keeping Martin's aloft.

Martin pulled back, his muscle memory taking over. He had been trained, practicing for such a thing. His mind was gone as he plunged through the boy, not realizing what he had done until blood soaked the hilt of his knife and his hand.

Coward he was, he ran without looking, without a glance back at the mother embracing her wounded son. A sight he never wanted to see once playing before him for a second time.

Then he tripped, plunging into the black, flaming mist, his brief scream silenced by the scourge pouring down his throat.

* * *

"'Ome, Cian, I will take you 'ome," Edda's voice was on the cusp of insanity, a horrific balancing act as she toted her son, the knife still in his belly. She could see flashes of Lowell as she scoured the bank of the river, looking for safe passage.

Weakly he pointed downstream. Weaker still, he spoke, "D-down there, it is shallow and calm. I like it there. Crossing is easier, too."

She hushed him and followed his advice, finding his happy spot and wading through it. In their wake was a trail of blood that the river troubled itself with ridding.

Through the forest and the plains to the cobblestone road, Cian grew paler, his skin beginning to gray as his lips did the same.

"C-cold."

"I will warm you by the fire, sweetin'."

Swaddling him in the blanket he left behind the same morning, Edda cradled him the same as she did when she first held him. She sat before the new, blazing fire and hummed songs to him as the bedding about him began to soak through with blood.

"Story, m-mama. Please?"

She felt as though her skin was breaking, sloughing off in sheets like slate.

She climbed the wall for this? She forgave herself only for her son to die?

His fingers were cold on her cheek as he wiped away a tear. "Mama?"

It was the right thing to do. It felt right, despite how wretched it felt in the end.

"Did I ever tell you about 'ow someday, we'd all be goin' 'ome?"

When he shook his head she told him about her dreams and the promising words of others within them. How someone with eyes like the ground beneath them would return them home and they would all be together once more.

As he faded, he smiled, listening to his mother. Her words dying away as she began to change into one who would forever protect her son.

There they stayed, the fire warming the Orphanage never burning out.

EPILOGUE

The threshold was worn by footstep and weather, the door hanging wide. From inside was a warmth like no other, a glow that few things in life can emit: a fallen star, a sunbeam, the smile of one who loves.

Stepping inside, the tale fully unraveled, told to Aiden through visions in his mind by way of another, by way of the world around him, through the ground, air and trees, through the magickal energy that encapsulates all. He fell to his knees and wept.

So welcomed was he, and so pained was his soul.

For how long he cried, he did not know, until he found the will to approach the figures in front of the forever burning flame.

A statue of mother and son, of Edda and Cian.

The boy remained wrapped in a red blanket, his skin gray. The woman's surface of swirling lines, deep red and yellow hues with spots of black. Gray dust and sheets of what was once her skin surrounded her from when she changed into the beautiful stone that lay beneath her surface.

To the touch, she was still warm.

Shifting his hand to the young boy, Aiden was overcome with grief, staring into the face that flashed before him when he walked up the cobbled path. With a pause, he brushed Cian's smooth cheek, letting out a gasping sob. "Cian, it is I you saw in your dreams. Those letters, I learned to read through them. I-I am quite good at it now." Letting his hand fall to the exposed fingers of his brother's frozen state, he sucked in a sharp breath before he found his words, "I will take you both home, I promise. It is not easy, but I have help."

Naïve hope filled him as he waited for a sign, a response, the hint of a smile. When none came, he stood to look around, knowing he needed a gem and an armlet. That was the way of their passage, he understood.

Up the stairs he found Edda's room, that which belonged to Camille once before. It was dusty, sooted and webbed. Closing his eyes, he asked for a whisper of guidance. A natural inkling bade him to the bed.

Underneath the pillow was the golden armlet, an empty socket at its center.

Aiden closed the door behind him, giving a brief walk to and around his brother Cian's room. It was too empty to gather much about the brother he hadn't known.

Across the hall, he walked until he found himself before a bunk bed, a blanket strewn across it. Lightly parting it, he crawled atop the bedding and was enshrouded in moonlight, the stars a brilliance he had been accompanied by for many nights, but not like this.

Here they were a wonder. Even more so since it was day when he walked inside.

He had no time to dally about, much as he wished.

Down the stairs and back to the mother and son he went. Settling next to her warming presence, he held a hand over the eye he knew to be false and asked for it to be given to him. It felt as though light itself seeped through his fingers before something heavy laid in his rough palms.

Despite its size, it was hefty, but he knew agates were always heavier than they appeared. He had picked up a few on his travels, but none so beauteous or created so fine by the world.

It was black at the center, like a pupil, surrounded by yellow and giving birth to white lines like the wings of a bird that rained down segments below it.

He place it over the armlet's opening and closed his eyes until he felt a pleasant warming once more.

He placed a kiss on Edda's forehead in gratitude and compassion, then to his brother with the utmost adoration and love a younger brother can feel for his elder.

Leaving the door open, he whispered, "Farewell. I will see you both again."

Striding back to the overgrown walkway where nature had taken over, the mist urged him in a new direction now, hinted at him a few times in the telling of Edda's story. It kissed at his heels as he thought of the two blind siblings he would meet.

To where the worship of the Sun began, and where the demonizing did too.

He began his long walk to the Monastery.

Acknowledgments

To my mom and stepdad, Rita and Rick, for giving me feedback and pointing out the flaws. My friend, Maddy, who edited my story simply because she wished to read it. Christine Foltzer for creating such a lovely cover and being patient with my newness to self-publishing. And Lauren, who gave me critique and helped me grow.

To everyone who not only bought my first book, but read it. Thank you for always asking when the next one will be out.

About Me, Rebecca Kropp

I was born and raised in Minnesota, surrounded by lush trees, plenty of birdsong, squirrel chitters, and coated in a beautiful blanket of white snow in the winter.

Being the youngest of three girls by near ten years, I found myself drawn to reading, playing plenty of games and creating stories of my own. Having so many stories in my head, I finally sat down to weave a web that continued to grow beyond what I imagined.

Here, I dipped my toes in a passion that seemed out of reach for reasons big and small, but overall, excuses. Here I found happiness, confidence, and a love for myself I could not fathom.

So, once more, thank you for taking part. I hope you enjoyed reading it as much as I enjoyed writing it.